The Presidents

Books in the
Detective Harry Lincoln Series

The Lincoln Logs
The Presidents

The second Detective Harry Lincoln Trilogy

The Presidents

Harold B. Goldhagen

Mountain Arbor
Press
Alpharetta, GA

This is a work of fiction. Names, characters, businesses, places, and events are either the products of the author's imagination or are used in a fictitious manner. Any resemblance to actual persons, living or dead, or actual events is purely coincidental.

ISBN: 978-1-63183-996-2 - Paperback
eISBN: 978-1-63183-997-9 - ePub
eISBN: 978-1-63183-998-6 - mobi

Library of Congress Control Number: 2021905764

Printed in the United States of America 0 4 1 3 2 1

♾This paper meets the requirements of ANSI/NISO Z39.48-1992 (Permanence of Paper)

Thanks again to my good friend of many years Mike Elia, and to my son Alex Goldhagen who helped put the polish on my manuscript.

This book is dedicated to retired Atlanta Police Major Kenneth E. Burnette. No better man or woman has ever worn the badge! Rest in Peace.

Beauties . . . and the Russian Beast

Prologue

A Coast Guard helicopter hovered over the fishing trawler. "Stand-by for one of our cutters en-route to your location," announced the helicopter's co-pilot over a loud speaker. The trawler had radioed the Coast Guard for assistance, giving their location by map coordinates.

Also on Lake Rockford in a rented schooner were two city detectives on vacation. It was one of those days when Mother Nature appears to love the world. The sky was blue, the same continuous blue approaching the horizon in any direction. Soft white clouds as though from dreams of the old master painters. It was early May, the balmy mid-morning temperature at seventy-three degrees. Homicide Detectives Harry Lincoln and his partner Floyd Washington had earned some time in paradise. They had left murder and mayhem for a few days, a well- deserved break from the violent urban jungle that was their home.

Their schooner sliced across the calm blue waters of Lake Rockford in the Monroe National Forest. It was the largest lake in the contiguous forty-eight states (other than the Great Lakes). Two hours out from the shoreline, the far off horizon was visible a full 360 degrees.

"Harry, there's a helicopter hovering about three miles out off our port bow." Floyd said as he scanned the water with binoculars. It was Harry's watch at the helm. "Yeah, I see a spec right above the water. Just for the hell of it, let's be nosey. We'll take a look, though it's probably one of those sight-seeing tourist helicopters.

Floyd was still watching through the binoculars as they got closer said, "No Harry, it's a Coast Guard chopper. There's a fishing trawler not moving beneath it." A short time later a Coast

Guard cutter appeared, came alongside the trawler and stopped. Coast Guard sailors and two officers then boarded the trawler.

Not wanting to get too close, Harry set the schooner in idle drift. They could observe activity on the aft deck of the trawler. Within thirty minutes' life lines were attached between both boats and two objects were transferred to the cutter. One appeared to be a full body bag, the other a very large anchor.

Harry radioed the cutter and advised it was the schooner lying aft of them calling. "Do you need assistance unidentified schooner?" The cutter answered.

Harry identified themselves as off-duty Zealand PD homicide detectives. "No, thank you cutter, but we'd like to follow you to your station to see if we might be able to assist you, if that is a body you have. Your station is in our jurisdiction."

"Roger that schooner, that trawler is following also. We have the body of a young female with what appears to be a gunshot wound to the head. The lake is federal jurisdiction, so as for now we'll take the lead. We'll see you at the station, and we welcome your offer."

"Copy that cutter. Out."

Later at the Coast Guard station, Harry and Floyd along with the two CG officers and several sailors from the cutter viewed the young woman's head down to her neck. "Good God," said one of the sailors. "This looks like something out of some fucking horror movie."

"It sure does," agreed Floyd. "I've worked homicide in Miami where we've fished a lot of bodies from the water, but this is a new one for me. A gunshot wound in the middle of her forehead, a metal collar around her neck with a chain attached, and an anchor secured to it."

Harry got on the phone and called Lieutenant McGee. "Lieu, its Lincoln and the time out you gave me and Washington for a few days in paradise took an interesting turn. A fishing trawler netted a naked female with a gunshot wound in her forehead from deep in the lake. She was weighed down with a heavy anchor. She looks young, maybe early twenties and could be from somewhere in Central Asia, possibly the Middle East. The Coast Guard has her now. Have you gotten any missing persons reports that could be her?"

"No. You both better get back, there's plenty to do here."

Zealand, Virginia a city nestled in the picturesque Blue Ridge Mountains. It's population comparable to the cities of Atlanta and Seattle. Enough to keep the 2,000 sworn members of the Zealand Police Department busy, without the frantic pace of New York City, Chicago or Los Angeles.

***

Lincoln and Washington had been dubbed "The Presidents" by their colleagues, and the media quickly picked up the nick-name. The Presidents had earned a following in the public eye. They were enjoying life out of their element, a life they had only dreamed about. But, sadly, in less than an instant on that fine day in May, their heavenly bubble burst.

CHAPTER

1

Three months earlier…

The Homicide Squad Room was filling up at eight in the morning as arriving day watch detectives took possession of the desks used by colleagues eight hours prior. This shared work space, littered with debris from scraps of paper, torn envelopes and unfinished report forms, to rumpled newspaper sports articles. A couple of old Playboy magazines were in the mix, generating the same smirks of displeasure among the several female detectives. All the litter, no matter what kind, was coated with the sticky remnants from coffee spills and donut crumbs that had accumulated during the shifts over the past several days. The usual banter and the kidding, the telling of the same war stories, over and over again, brought the decibel levels above what was suitable for the somber work and tragic events common in this space. The same light atmosphere prevails in all homicide squad rooms.

"Lincoln," roared Lieutenant McGee from his office across the squad room. "Grab your coffee and come in here."

Introductions were made as the three sat in the office of Homicide Lieutenant James McGee.

"Harry Lincoln, meet your new partner Floyd Washington." Three pairs of eyes caught each other. "Not a gag, not a bit. It's not April 1st" the lieutenant added.

Lincoln had not met nor even seen Washington before that moment. What brought Washington to that moment was a tragic event, a personal issue, he felt he could not very well endure where he had been. Floyd's wife, Lena Washington, suffered from inoperable ovarian cancer, eventually succumbing to it. Despite that, her death was not unexpected – it was hoped against for a long time. When she died, it devastated Miami Homicide Detective Floyd Washington. He felt that best way he could deal with it, was his work, but in a new setting. He simply had to re-locate to another city leaving behind a sterling reputation as one of their best. Remaining in familiar surroundings would be too painful.

He sent his resume to dozens of major cities around the country. Zealand, Virginia was one of them. The city personnel board, including several top police brass considered Washington's application. Two board members and a lieutenant from the police chief's office flew down to Miami to interview several of Washington's colleagues and his chain-of-command. It was not a difficult decision to hire him.

Harry Lincoln's current partner, Liz Kovak had requested maternity leave two weeks prior. The timing was right. Floyd Washington and Harry Lincoln would be a good fit, both considered top detectives by their respective police departments.

"Harry, show him around and bring him up to speed. Give him a rundown of our policies, probably somewhat different from Miami's. Also how the state laws of Florida may vary from ours." McGee didn't feel the need to instruct any further, knowing the caliber of both men. "Detective Washington, I am pleased to have you with us, as are the Chief of Police and the Chief of Detectives." Lieutenant McGee paused a moment and in a solemn tone, "We wish to express our sorrow and condolences from the entire department for the untimely death of your wife."

Floyd Washington replied with a quiet "Thank you."

Throughout the squad room, the front edges of each partners' desks butted up against the other with the partners facing each other as they did their work at their desks. Harry made the obligatory introductions as they made their way to the supply room, the equipment locker where incidentals, such as radios, keys for their assigned detective car, a pair of handcuffs and a can of pepper spray. Most important of all, a bulletproof vest, necessary for day-to-day duties. At the armory Detective Washington was issued a 9mm semi-automatic service weapon plus fifty rounds of ammunition and two extra magazines. Also issued was a tazar. The last piece of essential information on the tour was the most expeditious route to the men's restroom.

As Floyd finished arranging his desk, Harry noticed that he placed in a prominent position a gold framed photo of an attractive woman.

Outside in the detective parking lot, the two entered their assigned black Ford crown 'vic' and upon leaving police headquarters, headed for midtown. Located just east of midtown is Mike's Tavern, a favorite lunch spot for a cross section of the city's population, including cops and firefighters. Harry had lunch there most days. Although he mentioned this to Floyd, they continued on for a few blocks to a small café; a place for lunch and some private talk without interruption.

"I'd like to express my personal deep sorrow and sympathy for what you must be going through. On a more pleasant note, I'm glad we have a guy of your caliber. From what little I've heard, you're just the professional we want and need. The word is that you are a competent, thorough, conscientious detective, straight as an arrow with a track record to be envied."

"Harry as I looked around the department earlier I noticed how diverse it is: Race, nationality, gender and ethnic origin. I assume that religion is included." Floyd continued, "I grew up in a racially segregated state governed by the Jim Crow laws, surrounded by a dozen or so similar states ruled by that same Jim Crow. That's all in the past. Now before we get started, do you have any problems working with a black partner?"

"No." Harry said emphatically. "That's the short answer. The long answer is "Hell No!" Harry continued, I admit that I have my biases just like everyone else and they are pretty general: Politicians, celebrities, TV hucksters, and TV cop shows which I believe are insulting to real cops. But, I don't feel any bias or prejudice towards people because of their race or any of those others whom you pointed out when talking about diversity. I had a black partner, an older veteran, when I still worked in uniform who taught me a lot and kept me alive on several occasions. He died of cancer a few years ago... I cried like a baby... I am very happy that I will be working with you...I look forward to being your partner."

Harry switched gears and got down to work. "There's nothing heavy at the moment, no 'whodunits' a few domestic homicides and, as always, there are the boys on the street corners showing each other how tough they are. Homicides due to gang activity are always happening because of local turf wars... the personal beefs keep the bullets flying. I'd imagine it's the same in Miami."

With lunch finished, Harry suggested they go back to the office to see if McGee had any words of wisdom for them. "He comes on pretty strong sometimes. Beneath all that bluster he's not a bad guy."

CHAPTER

2

The luxurious penthouse overlooking the City of Zealand was one of five around the globe owned by a Russian multi-billionaire, Boris Zherkov. Zherkov is physically average size, humorless man of middle age with closely-cropped steel-grey hair. He was feared by those who knew him. Boris Zherkov was an ex-KGB colonel, a holdover from the Cold War who started gathering rubles by demanding sizeable bribes.

At the peak of his military career Colonel Zherkov was known as a brutal, merciless man among his colleagues. When poor souls were brought to the cells in the basement of Moscow's dreaded Lubyanka Prison, accused or suspected of some crime against the state, they would rarely if ever emerge in the same condition. Bones broken, finger nails, toe nails pulled out, or teeth extracted. He would have a man suspended from the ceiling from cables attached to sharp hooks driven through his palms, a ten-pound-weight hanging from his testicles, for hours.

Women prisoners were strapped to an examining table naked, legs spread wide, feet locked into stirrups. She would be brutally gang-raped by every guard in the building, then turned over face down, and anally raped by those same guards, while Colonel Zherkov put out lit cigarettes all over her body.

After the colonel was satisfied that every bit of information concerning subversive activities, and the names of those connected to them had been exhausted, or they pleaded there was nothing to confess to and begged for mercy. The battered, mangled and half dead prisoner was then taken from this chamber of horrors and dragged down a narrow corridor to, the unfortunate was told, a waiting cell. In most cases, without warning two bullets were administered from behind into the base of the skull. Another subversive removed from Mother Russia.

***

When Zherkov left government service he went into business. He practiced the capitalist system of supply and demand. His main commodities were illegal drugs: cocaine and heroin. Within a short time, he saw that huge profits could be made from illegal guns as well. Particularly the Russian made KalashnikovAK-47 assault rifle. This very simple and dependable weapon was in demand all over the world. It was a struggle to fill the mountain of orders, but Zherkov solved his problem by stealing from warehouses and hijacking trucks.

From the drugs and guns, he was well on his way to making his fortune.

Then Zherkov saw that he could make more at a lower cost… human trafficking. It turned out to be his most profitable enterprise. Scour the slums of impoverished countries, find girls and young women barely scratching out an existence, offer them jobs making more in a month than they made in a year. An agreement would be worked out where the trip to one of four different cities around the world would be financed by Zherkov's "company" and in time reimbursed by the woman through a small but regular percentage of her wages. Thus, the ruse he used to entice these women into his power.

Boris Zherkov had "crossed the Rubicon" … committing his fortune to sexual slavery.

CHAPTER

3

Floyd had just returned to his apartment when his phone rang. "Detective Washington this is Liz Kovak, Harry Lincoln's former partner. I apologize for calling you at home. After speaking with Harry, who had said very nice things about you, I thought I'd give you a heads-up. I left the police department to have my second child, to be a stay-at- home mom and raise my family. Harry Lincoln is a great partner. You are lucky to be working with him. From what I've heard you'll be two of the best. But, as good as he is, he has a major weakness -- his hair-trigger temper. I've been with him on several occasions when he's lost it, albeit for good reason, I thought he might kill some no good bastard but I was able to save him from himself.

Floyd replied, "Sometimes I feel the same way, unfortunately we won't have a cooler head like yours around to save us both. I'll keep that in mind and when situations come up I'll try to keep my feet on the ground. And both of Harry's also. Okay?

"Please don't tell him that I called. Goodbye Floyd and good luck."

"Goodbye Liz, I'm glad you called. Thanks."

"Patrolling the streets of any low-income, high-crime area of a city is not much different from patrolling the same kinds of streets in any city. As I've already mentioned, currently we have no 'whodunits,' just the usual domestic murders, street corner killings and gangland homicides." Harry explained to his new partner. "The only requirement is to get all the essentials; a rap sheet if the identity of the perp is known. Whether an arrest been made.

All witness's statements, plus all physical and forensic evidence. Then forward the complete package to the D.A.s office. I suppose it's the same in Miami?"

"Yeah," answered Floyd. "Except here the heat is not unbearable, low humidity and no palm trees."

"I'd like you to meet one or two of my most reliable C.I.s. I'm sure you had a few of your own in Miami. In time you'll develop some here, but this might give you a start," Harry said as he dialed the cell phone to one of his better confidential informants.

"Ham, can you meet me in about fifteen minutes? I want to acquaint you with my new partner."

"I'll be there."

***

Sitting in their unmarked detective car a short time later at the usual meeting place, Harry was introducing Floyd, suddenly there came a piercing sound from the police radio, "Detective radio 199 calling Homicide 134 and 136."

"134, go ahead 199", acknowledged Harry.

"199 to Homicide 134, at Zealand Memorial Hospital ER, Signal 51" (person stabbed).

"134, copy that"

***

At the hospital the detectives crowded into the trauma room as doctors were working frantically returning the intestines that had burst out of a large gaping cut across a young man's abdomen.

"Once we put these back where they belong and sew him up, he should be okay detectives."

"Thanks Doc," said Harry as he and Floyd left the trauma room to find the responding officer.

The cop's report was simple enough. "It was nothing more than a lover's triangle, only the husband with the butcher knife didn't think it was very romantic. He came home unexpectedly and found his wife in bed with the victim. He dashed into the kitchen, grabbed the knife and before the victim could scramble into his pants; the husband sliced him open pretty good. His guts were coming out." The cop turned everything over to the detectives.

After reading the husband the Miranda Warnings, they booked him into the jail then turned the knife as evidence over to the Property Section. Harry and Floyd returned to the office to complete the report, with the: who, what, where, when and how. Along with all the other paperwork that goes to the DA's office.

After completing the tedious details that constitute the official crime folder, Harry observed it was time to call it a day. Joining the exodus of the departing day watch detectives, Harry and Floyd paused momentarily in the parking lot when they got to their cars. Harry asked, "I've got a loft here in the city near the river, where are you staying?"

"I've rented an apartment until I can find something more permanent, maybe a condo or townhouse."

"If you don't have any plans, how about meeting to grab a bite at Mike's Tavern, the place I pointed out in midtown this afternoon? Nothing fancy, but the price is right. We have an unwritten rule in the squad: We all pick up our own checks, keeps it less complicated."

Floyd said he could make it about 7:00 p.m., there were a few things he had to take care of at his place. "If that's okay I'll see you then." Harry agreed, and the two separated.

Harry went to his loft to relax before dinner. After a quick refreshing shower, he put on a comfortable pair of jeans and a sport shirt, relieved of the annoying tie, he made a phone call.

"Hi Jessica, I know this is short notice but if you don't already have dinner plans, or other plans for the evening, how about meeting me at Mike's for a burger and a brew. I want you to meet my new partner, Floyd Washington."

"Oh Harry are you serious, 'Washington?' You had better have a sense of humor because of all the kibitzing coming your way."

"Yeah Jess, it's already started."

"Well in that case I would be honored to dine tonight with the Presidents."

CHAPTER

4

"Harry, would you mind if I cancelled dinner for tonight, and changed it to tomorrow night? I just have too much to do here getting squared away." Floyd's voice on the phone was apologetic.

"Not at all, is there anything I can do to help?"

"No, it's just all my personal stuff has to be unpacked and put away. But thanks."

"Okay, see you in the morning. Dinner has been moved to tomorrow night."

***

They lay side by side, on their backs, both waiting for their racing hearts to return to normal. After dinner out, Harry and Jessica had returned to Harry's loft each leaving a trail of clothing from the front door to the bedroom. With fresh sheets beneath them they connected, Harry thrust deep and hard; Jessica, matching stroke for stroke thrusting upward with equal intensity. It was over for both quickly and simultaneously. Harry was thankful for the loft's soundproof walls. As they were recovered, Jessica managed to say, "Harry it isn't fair, here we are on our fourth date and I'm already in love with you. You give me this long speech about not looking for a long relationship with you, and then prove to be the kindest, most considerate, loving man; not to mention the most passionate lover I've had."

"As I've told you before, I'm not looking for the domestic life, to get married and have a family. When I start to see a woman exclusively, I think it's only fair to let her know this up front, so if that's what she wants, she doesn't waste time with me. Now let's jump in for a quick shower. Then I'll take you home."

"Harry, why don't we stay here? Spend the night since we're already nice and cozy?"

"I've got an early morning squad meeting and I can't chance getting tied up in morning rush hour traffic after dropping you off. Lieutenant McGee doesn't tolerate being late for his meetings. Plus, I don't want to set a bad example for my new partner."

"Speaking of your new partner, how are you two getting along? Are there any issues with the black/white thing? Is he dating anyone yet? Is it too soon after he lost his wife?"

"We are getting along just fine, no problems. And Jess, I don't know anything about his love life."

"Jessica, Floyd and I are meeting for dinner tomorrow. Why don't you come with us?"

"I thought when I dine with the "Presidents" maybe we could include Lisa, make it a foursome?"

Harry remembered the case he handled six months' prior: Lisa Daniels and her boyfriend were kidnapped from a park by two black thugs. She was taken to an abandoned house and sexually assaulted. Her boyfriend, shot and killed.

"Jess, after the terrible ordeal that Lisa endured at the hands of those two animals -- the kidnapping, the multiple rapes and sodomy, the physical injury and the degradation. I'm not a goddam psychologist, but I believe that none of that has been forgotten. And surely not the cold- blooded murder of her boy friend. Those horrors she'll re-live every time she sees a black man."

"My sister Lisa never had a racially prejudicial bone in her body." Jessica insisted.

"No, not until that night. And how do you suppose she'll feel sitting across the dinner table from a black man now? I think it's a bad idea."

"So what you are saying is that she has to endure that tragedy during the entire rest of her life, right? Who better to help start to change that is for her to be with than the two of us and the honorable and trustworthy black man, Floyd Washington? I'll run it by her and get her reaction."

"Okay Jess, keeping in mind that no one likes to be blindsided, I'll see what he thinks about being the object of this racial exercise, this social experiment officiated by the two of us. If either objects, we call it off. No need to ruin a possible future friendship."

***

"Okay ladies, knock off the chatter and listen up," bellowed Lieutenant McGee, bringing the squad room into instant quiet. "We're in a rare situation that we don't find ourselves too often. No current 'whodunits,' no serial killers or rapists, just our every-day smoking gun murders and identifiable rapists, every case a slam-dunk. Be damn sure all perpetrator and witness statements, physical and forensic evidence, and everything else that's needed are in those files before they go to the D.A.'s office. I don't want to get a phone call from some irate ADA bitching about not being able to prosecute because this or that is missing.

The meeting broke up with everyone happy that their working lives, however temporary, now consisted of eight hour shifts, two off days, just like the other squads.

CHAPTER

5

Ivan Bluvich was a "talent scout" a recruiter for Zherkov Enterprises. He traveled to various third world countries searching for girls and young women to bring to Boris Zherkov. There was no shortage of women, but very few met Zherkov's requirements – attractiveness, allure, sexually appealing. They had to be able to appear to exude the ability to entice men of means who are looking for temporary feminine company to engage in their sexual fantasies. They would soon be forced into sexual slavery.

***

Ivan Bluvich recognized the main train terminal as the train pulled in slowly bringing him once again to L'viv, Ukraine. He had been there many times when Ukraine was still part of the now defunct Soviet Union. During those times, it was one of the satellite countries ringing Russia's western border, forming the "Iron Curtain." Today, though it was again an independent nation. Bluvich got off the train, carrying his one small piece of luggage, and left the terminal. He got into a taxi, instructed the driver to take him to the Empire Hotel where he was to meet his Ukrainian contact, Vitali Goraya, who lived in Ukraine's capital city of Kiev.

Goraya also worked for Boris Zherkov. He was responsible for scouting Eastern European countries to find women and girls who met Zherkov's qualifications, who were likely candidates, and then to notify Bluvich.

Entering the lobby Bluvich was intercepted halfway to the desk. "I've already registered you, you just need to give your passport to the desk clerk" said Vitali Goraya. "Let's go into the bar, I know you're thirsty from that musty train."

The bar was almost empty and they sat at a rear table. The waiter brought a bottle of vodka, two glasses, then left. "I'm telling you Ivan," stated an excited Vitali Goraya. "This one is gorgeous, like one of those fucking American movie stars."

"And when do I get to see this beauty, Vitali?"

"Tomorrow morning we'll drive down to this village where there is a large collective farm, about an hour and a half from here. First, though, let's have something to eat, get you settled in your room, freshen up and maybe take a shower to get off all the grime from the train. I've arranged for you to have some female company tonight."

***

The following morning the two met in the hotel's restaurant where they discussed the plans for the day. They ate a hearty breakfast of pickled herring, smoked salmon, whitefish and sturgeon, a variety of cheeses, hard-boiled eggs and pickles, all served with dark coarse bread. It was then washed down with hot tea, spiked with a touch of vodka.

"We will drive, at most two hours south from here, almost to the Romanian border, to the village of Kosiv, in a valley surrounded by the Carpathian Mountains." Vitali mumbled, stuffing his mouth with food and talking at the same time, spitting bits of herring and cheese onto the table.

Ivan impatiently said, "Let's finish up and get on the road."

***

Leaving the hotel, Vitali had to drive slowly and cautiously to avoid hitting one of the many "Babushka Women" who early each morning scrub down the cobbled stone sidewalks with long handled scrub brushes and pails of soapy water, a long tradition from Eastern Europe's large cities to small villages. The four-lane highway leaving the city was as smooth and modern as any city, but shortly it narrowed into a two lane road. Traffic was sparse, but the further they drove, the more pot holes Vitali had to avoid. The road surface got worse as they drove, until the pavement was gone, replaced by a dirt and gravel road.

"You wanted independence? Here's your independence." Ivan said with some glee in his voice. "Your countrymen can't even pave their roads, no more Russian rubles."

They were now only seeing the occasional old, slow truck. These vintage trucks were difficult to pass because of the narrow road. Soon the dirt and gravel road became so bumpy that Vitali had to drive much slower, and wagons and carts pulled by mules and oxen replaced the old motor vehicles

"You know my friend," said Ivan with a tone of superiority, "this is like we've traveled back one hundred years in time. There is an American movie called, *'Fiddler on the roof'* that I feel we have fallen into."

Vitali felt the sting of the insults and quickly changed the subject. "So the prospect you are going to meet. This twenty-two-year-old woman works in the fields of the collective farm picking potatoes, onions, cabbage, beans, tomatoes and whatever else needs harvesting. She's been doing this ever since she was a child." Vitali wanted Ivan to know as much about her as he could tell him. "She lives on the farm in kind of barracks with most of the other female workers."

"What is her name? Does she not have a family?" Ivan asked, wanting answers to these and other questions before he met her.

"Her name is Olya Timko. When she was six years old she was first traumatized the night the KGB broke into their house and arrested her mother and father on some charge against the State. They were sent to a gulag somewhere in Siberia. Olya never heard from them again. Olya, an only child, was taken in by a neighbor, not out of kindness or pity, but to get a free house maid. No love, tenderness or understanding was shown. The frightened six-year old girl cried herself to sleep at night.

All she had was a life of drudgery for a year because the mistress of the house always carried a thick hickory switch which she would use liberally on the domestic help when she found one of her strict rules had been broken. Little Olya was told by the household cook, of this nearby farm that was always looking for workers to pick the crops in the fields. The cook also said that all the girls and women slept in one very large room, and they ate together in a larger room with all the other workers. And now comes the best part," said Vitali. "This little seven-year-old girl walks by herself in the blistering heat for over six hours, and presents herself in the farm's office, saying she wants to go to work. And she's been there ever since."

I know the foreman; we went to the same school in Kiev. I come here occasionally to have lunch with him. There is a huge dining hall where all the workers and the bosses eat. The last time I was here was the first time I saw her. How do they say in the American movies? 'She knocked my eyes out.' I made inquires about her, and that's when I called you. My foreman friend is the one who told me her story. You can ask him for more details if you need." Vitali was anxiously anticipating seeing her again, but this time speaking with her.

"Mr. Zherkov will be very pleased to get her, she is a ravishing beauty. I have not yet approached her as my orders are clear, when I find one that Mr. Zherkov might be interested in I'm to notify you." Vitali followed orders. He did not want to make Mr. Zherkov angry. He had seen the man's anger unleashed in person once against a colleague for refusing to follow orders.

Upon arrival at the farm, they went straight to the office to meet with the foreman. "Andre, this is Mr. Zherkov's right hand man Ivan Bluvich. Ivan, may I present Andre Krakov, the overseer of the farm. Andre and I have known each other for many years."

"I am very pleased to meet you Ivan," said Andre, shaking his hand. "I understand from Vitali that you are here on business for Mr. Zherkov. How can I help?"

"Olya Timko", said Ivan. "We would like to speak with her in private."

"The whole crew is eating lunch right now. Please be my guest and have lunch as well." Andre said. "When lunch time is over, I will have one of my men bring her to the office instead of returning to the field. I hope you are not going to take her away from us, she is one of our best workers."

"It's not what we want its what Boris Zherkov wants," Ivan reminded them.

***

Olya Timko entered the room as she was told. She saw the foreman with two strange men. "Come in Olya," Andre said. "I want you to meet these men who want to talk to you about a position away from the farm."

After the introductions, Ivan spoke up. "We represent Zherkov Enterprises, a worldwide company with the home office in Moscow, Russia. We place select people for domestic work in very wealthy homes. We have an opening for a governess with a very loving family in London, England. This job is to look after and take care of two young children, a one-year old baby and a three-year old child. A tutor will come every day to help you learn English."

Olya just sat and listened. She had learned to be wary since being on her own as a small child. "I like it here on the farm," she said. "Mr. Krakov and everyone else have been very good to me. I work hard and I am treated kindly. This position that you are offering and the family that I would be working for sounds like something I have dreamed about. I love babies and young children, but I only have your word on this, and I don't know you two gentlemen."

"I don't blame you for being cautious. You are a very smart

woman," Vitali said, Speaking up for the first time. "I have known Andre Krakov for many years, we went to school together. He can vouch for me as an honorable man, and Zherkov enterprises as an honorable company. Mr. Bluvich holds a position high in the company."

"Let me bring up another matter." Ivan said. "I understand that your weekly salary is thirty Hryvnias, plus a place to sleep and meals. After a money exchange, that would equal three Euros. The rate of exchange is ten to one. This position in London pays five hundred Pounds each week and with the exchange that would be five thousand Hryvnia. You will sleep in your own room and have your own bathroom in the luxurious home. You will be provided a passport and the required visas plus airfare to London. You will also be advanced enough money for the things that you need, and when you are settled in, you can reimburse that loan in small amounts as you get your pay each week."

Olya was so overwhelmed with the money, and everything else, that she was speechless. But she was also very skeptical.

"Think it over for a few days, and let Andre have your decision. But don't wait too long. We have to fill that position soon," Bluvich said.

They all got up and said their goodbyes. Olya went back to the fields. Andre walked to the van with them, promising he would stay in touch. Ivan and Vitali headed back to L'viv where more female company and a couple of bottles of vodka awaited them. These females were common prostitutes found anywhere in the world, hardly in the same class of women that Boris Zherkov had Bluvich searching for all over the globe.

CHAPTER

6

Boris Zherkov conducted his illegal enterprises in the same businesslike fashion as some of the most profitable legitimate companies. The difference was the motivation applied: raw fear and brutal beatings, plus the drugs needed to quench the unbearable pain and misery suffered by the hopeless addict, as opposed to positive recognition, monetary bonus and promotion. Zherkov Enterprises, like the more successful companies, had structure and a business plan that included separate divisions, with a strong chain of command in each. Each prospective woman was told she would be living in some glamorous city around the world. In fact, they all would be brought to Zealand, Virginia in the United States to serve Boris Zherkov in their captivity.

Ivan Bluvich reported directly to Boris Zherkov. "I have two pending, one a sixteen-year-old Malaysian girl, the other a twenty-two-year-old Ukrainian woman. They are both beauties, and I know you will be very pleased with them," boasted Ivan on the phone to his boss. "I have a strong feeling that both will accept our "generous offers."

"Well done Ivan. Keep at it and always remember quality over quantity. We don't want to offer our distinguished clientele unexceptional, below par company. Let me know when we can expect these latest two."

***

Zherkov Enterprises certainly did have "distinguished clientele:"

politicians, business leaders, judges, prosecutors, top police officials and so on down the line. Whenever these elite of society wanted female companionship, not just the ordinary prostitute, but someone of exceptional beauty to cater to their whims, their fetishes, their sexual fantasies, they called on Zherkov Enterprises.

"Bring her in here," barked an impatient Boris Zherkov into the phone. He was sitting comfortably in a leather club chair in his private suite within the compound; this very secure compound with a picturesque view of the river where his female "employees" and staff lived. When he had the first face-to-face chat with his most recent female "employee," Zherkov preferred this informal seating area in his spacious suite, not sitting behind his large mahogany desk.

"Come in and have a seat on the couch. My name is Boris Zherkov and I own Zherkov Enterprises, the company where you have been employed for the last month or so." She sat visibly frightened. "I understand you are from English speaking Bermuda which means we can speak with each other without an interpreter, as I speak several languages, including English. I also understand that you know why you are here and what is expected of you."

"Please Mr. Zherkov," pleading a shaken and crying Alice Rawlings. "I can't do what that woman who brought me in here told me I would have to do. Please Mr. Zherkov, I'm begging you please let me go back home"

"That I can't do," he said. "I have too much invested in you. And how could you get there? You don't have any money and I have your passport and visa. If I let you go and somehow you managed to get there, would you go back to that restaurant and wash pots and pans, living in that filthy hovel? And how would you pay for your new heroin habit? No, you will stay here and do as you are told."

***

A month earlier the private jet with Alice Rawlings aboard

landed at a small airport where a car was waiting on the tarmac. She was treated no differently than the dozens of other girls and young women sent to Zherkov Enterprises by Ivan Bluvich. Once in the car she was offered a glass of fruit punch spiked with a heavy tranquilizer drug, which sedated her before they arrived at the compound. While unconscious, the men in the car shot a syringe full of heroin into the artery in Alice Rawlings' arm.

Alice woke up confused and with a painful headache. The last thing she remembered was riding in a car with two men after the plane landed, but now she was lying in a bed in a small room. *What happened,* she thought to herself, *where am I and why am I here?* She struggled to get up and out of the bed, but could not stand without holding on to the bed post. She found it strange that the room did not have a window. After a few minutes she noticed a door that connected to a bathroom, and then a second door. *This other door must be the way out,* but after she wobbled across the room, she found it locked. She knocked on it and called out, but there was no response. Alice Rawlings began to cry.

The routine was the same for all the women brought to the compound: Locked in a room alone, her only contact was one of three different men who brought her meals. The women all asked the same questions concerning their situations. The men ignored the questions and did not respond. All three men came in once a day every day, two to hold her down, while the third inserted the needle into her arm, releasing the heroin.

It took no more than a few weeks to turn a woman into heroin addict. When one had become hopelessly addicted, a woman from Zkerkov's "staff" came to her room. "My name is Olga Aslof and I will help to get you settled in. I can answer your questions. Since you arrived, you have been asking, 'Where am I? What am I doing here? What is going to happen to me?' 'When am I going to move in with that nice family to help with the domestic work'? "Here are the answers: There is no nice family for domestic work. We are now your family, and you will work for us... But you will not be doing domestic work. You will move to another room where the windows will let in plenty of sunshine and the door will not be locked to keep you in. You will be able to walk around the compound whenever you want, meet the other women and girls who are in the same circumstances as you. You will eat your meals in the main dining room with all the others.

When you are needed you will be taken to visit very important clients, and you will entertain them in any way that they desire. And yes, that means sex. Any type of sex. If any of these clients report their dissatisfaction with you, you will be severely punished. You will be stripped naked and beaten with a thick leather belt. If you are reported a second time, in addition to the beating, your drugs will be withheld. And if you think the beatings were painful, you don't know what pain is until you have experienced withdrawal pain from heroin.

Soon you will be taken shopping for a new wardrobe. You will be taken to the beauty shop. We want you to be attractive and appealing to these very important clients. We will supply you with birth control pills, which you will start taking immediately to safeguard our investment in you; we cannot allow you to become pregnant. A doctor will come to the compound every month, and you will be examined for cleanliness to be sure you are disease free. You, and some of the other women and girls here will participate in a tutorial, taught by me. I have been here for a very long time. You will learn the finer points of sex, things that you might not have experienced or even thought of before. You will be schooled in the fine art of Kama Sutra. You will learn how to satisfy any man's sexual appetite. On occasion the client will be a woman so I will also instruct you on the finer points of pleasuring her. You will live very well here, not like from where we rescued you. Shortly you will be taken to meet with the boss Mr. Zherkov who likes to chat with all the new-comers. It will be in your best interests to smile, be friendly. Don't be negative… Now let's get you moved into your new room.

CHAPTER

7

"I was okay with it, but I wondered what went on in her mind when she looked at me across the table," Floyd said to Harry as they settled into the squad room the morning after the dinner with Lisa and Jessica Daniels.

"I spoke with Jessica earlier this morning. She told me that Lisa was glad we got together. She said that meeting you was a good first step enabling her to get over her fear of black men. So I guess we did a good thing." Harry assured Floyd.

"Lincoln, Washington," called Lieutenant McGee from across the room. "Go to 349 Rogers Street in the Sixth Precinct on a domestic homicide. Sergeant Hayes is waiting for you."

***

The detectives arrived at the Rogers Street address. Sergeant Hayes was standing on the front porch. "Thanks for getting here so quickly. But before you go inside let me give you the history behind this homicide. We've answered calls here before, mostly domestic violence. The husband sits around and drinks all weekend. Sundays he watches his favorite football team play. When they lose, he goes into a rage. When his wife says or does something that he doesn't like, he beats the shit out of her. Then she calls 911. We get here to arrest him but we usually have to fight him. The next day in Municipal Court, she refuses to prosecute him and so he's released. The next weekend it's the same all over again. Today was different. Today, after he beat her, he lay down on the couch. She got a baseball bat and beat him so badly that she killed him. Her name is Gertrude Hardee; your victim on the couch is Thomas Hardee. Okay, let's go inside."

"Has anyone advised her of her rights yet Sergeant?" Harry asks before they go in.

"No, she met us at the door and told us what happened. None of my officers questioned her, including me."

The three enter the house, Mrs. Hardee was sitting at the kitchen table. The detectives identify themselves and Floyd sits down and reads her Miranda rights. "You have the right to remain silent" ...He begins. She says she understands and is willing to tell them what had happened.

Mrs. Hardee repeats what she had already told Sergeant Hayes, and adds more. "That sorry bastard husband of mine watches his favorite football team every weekend and starts drinking in the morning. By the time the game's over he's drunk, and if his team didn't win he's so angry, that he takes it out on me. Well today I'd had enough. When he was finished with me he plopped down on the couch in a drunken stupor. I got the baseball bat that he keeps in the bedroom and gave him back what he's done to me for so long. And you know what? Those sorry god-damn wimps on that football team of his don't ever win!"

Harry got on his radio: "Homicide 134 to detective radio 199, start a crime scene unit and the medical examiner to 349 Rogers Street in the Sixth Precinct."

"Detective radio 199, copy that."

The detectives stepped out onto the porch to wait, and have a chat. "Harry, it looks to me on face value that this is a classic case of justifiable homicide," observed Detective Washington, but like they say, we are not the judge or jury.

"I see it the same way Floyd," agreed Harry. "After the crime scene techs get through and the medical examiner gets here and takes charge of the body, we'll take her downtown, turn the bat over to Property, get a written statement and then book her in on a voluntary manslaughter charge with a recommendation of self defense to the DA's office."

***

Detectives Lincoln and Washington had left Gertrude Hardee to be booked. As they were leaving the city jail they received a call to meet Mr. Alan Traken at 3301 Forrest Road, Apartment 2B, in the 2nd Precinct. When they arrived, they met with a distraught Mr. Traken. "She hasn't come home yet, and she's not been seen or heard from since yesterday."

"Who is she, and how do you know that she hasn't spent the night last night with one of her girlfriends?" Harry asked, attempting to calm him down.

"She is my girlfriend. Her name is Shirley Duncan. Her friends had a birthday party for her at her favorite restaurant last night. She didn't show up and all of her girlfriends were there. She never showed up! I checked with all the area hospitals to see if she was there. I checked with the police department to see if they might know something."

"Mr. Traken," Detective Washington offered, "there are dozens of reasons for her not to come home for one night, or to miss the party, most of which would not suggest foul play."

"But, that's not like her. All her friends agree that she wouldn't just disappear without a word to anyone. This is her apartment; I have a key because I occasionally come over to spend the night."

Harry and Floyd inspected the apartment, looking in the closets and dresser draws and finding everything clean and neat. In the bathroom were her personal things, including birth control pills, toothbrush and other toiletries. The usual range of cosmetics on the vanity, plus a full set of luggage was in a closet. They found nothing to suggest that Shirley Duncan had packed up and left for any length of time.

"Where does she work? What does she do?" Harry asked, thinking that there might be something to this and that they better get on it right away. Floyd had the same thought and was glad to hear that Harry was moving in that direction.

"She is a pharmaceutical's rep; she calls on doctors in the metro area and beyond."

"Do you know what doctors she was supposed to call on yesterday?" Harry asked.

"No, but in the second bedroom that she uses as an office, that large calendar on the wall is her schedule each day for the month."

When they looked at the calendar it showed the names and address of six doctors scheduled for yesterday. "Mr. Traken, when an adult is missing, we usually wait forty-eight hours before starting an investigation. But due to the circumstances in this case, we'll look into it right away." Harry assured Alan Traken.

"One more question before we leave you." Floyd asked, his note pad still open in his hand. "Does she have any mental issues such as: bi-polar or maybe schizophrenic paranoia, anything like that?"

"Shirley Duncan has no such issues, mental or physical. She is healthier all around than most people that I've ever known. She wouldn't just disappear without a word to me or anyone else; I feel like something bad has happened to her." Alan Traken said as he began to sob.

The detectives left, both thinking that he might be right.

CHAPTER

8

After being home for less than a week, Ivan Bluvich received a call from Rui de Silva, Zherkov's man in Brazil. "Ivan, come to Brazil and you won't be sorry that you did. I can't offer you Sao Paulo, or Rio, but you'll be glad you made the trek to the northeast city of Caruaru. When you see this very pretty buxom young woman, you'll agree she is a strong candidate for Zherkov Enterprises, and will surely please Mr. Zherkov.

***

Three days later Ivan Bluvich de-planed the Varig 767. de Silva was waiting for him next to a black Mercedes on the tarmac. Leaving the airport, they drove the twenty-odd miles directly to the fruit packing plant where Maria dos Santos stood at her station packing fruit, along with dozens of other men, women and children. Maria started there at the age of eight. Now ten years later her three younger siblings, mother and father, toiled there with her for twelve hours each day. Their pay was based on volume, and none of them made more than six Brazilian Real (three U.S. dollars) per day.

Bluvich and de Silva followed as the dos Santos family walked home after work. They lived near the outskirts of the city in a wretched hovel amongst hundreds of similar structures, each barely standing in a combination of dirt, mud, garbage and raw sewage. They knocked on the only door, introduced themselves, and spent an hour explaining the opportunity that awaited Maria in Lisbon, Portugal as a governess for the children of an upper middle class family. "You will live in a large modern house and have your own bedroom with a private bathroom."

Maria tried to imagine it, but she had never known indoor plumbing with hot and cold running water.

"We will return here tomorrow for your decision." Rui de Silva continued in their native Portuguese. "And, remember, this is a once in a lifetime chance for Maria to get out and have a better life. She will be able to send home more money than you have seen at once as a family."

***

When they reached the downtown hotel, Bluvich received a message from Boris Zherkov. As soon as business was concluded in Brazil, he was to proceed to Senegal and meet with Mustapha Gadio, the local contact for Western Africa. Ivan and Rui ate dinner at the hotel restaurant and discussed Maria dos Santos. The two were all but certain they had her. They would meet with Maria the following morning at work for her answer. But, tonight Ivan was in need of some relaxation. de Silva arranged for two women to visit Ivan in his room for his favorite sexual treat; a ménage a trio.

The next morning, Maria dos Santos became the newest addition to the Zherkov Enterprise's stable. Ivan Bluvich boarded a plane alone for the long flight to the west coast of Africa. As the plane leveled off at thirty-five thousand feet, Ivan ate and enjoyed a special meal and complimentary wine served to passengers in exclusive first class accommodations. He congratulated himself on the successful outcomes of the last three candidates. Boris Zherkov would be pleased.

CHAPTER

9

"She made her first three appointments in the morning," Floyd said, reading from his notebook. "She never showed for the next one after lunch, so if there was some kind of foul play, it would have been between numbers three and four on the list."

"And because both doctor's offices are in the same medical building, we'll start there," replied Harry, thinking out loud. "I guess she would have parked somewhere in the attached multi-level garage."

Alan Traker was contacted to see if he had heard from Shirley. He had not. "Mr. Traker, what is the make, model, year and color of her car? Do you know the tag number?" Locating Shirley Duncan's car would be the first step. Traker was able to provide the vehicle information.

The parking decks were searched… Her car was not found.

A statewide lookout was broadcast over all ZPD channels, all Metro PD's, Sheriff's Offices and the State Police. *"Be on the lookout for a white 2005 Toyota Camry 4DR bearing Virginia license plate 1-13766. This car is wanted in connection with the disappearance of Shirley Duncan, WF26, 5'3"120lbs, brown hair, brown eyes. Any info, notify Detectives Lincoln/Washington, ZPD Homicide.*

"Lieu, because of everything we've been able to learn about this missing woman, it was our judgment the forty-eight-hour SOP should be suspended." Harry explained during the initial briefing in Lieutenant McGee's office. "We leaned on the boyfriend, Alan Traker heavily. Both Floyd and I feel that he's on the level. His movements and alibis checked out for the twenty-four-hour period previous to her disappearance. We've interviewed many of her friends and, in the course of the routine canvas, spoken to neighbors and acquaintances. The doctors and their staffs could not add much, except that those in the office of doctor number three on the list of appointments were the last to see her, as far as we know right now."

"Harry," Floyd said as they secured their equipment and the case file for the day. "Tomorrow let's spend some time in the parking decks talking to folks as they come and go. Maybe we'll get lucky."

***

On his way home at the end of the watch, Harry made two stops. The first was to see Ham, his long time and very dependable CI (confidential informant). The other was to meet Mule, a secretive CI whose relationship with Harry was known to no one. Their street level networks had proven invaluable in clearing cases to which Harry Lincoln was assigned. There would be many more pairs of eyes looking for Shirley Duncan's car.

He made a third. "Hi Jessica, I'm on the way home. If you're not busy this evening, would you like to come over and share a pizza with me?"

"I'm not busy and I'd love to. Shall I pick one up on the way?"

"No Jess, I'll order one to be delivered, I know how you like yours."

"Okay, I'll leave in about five minutes and should get there about the same time as the pizza."

Jessica Daniels was one of the people Harry Lincoln invited over to the loft. It was his private place that only a select few had visited. Harry and Jessica were hungry and almost finished the large pizza. With two slices of pizza left and most of the Chianti gone, Jessica suggested they relax in the warm water of Harry's Jacuzzi.

It was relaxing and exciting at the same time. They faced each other as they reclined on opposite ends of the tub. Harry was mesmerized by the dark shadow-like triangle shimmering beneath the surface of the clear water, distracted only by two perfect hard nipples bobbing out of the water. Jessica also observant gave him a knowing look and said in a sultry whisper, "periscope up."

Now dried off and snuggling in Harry's bed, happy to be kissing and caressing ending up in some awkward contortions. They were in no hurry. After exploring every inch of each other, they connected with the passion that had been building all evening, with him driving deep, her stretching and reaching up, which led to a simultaneous climax so intense, it would be difficult to duplicate for the rest of the evening.

Driving home later in the wee hours, Jessica thought. *Of the good men I've known throughout the years Harry Lincoln rates at the top of the charts. But, there will come a day because of his noble logic when I'll have to give him up.*

Harry stayed in bed and eased into a satisfied sleep with the taste of her tender good night kiss still on his lips.

CHAPTER

10

As the plane made its final approach, Ivan Bluvich looked down at the blue/green water of the Atlantic Ocean. The Dakar airport started at the water's edge, the western most point in Africa, in the lush country of Senegal. "It's been too long since I've seen you Ivan," boomed a giant of a man in French, as he gave his visitor a welcoming hug. Mustapha Gadio, at nearly seven feet tall almost always had a smile on his face.

"You must have found something outstanding my friend, Boris Zherkov himself ordered me here."

"I most certainly have, but it can wait until tomorrow. Tonight allow me to show some hospitality, Senegalese style," the big man said, his white teeth gleaming.

After checking into the Imperial Hotel in downtown Dakar, one with an unmistakable European touch, they ate an expertly prepared exotic seafood dinner, some of the best tasting creatures, some Ivan had never heard. After complimenting the chef for the excellent meal, they drove an hour to the tiny, African village of Rafique. With the ritual of meeting with the village elders completed, Mustapha led him to a barnlike structure. Once inside, Ivan saw mats, cushions and blankets set in a circle around an open space. Of the several hundred villagers, only about fifty were admitted.

A small choral group gathered in center and began to sing the music of Senegal as only Africans can. The deep base, rich baritone and melodic tenor blended in harmony. Ivan Bluvich knew he was in Africa. The singing ended, the dancing began, the male dancers dressed only in loin clothes, the women topless. Ivan intently listened to and watched the entire performance. When it ended he stood and applauded as loudly as if it been the Bolshoi Ballet in Moscow. Mustapha beamed with pride.

"Now my friend, if you will come with me I'll show you to your hut where you will spend the night, and tomorrow you will meet the most beautiful woman in all of Senegal, maybe on the whole of Africa. In the meantime, the two women in your hut will ensure that your night is comfortable and pleasurable."

The next morning, he and his two new intimate friends shared a refreshing shower. Mustapha came by and brought him to the larger building, where they ate breakfast, before driving back to Dakar.

"Her name is Awa Senghor. She's twenty-eight years old, and right now she's out of work. The fish processing plant where she worked for the past five years has shut down." Mustapha told Ivan. "There's not much work here for a woman her age. She was lucky to have that job making the equivalent of thirty-seven U.S. cents per hour. Like most families in Senegal they all live under one roof. Too many children and all those mouths have to be fed. Awa has six siblings and is next to the oldest. Her older sister is married with three children and a husband, all five also live there. The house, as you can imagine is over- crowded to the breaking point. It's not much. All but the youngest children must work to get by. But, when you see her my friend... Well you will see... They are expecting us."

A pre-school young girl opened the door, letting the two men enter. There were several other children in the large room just inside the front door. Only one adult was in the room, and she said that she was Awa's older sister. All the others were out working.

Awa entered the room from a different part of the house. To Ivan, she looked like a picture out of a high fashion magazine, better he thought, because her bones were not protruding against her smooth rich ebony skin. Her hair was cut close to her head.

She was tall and slender with just enough flesh on her frame to feel comfortable to someone holding her in a loving embrace. She looked like a magnificent sculptured statue without the sharp angles. Rembrandt could have painted her face. Awa Senghor defined beautiful.

Introductions were made, and although the official language in Senegal was Serer, most of its people spoke French. Ivan's French was not fluent but passable enough to converse. Ivan then recited the scripted lies about the company before saying, "We would like to place you in a top modeling agency in New York City in the United States. The pay for top models is very high. You could make enough money in a short time to buy your family a nice big house in a better section of Dakar, and to send enough home that your family will no longer have to work."

"Mr. Bluvich," Awa said, "that all seems like a dream, but how do I know what you tell me is true? And, if it is, how would I get to America? I have no money and I don't even have a passport."

"You've known Mustapha since you started working. He and I have known each other for several years, and he will vouch for me. This is your opportunity for you and your family to no longer live in poverty." Ivan placed a business card in her hand. "You can call the home office and speak with the owner, Mr. Zherkov himself at this number. We will get your passport and any visas you may need. And we will advance you enough money for travel and to live on until you start getting paid. You can then pay us back a little each month. Speak it over with your family tonight, and give me your answer in the next couple of days. Here is my card; I will be at the Imperial Hotel."

CHAPTER

11

It had happened so suddenly she wasn't quite sure what happened. Shirley Duncan was confused and very frightened. It slowly began to come back: *"I'd left my last appointment for the morning and was going to get some lunch. As I was getting into my car this man pushed me in and got in beside me. He told me not to make a sound and if we saw anyone not to make any motions. He showed me this big knife and said if I did, he would stab me in my chest. I must have fainted for just a minute or two, because we were still in the garage and he was asking me about ATM's."*

Thirty-eight-year-old Eddie Banks was a predator, always looking for the easy score. Stealing cars was his thing. He drifted from place to place, stealing instead of working. His luck ran out twelve years' prior in Ft. Lauderdale Florida, when he boosted a car and a woman with it. Eddie Banks was caught and sentenced by a Florida jury to thirty years for kidnapping, rape and auto theft. But, street-smart Eddie had been around and knew how to work the system. He attended classes, received his GED (high school equivalence diploma) and stayed out of trouble. Eddie Banks conned the Florida Parole Board into releasing him after serving eleven of his thirty-year sentence. The conditions of his release were: find a job, report to his parole officer once a week and not leave the state.

***

Eddie Banks was casing the parking decks, looking for a car to steal, when he spotted Shirley Duncan getting into her white Toyota. He forced his way in behind her and rendered her mute with stark terror. He went through her purse and found her wallet. Sixty-three dollars in cash and several bank cards, "Which one of these cards works in the ATM machine?"

Frozen with fear she pointed a shaky finger as he drove out of the garage. Stopping at the first ATM he saw, he asked for her PIN number and how much the machine would give.

"The most you can withdraw is two hundred dollars. But if you stop at another one you might get another two hundred. You can have the money, my car and anything else! Please don't hurt me! Please!"

"This key that was hidden in the back pocket of your wallet, the one with the number on it. What's it to?" Shirley Duncan began to cry. "It's my safe deposit box in the First National Bank downtown. You can have it all, just please don't hurt me, I'm begging you."

***

Two days later, from mid-morning to mid-afternoon the detectives questioned people as they pulled in to park, and those as they left. "Did you happen to notice a young woman driving a white Toyota here in the garage two days ago? If you did, did you notice anything unusual about her or the car that might have caught your attention?" All the responses were negative.

When they spoke with the garage cashier she said, "I see that car with that girl in here all the time. We always say 'hi' to each other when she's leaving. The other day, the day you are asking about, there was a man driving. She was over in the other seat. She didn't say anything. She had this strange look on her face. And she was shaking, like she was cold or scared."

"Can you describe this man?" Floyd asked.

"He was white, maybe late thirties, early forties."

"Was he wearing glasses, and how about facial hair?"

"No glasses, but he looked like he hadn't shaved for two, three days. I did notice he had some kind of tattoo on the side of his neck, but I couldn't make out what it was because his shirt collar covered most of it."

"Can you think of anything else?"

"No, he just paid the ticket and drove out without a word."

"You've been very helpful, thank you very much." Floyd said as he wrote her name and contact information in his note pad.

"What's this all about," she asked. "Did something happen to her?"

"We're not sure; she's been missing for two days now. Here's our cards if you think of anything else call us day or night."

***

Harry dialed his cell phone "Mr. Traker, this is Detective Lincoln. Did Shirley use ATM's? In which bank was her account?"

"Detective Lincoln, Shirley used The First National Bank for it all: checking, savings, credit and debit cards. She even has a safe deposit box. When her mother passed away she left Shirley quite a bit of expensive jewelry. I advised her to rent a box to keep it safe."

At The First National Bank Harry and Floyd identified themselves to Mr. Wardling, the Bank Manager. "Mr. Wardling," began Floyd. "We have reason to believe that one of your customers, Shirley Duncan, has been abducted. The abductor might have used her card to withdraw cash from your ATM. If so, we'd like to see if his photo was recorded in the withdrawal."

"Certainly detectives, I'll send for copies of those transactions right away. It should only take a few minutes. While we wait, can I get you gentlemen some water, coffee or a soft drink?" They both declined.

"That's Eddie Banks!" Floyd exclaimed, louder then he intended, when the photos came in. "I caught up with him and turned him over to Ft. Lauderdale where he was wanted for several felonies. He's a petty thief and car booster who operated all over South Florida. He went big time when he car-jacked a woman, took her to the woods and raped her. He received a long prison sentence; I'm surprised he's out."

"Mr. Wardling, you've been a great help as you can see" Harry said. "We need your help again. Ms. Shirley Duncan uses The First National Bank for all her banking: credit and debit cards, checking and savings. Please text either of us if and when you hear of any activity on her accounts. These are our numbers to use any time of the day or night. And, one other thing, she has a safe deposit box here. Should anyone come in and ask for access to the box, call 911 immediately telling the operator who and where you are. We will notify the emergency operators to be aware of your call, and to dispatch cars right away."

CHAPTER

12

She is going to a better place, where she will be waiting for you to join her someday…

Those words kept ringing in his ears. *I thought about it, and thought about it. I've always heard about cops 'eating their guns' for one reason or another. I had the best reason, but if I did it, would I really be with her again? Maybe I would, nobody knows. Maybe those words were just meant to comfort me. Being alone is not good, so Floyd Washington, start meeting people make some friends. I feel the best when I'm with Harry, he's a good partner and would be a good friend.*

Floyd Washington was still grieving, but kept it hidden when around other people. The hours he spent in his apartment alone were the hardest. The hole in his heart belonged to Lena after she left him, it hurt so much. What saved him from doing something irrational was spending so much time with Harry Lincoln, working on this missing woman; he felt so much like his old self again, anytime he was with Harry.

***

"Hi Harry, its Floyd," he said into the phone, "I hope I'm not disturbing you if you've got company."

"Not at all Floyd, I'm just relaxing and catching up on some reading. What's up?"

I just thought if you weren't busy maybe I could meet you at Mike's Tavern for a couple of cold ones?"

"That sounds great; I've been sitting on my ass since I got home. How about thirty minutes?"

"Copy that."

***

Making their way to a table Harry waved to a couple of off-duty firefighters. They had no sooner sat down, each ordering a beer, when two men came over and sat down. "Well Lincoln, we heard you had a new partner, some hot shot from Miami."

"Detective Floyd Washington, let me introduce you to two of our finest. This is Captain Edward Boling and Lieutenant Bryan Wadsworth."

"We've been waiting for someone to come along to show up Lincoln, knock him down a peg or two" Captain Boling quipped. And, wouldn't you know it would be Washington"

Lieutenant Wadsworth added, "With the combo of Lincoln and Washington, the bad guys in this town don't have a chance."

"Captain, Lieutenant I'm glad and honored to meet you both. And, from what I've heard about Detective Harry Lincoln, I'm hardly that guy."

"All kidding aside, we've heard about you and we're damn glad to have you here," Captain Boling said shaking Floyd's hand. "So, welcome and if we can do anything to assist you just holler"

After the two left Floyd told Harry that he'd gotten that kind of reception from everyone since he'd arrived. "If all the bosses are like that, this will be a dream job."

"Just remember, when you have a reputation, they'll expect performance and results 'above and beyond' from you."

They both ordered and started to eat.

"Harry, let me change gears for a minute. We both live alone, but I don't seem to handle it well. Maybe it's because I've lost my wife recently. Maybe it's being in a strange city, and a new job. When I'm off duty and I'm in my apartment by myself, I get to thinking about her and how much I miss her. I get melancholy and depressed, then start feeling sorry for myself. That causes me to have crazy thoughts. The reason I'm telling you this is that you also live alone and have tragically lost your dad with whom you were very close. You seem to be a stable and contented guy. What's your secret?"

"No secret Floyd," Harry replied gently. "Unlike you I've lived in this town all my life, although I know many people here, I'm kind of a loner. I don't socialize much, although I've had different girlfriends through the years. I don't let them in too close. I discourage domestic talk. I'm married to my job and want to keep it that way. That doesn't mean I don't like women, but I don't jump into bed with any pretty woman with great tits and a terrific ass. What I mean is I like being with her after the sex is over, have intelligent conversations, and I truly have to like her. But, to be fair I always let them know at the beginning that there is no future with me. When I get home after whatever watch I'm working I bring something in to eat, and sometime I cook a little something. Sometimes my current girlfriend will cook a meal at my loft or at her place. When I'm home alone I enjoy the solitude. I relax listening to classical music while reading a book. I watch very little TV."

"My likes are about the same as yours Harry, I like classical music, and I always have a book or two that I'm reading. I'll make some friends in time, but I'm not looking for a woman. It's just too soon; I'd feel like I was unfaithful. I'll probably feel better when I find a nice townhouse and get out of that apartment."

"You'll be okay Floyd. I've found the best medicine is time; it helped me bounce back from my tragedy. Speaking of time, it kind of slipped up on us. Let's get out of here. See you in the morning partner.

Let's find Shirley Duncan."

CHAPTER

13

They were not held by heavy chains in cages or electric fences topped with razor wire, not even sub-terrain and windowless stone cells. Escape was possible from those kinds of prisons. There was no escape for these girls and women, for just the threat of missing the next administered dose of the drug would make them anxious. They had been shown the consequences of not getting the drug for an extended period. They became physically ill and the longer it went, the sicker they got. Then the pain started and increased with each missed dose. They had to have the drug; they would beg, and as the pain got unbearable, they would start screaming to make it stop. At this point they would scream and beg, hitting their heads against the wall managing feeble promises to do anything for a man, or woman, to please him and make him happy; if only they could have the liquid gold.

The large compound, where all the women were housed was surrounded by a wall with a gated entry point guarded by Zherkov personnel to keep out the curious. It was equipped with the amenities of a country club: tennis and volley ball courts, an indoor swimming pool with a fitness center, and a spacious lounging area. It was listed at City Hall as a non-profit facility for displaced foreign women and girls run by a Russian philanthropist. Of the five Zherkov enterprises offices around the globe, Boris Zherkov chose the United States as the best location for the compound. There were less official eyes and questions. His office was several miles from it, high up in a downtown office building.

There was hardly a prison more secure, as were these iron bars a derivative of the poppy seed, with escape barely contemplated. There were punishments for unsatisfactory performance. The women were delivered to their "assignments" by two of Zherkov's men. When the women were returned to the compound, the men asked the client if his expectations were met. Once a dissatisfied state senator said the woman didn't have anything to say, and moved with no more emotion than a robot. She failed to give anything, especially not what one would expect from a Zherkov girl who was set apart from the ordinary high-class call girl.

Boris Zherkov himself made an example of her with the rest watching. The women were brought into a very large gymnasium where this unfortunate woman was lying spread eagled on her stomach over a large barrel like object, her wrists and ankles tied to metal loops on the floor. She was naked, begging for him not to beat her. Zherkov walked over to her holding a heavy leather belt. "This very important client was not pleased. He said he might as well have gone home to his wife. He said this Zherkov girl was worse. This will not happen again from any of you, and if it does this is what you can expect." With that he began to beat her. He lashed her very hard with the belt, and kept lashing her despite her loud screaming and begging. He stopped when she passed out. The only sound to be heard in the room was Zherkov's heavy breathing.

Leaving the gymnasium, going to an adjacent office, Boris, the sweat glistening on his face, sat with Victor and Olga. "I needed one of them to make an example of while all the others looked on." Boris told them, his breathing not quite back to normal. "Olga, when she's able to function again and fully recovered we'll keep her here to service the staff and keep them satisfied. She can no longer be sent to any client because of the scars from the beating that will always show on her back all the way down to the backs of her legs. You have a talk with her. Tell her that if she does not perform for our staff, she will not get her daily dose and pain will be her life. And for the rest of them we can't allow this to happen again. Remember that our business depends on word of mouth. Our reputation must be protected."

CHAPTER

14

"Homicide, Washington," Floyd said answering the phone with the blinking button. He no longer felt awkward in the noisy squad room, more and more, he felt like he belonged. He was treated with respect by the other detectives in the squad; the word was out about his record in Miami. "What makes you think it was a body?" Floyd asked the caller.

"From the way it was wrapped up in something, and the way he was carrying it?

What kind of car was it? Did you see the tag number? What's the name of this road and where is it located? Okay we'll find it; my partner and I will come out and check on it. Can I have your name sir? Thanks I've got it. You're going to wait there for us? We would appreciate that very much. We're leaving from downtown it should take us about twenty minutes based on the traffic. We'll see you out there, thanks for calling."

Floyd repeated the information to Harry and a few of the others who were within earshot, including Lieutenant McGee. "That caller said he saw a man take what he thought was a body out of the trunk of a car and carry it into the woods. He said it was a white Toyota, but he didn't see the tag. He said it was a two lane back road. Windy Mountain Road, almost out of the city"

"Yes, I know Windy Mountain Road and it is a back road, not much traffic. If he's going to wait for us we'd better go and see what's what," answered Harry, gathering his equipment. The lieutenant gave a nod as they went out the door.

***

There was nothing on either side but dense woods as Harry and Floyd cruised slowly along Windy Mountain Road. At the approximate location, they saw a pickup truck parked on the shoulder. Harry pulled up behind it. They both got out. A man got out of the truck, walked back to them and introduced himself as Albert Reese, the same name he gave to Floyd over the phone.

"I leave early for work to beat the heavy traffic and use this out- of- the- way road to skirt around one of the freeway bottle-necks. It was dark this morning when I saw this white car, I think it was a Toyota parked somewhere along here. I saw a man take what I think was a body out of the trunk and carry it into the woods."

"Did you actually see a body? Can you describe the man?" Floyd asked.

"No, I never saw a body, it was all wrapped up in something, and the way he was carrying it made me think it was a body. Maybe I'm watching too much TV. But, like I said, it was dark and as I drove by slowly I just got a glimpse of him. I think he was a white guy, and I wouldn't know him if I saw him again. I've got to get to work now. I've called my boss and told him I'd be a little late, but I've got to go."

"Mr. Reese you've been a big help, and we appreciate it very much." Floyd told him. "Now if I can get your address and phone number, should we need to contact you, and we'll enter your name along with the information into our report. Here's our cards with our numbers should there be anything else you might think of, call either of us day or night."

Albert Reese gave them his contact information and then left.

"Well partner," said Harry. "Let's have a look."

***

They trampled around in the thick underbrush for almost an hour with no sign of anyone being there nor anything being disturbed. Hardly dressed for the terrain, they each had some cosmetic damage to their dress shoes and noticed small threads pulled from their suit pants. "We gave it a pretty good cursory look," Harry said, once they were back on the road, brushing leaves and briers from their suits. "We'll need some more help; I'll call McGee to see if he can get some recruits out here from the academy. Mr. Reese saw the man carrying whatever it was into the woods on the right side of the road. What if after Reese left, the guy changed his mind, and decided to cross over to the other side of the road?"

***

An hour later Harry flagged down the police academy bus at their location as the motorcycle units that Floyd had requested detoured traffic from each approach on Windy Mountain Road. Two academy classes of thirty each, totaling sixty police recruits were gathered in a formation on the road, accompanied by their instructors. Harry approached them and began his briefing.

"I am Detective Harry Lincoln and this is my partner Detective Floyd Washington. We are investigating a kidnapping and possible homicide. You will be looking for the body of a female." Harry began his instructions. "She may be lying on the ground, or she might be buried. If you see freshly dug dirt, it could be her. As you can see the road is heavily wooded on both sides. You will be divided into squads with an instructor in charge of each squad. Your instructors will place you on each side of the road. Once you are in position you are to stay no more than six feet from those on either side as you walk slowly. If you see anything that does not grow out of the ground, stop. Do not touch it, do not pick it up, do not step on it or walk through it. Call your instructor over. And he or she will notify one of us. Your starting point will be that motorcycle officer down there. You'll stop at the second motorcycle officer up at the other end." Floyd then briefed the instructors on where and how to deploy their people.

After the first twenty-five minutes an excited voice from the thick underbrush shouted, "I've found something, I've found something!" Harry and Floyd followed the shouting, the relentless brambles ruining two suits until they came upon six or eight members of the search party standing in a circle. In the center was a length of fresh dirt with the back of a woman's shoe sticking out from it.

Harry ordered everyone to step back about twenty feet, and had the instructors to add more recruits to form a circle around the shoe. Harry carefully used the tip of his finger to brush back enough dirt to see a foot inside the shoe. "Floyd, get a crime scene unit out here and put in a call for the medical examiner. I'll call Lieutenant McGee to brief him." He then addressed the Academy personnel, "No one is to enter your circle without first clearing it with Detective Washington or me."

***

The crime scene techs arrived first, Lieutenant McGee a few minutes behind them. Harry spoke with the sergeant in charge of the Academy detail. "Sergeant Hammond, have your people to stand down now and load them back onto the bus for the trip back. We'll keep that recruit with us, the one who found the body until we return to the office, so he can make his written statement. We'll see that he gets back to the Academy"

When the recruits were all seated, Harry and Floyd boarded the bus and stood up front. "Detective Washington and I want to thank all of you for helping us find the victim. Without the cooperation like you gave today, this case might not be cleared. One day some of you may be standing up here like we are; then you'll understand."

CHAPTER

15

Boris Zherkov had it all: Money, power and his pick of some of the most desirable women in the world. Power was his aphrodisiac. As each new fledgling was brought before him; their indoctrination complete, the unmerciful heroin addiction sealed, he would personally inspect her. "Drop the robe and turn around very slowly." Naked, she did as she was told; she had seen some of the punishment for disobeying. Boris Zherkov the businessman had to be assured that his commodities maintained their high standards.

When Boris felt the need of feminine pleasure and comfort, he chose one from his "stable." On occasion he would summon Olga and instruct her to prepare one of his beauties for an evening of sex to please him. He rarely, if ever became emotionally involved with or attached to any of the women under his control.

There was an exception. Awa Senghor! What was it about this twenty-eight-year-old Senegalese woman? She was the latest to have her initial interview with Zherkov and to be inspected by him. Was it the ebony color of her skin? The beauty of her face? Or maybe her exquisite female form? But, he was surrounded by so many attractive and appealing women. After giving it a lot of thought he realized what made her stand out from the others: She possessed a stately, regal air. As far as Boris Zherkov was concerned; Awa Senghor was royalty.

"Olga, this African woman Awa Senghor is to be given special treatment. Move her into the best room in the compound. Take her to the spa to have her pampered, from a full facial to a complete body massage, a manicure and pedicure. Then go shopping and get her a complete wardrobe of western-style clothing with straight skirts two to four inches above the knee. And most important of all, get her some very sexy lingerie. I will make my car and driver available to you. You will not let her out of your sight. Another thing, don't send her on any assignments, unless I tell you otherwise."

***

Boris answered his private line. Few people had it, few very important people. "Boris, this is Ed Knowles, is this line secure? Can I speak freely?"

"Yes, of course, but I understand the Chairman of the Public Safety Committee using caution. What can I do for you?"

"Several months ago you sent a woman to make me happy. She certainly did. I'm calling on you again, but this time my request is somewhat different. This time my wife wants to be included along with me. We are not your ordinary married couple, and be that as it may, our request is rather unusual, but I don't want to go into it over the phone."

"I will send my personal assistant Olga Aslof to meet with you and your wife. You may speak freely to her, as I am the only one who will know of your conversation. She prepares the women for their responsibilities. Explain your desires to her, and your wife's. We will see to it that they are carried out implicitly.

***

The next morning Olga reported back to Boris with a bizarre, although not unexpected request. Knowles and his wife would require a young, somewhat inexperienced teenage girl, and a very experienced woman. They were to engage in four-way sex. The client and the more mature woman would be engaging in more traditional sex, but she would please him in two ways. The young girl would be tenderly placed by the wife in just the right place and position and then coaxed into giving pleasure.

Olga chose the young girl from the South Pacific Island of Fiji and the woman from Portugal. Olga told them exactly what was expected of them. Boris threatened that if they did not do exactly as they were told, that if the client wasn't completely satisfied, that very painful punishment awaited them. He said to the selected women. "But, in the meantime, just before you both leave the compound for your assignments; I'll have Olga give each of you a jolt of our liquid gold to put you in the mood, and to keep you mellow."

***

The following day the restricted number was dialed again. "Boris, it's Ed. You've come through again. I've not seen my wife this happy in years. As for me, you've made a friend. Please let me know if there is any way I can be of service to you."

"Thank you for calling. It's always good to hear from a satisfied client. I'll be sure to pass on your kind words."

CHAPTER

16

She lay on her stomach under four inches of dirt and leaves. Her clothing was in disarray. Shirley Duncan was left hastily in a shallow grave, void of any dignity. When the medical examiner carefully turned her over, Shirley's eyes were open looking at those around her. Her open mouth was stuffed with cloth.

Later at the morgue, the cloth removed from Shirley's mouth was determined to be her panties. They were packed so far down her throat; the airway was clogged causing her death to be from suffocation. The autopsy also revealed that Shirley Duncan had been beaten and raped.

***

"Homicide, Zaklinski," answered the familiar voice over the phone.

"Hello Zak, this is Floyd. How's everything in the land of palm trees?"

"Well how the hell are you? Don't tell me you want to come back and you're calling me to put in a good word for you?"

"No, nothing like that, this is strictly business. Actually I'm pretty happy here, everyone is treating me well and I have a great partner.

"Floyd, I'm almost afraid to ask… what kind of business?"

"Eddie Banks!"

"Unbelievable huh Floyd? We heard those geniuses on the parole board let him out. What has Eddie gone and done now?"

"Zak, we believe he's responsible for a kidnapping, rape and homicide here. The victim's car is missing, and you know how Eddie likes cars. Anyway, we've entered all the details on NCIC. I thought I'd give you a heads-up in case he returned to his old stomping grounds."

"Okay Floyd, I'll nose around and let you know if I get a nibble."

"Thanks Zak. Take a break from the heat and humidity sometime and come visit us. See how the other half lives. So long pal, it was good talking to you."

***

Harry and Floyd spent any free time, while on duty, looking for Shirley Duncan's white 2005 Toyota, license plate Virginia 1-13766. They rode the main surface streets, side streets, back alleys, multi-story parking decks and open ground level parking lots. They looked odd hours, day and night whenever they could. In addition to entering Eddie Banks and the car with the tag number, into the National Crime Information Center, they distributed all the relevant information to the news media.

***

"What's the matter Harry?" Jessica asked a silent and morose Harry Lincoln, who for the last fifteen minutes had just sat and stared into the fireplace. They had been out to dinner, a quiet dinner where her attempts to make conversation were met with short answers and low grunts. On the drive back to the loft she no longer tried. She went straight into the kitchen to brew some coffee. He went into the living room without a word. In a short time, she carried a tray with two mugs of steaming coffee and some pastries. "Please tell me what's been troubling you all evening. Please Harry don't shut me out, talk to me."

"The medical examiner gently turned her over and she lay

there in the dirt, looking at me as if to say, 'Look at what he did to me, don't let him get away with it. Get him detective and make him pay.' Jess, that look, her eyes, her pleading eyes have burned into my soul."

"He won't get away with it Harry, I just know he won't. How many times have you cleared your cases when you didn't know who the bad guy was? This time you know who he is, and Floyd has even arrested him before. Yes, Harry, you and Floyd will get him; he won't get away with what he did to that poor woman. What you need now more than anything is a good night's sleep. Come to bed Harry and let me hold you and rub your back until you fall into a nice restful sleep."

CHAPTER 17

It was a virtual Tower of Babel; this restrictive compound where attractive women and girls were jolted into frightful reality. When they were finally told where they were, and what would be expected of them, most didn't quite understand because of the language barrier. English, Spanish, French and Russian were the predominant languages spoken. Those who could not comprehend had to do the best with gestures. What made communication manageable were the few staff people who could translate in several different languages.

Olga Aslof confided in Awa Senghor while out shopping with her. "All the women get a few new outfits, some lingerie and a makeover at the beauty shop. But, nothing like his instructions concerning you. Mr. Zherkov must be saving you for his exclusive use and that hasn't happened before." Awa looked at her but said nothing. "Although," continued Olga, "I don't know what kind of lover Mr. Zherkov is, you might be better off than the others. They must go to anyone, even if they are filthy pigs. Sometimes the client is a woman. They must satisfy whoever they are sent to, or be punished."

Later that evening Olga came to Awa's room. "I'm to bring you to Mr. Zherkov's private suite where you will have dinner with him alone. You are to bathe and then dress in one of your new outfits with the jewelry we selected today, and especially your new lingerie. He wants to see you dressed in western-style clothes. I will help you get ready as I'm sure these clothes are different from the clothing of Senegal."

***

Olga knocked softly on the door. Zherkov answered to come in. As the two women entered, Awa was silently awed by the richness and splendor of the suite. "Olga, give us about thirty minutes and then let the staff serve dinner." Awa was still standing in the foyer as Olga left. "Come in Awa. Have a seat on the couch by the fire," Zherkov managed to say in halting French, with enough confidence that she understood him. "Yes, Mr. Zherkov," immediately doing as she was told.

"Awa, when we are alone here in the suite, just the two of us, I want you to call me Boris. Any other time you are to address me as Mr. Zherkov." He went to the well stocked bar and returned with a bottle of wine and two glasses. "This is a mild French wine; have some it will relax you before dinner."

"I've never had wine before," Awa said, "but I'll need something other than wine to relax me, Mr… pardon, Boris."

"Drink the wine first Awa. The liquid gold will be dessert so you will be very relaxed and extremely mellow."

Dinner was brought in by the kitchen staff and served in the private dining room within the suite. After coffee and sweets were served, they were alone. Boris felt free now to tell her what was on his mind.

***

"Awa, you've been here long enough now to know what we do and how we conduct our business," Boris said in a gentle tone looking directly at her. "By this time, you would have been expected to do the same. However, I have decided to make an exception with you. I said we have many attractive women and girls, but I did not use the word beautiful. You are the only beautiful woman here. I could make you my exclusive woman and you would have to serve me in any way I desire. But, I can have all the sex I want, any way I want it, from any of those very attractive women and girls here. Because your beauty is regal and I see it as royalty, no man will touch you, including me. I just want to look at you, all of you. You will be a feast for my eyes, and my eyes only. My eyes are ravishing you now in your stylish new clothes which enhance your beauty. Now delight me in your lingerie and then display for me your impeccably rich ebony body."

Boris paused and stared as she stood by the fireplace. He opened a draw of an end table, produced a full syringe, and very quietly punctured her arm, emptying the contents. Within a short time, Awa Senghor was floating without a care in the world. The feeling of well-being was indescribable; almost like being a real Queen. *"Did I hear right? Did I understand him in his broken French to say that I do not have to give sexual pleasure to any strange man or woman that I'm taken to, like all the other women here? Surely I must be confused when right after he tells me of my beauty, he then tells me that I don't have to have sex with him, he just wants to look at me dressed and undressed. I feel so good right now; I'm in the mood to be admired, so I'll let him admire me. And if the sight of my naked body excites him that much, the way I feel right now I might enjoy it."*

She undressed slowly walking around the suite until she stood naked before him. Not a word was spoken as she turned around striking several poses allowing him to look at different angles. Boris broke the silence saying, "That was just what I wanted. You may get dressed now and go back to your room." He added the final touch as he zipped up the back of her dress.

"Good night Awa."

"Good night Boris."

CHAPTER

18

The following morning, Harry and Floyd went directly to see Lieutenant McGee to brief him on the progress of the Shirley Duncan case. "It's just a matter of time Lieu," Floyd assured him. "If I know Eddie Banks, he'll surface somewhere; he can't stay out of trouble for long."

The words were no sooner out of his mouth when someone hollered in from the squad room, "Floyd line three, Miami Homicide."

Floyd picked up the phone on McGee's desk. "Washington speaking, hi Zak what's up?"

"Eddie Banks, Floyd. A couple of cops nailed him running out of a store with a six-pack of beer. They were double parked across the street writing parking tickets. He was still driving her car, but now it has a stolen Florida plate."

"Hold on a second Zak." Floyd repeated the message to Harry and Lieutenant McGee. The three of them looked at each other as if to say, 'This doesn't even happen on those dumb TV cop shows.'

Floyd got back on the phone. "Zak, hold on to him on our felony warrants and we'll let you know soon how we're going to get him back here. Thanks Zak, and if I come down after him, those two cops get lunch on me."

Lieutenant McGee spoke up. "I'll run it by the boss to see if he'll approve you both flying down, and driving him back in her car. The Chief of Detectives has that authority, and if he agrees, I'll send you both."

***

As soon as they de-planed at Miami International, Harry and Floyd were greeted by Detective Dennis Zaklinski. Introductions were hastily made and, while on the way to police headquarters, a laughing Detective Zaklinski retold the unlikely story of Eddie Banks' capture. "Floyd, Harry not even Hollywood would have the balls to think the public would swallow shit like that. And to think we get paid for utilizing these latest high-tech crime-fighting methods."

"Zak," quipped Floyd. "How smart was I to leave this highly advanced law enforcement agency, and immerse myself back into the nineteenth century?"

"It was just something that won't happen again while I'm still around," Zak said as the laughter ended. "We'll go straight into the courtroom where the judge will hold the extradition hearing."

***

An hour later, the hearing over, Eddie Banks was now the official and legal property of Detectives Lincoln and Washington. The four rode in Zak's unmarked city car with Floyd in the front passenger seat, Harry and Eddie Banks in the rear. Banks was directing them to a Miami suburb. "It's in that vacant lot behind this abandoned gas station," he said.

Zak and Floyd got out and rummaged around in the overgrown lot. There was no conversation in the back seat from Harry and Banks.

"Here it is, I found it," shouted Floyd holding up a bent vehicle license plate and returned to the car. He straightened it out and there it was… 1-13766. Later Harry and Floyd admitted as they first stared at those numbers, they both felt chill bumps.

"Lieutenant," said Harry into the phone. "We've got everything we came down for. Banks did not fight extradition; the hearing was very quick. Shirley Duncan's car has been secured in their restricted lot, no one has been in it and we have her license plate. We think it best if we have it trucked up there instead of driving it and contaminating the interior of any forensic evidence that might be needed in court. They said they would process it for us, but that might mean flying up some of their people for the trial."

"Good thinking guys, I'll get it cleared with the boss. Use your department credit card for a rental car to bring that mutt back, the TSA won't let you on a plane with him. Use it for any other expenses related to transporting the car. Be sure to seal her car really good before it goes on the truck, and tell the driver to stay out. If it has to be entered to release the parking brake or to be put in neutral, anything of that nature, you guys do it very carefully."

CHAPTER 19

"Hello, Boris Zherkov speaking how may I be of service?"

"Mr. Zherkov you've told me in the past that this number is secure, but with recent technological advancements I'd prefer not to use names or discuss business over the telephone. On our previous meeting you directed me to a small out-of-the-way café where we had a three o'clock cup of coffee and no one paid any attention to us. I would like to meet you at that same place, say tomorrow afternoon at three o'clock. And, please come alone; I shall also be alone."

The following afternoon at precisely three o'clock Boris Zherkov pulled into the gravel parking lot adjacent to an older café in disrepair. He parked his black Mercedes 550 next to a grey Lexus LS 460. Two older pickup trucks were the only other vehicles in the lot. Inside, sitting at a booth in the rear, a well dressed man in his early fifties made eye contact with Zherkov and motioned to him with a slight nod.

The president of The Citizen's National Bank stood and they shook hands. "My name is Morris Collins. We've done some business not quite a year ago."

"I remember you Mr. Collins," said Boris. "And, as I recall my services were satisfactory."

"I was completely happy and satisfied with what you provided at that time. That was only for me, but you assured me that the number could increase substantially and they would all perform at that same level."

"That is correct. We do have the quantity, but more importantly, we guarantee quality."

"That is most imperative Mr. Zherkov. I have had high-class, expensive call girls in the past. None of them compare with the level of quality and satisfaction to the woman you provided me with last year."

"Just tell me what I can provide you with this time and it will be done." Boris almost shouted with anticipation.

"Let me explain," Mr. Collins said talking slowly and softly. "I want to give a private party for seven of my best customers. They are not only my best customers, but also some of my best friends and we talk intimately. Some are married as I am, but I know that all of them have hired call-girls in the past. Their tastes and preferences are widely varied, ages ranging from mid-teens to mid-thirties. Most of them prefer white women, but a few like women of color from different nationalities. From what I remember of our conversation last time, you are in a position to accommodate the eight of us."

"I can gladly fill your requests and any others you might have Mr. Collins. When is this party going to be? Where are you going to have it? Also, give me a list of the different types the eight of you will require."

"I'm thinking about a week from now. I'll have to be sure they will all be available. As far as where to have it, I'm not sure if we should have it at a hotel or if your facility would be more appropriate. One more thing Mr. Zherkov; we may want to be entertained by the women putting on a show for us amongst themselves and possibly a couple of ménage au trios."

"That sounds like a very interesting and entertaining party Mr. Collins. When you decide on the date, let me know as soon as you can. My place is appropriate and I will be glad to make it available for you. Also, get that list of the variety of women to me and I guarantee that the wishes and desires of you and your seven friends will be fulfilled. When you have it all together, call me at that same number and we'll meet here."

CHAPTER

20

"Yes Lieu, it was a long tiresome, uneventful drive and we're beat. We took the rental car over to their PD garage before we left and had them take the rear seat interior door and window controls off. Before we turn it in, we'll take it to our shop and have them to re-attach the controls. When we stopped at a rest area, we had him piss into a jar. One of us went inside to empty and rinse it out. We had no conversation with him on the way back, and the only questions we asked him when we stopped at a fast food joint were whether he wanted a hamburger or a chicken sandwich." Harry explained.

"We didn't want some defense attorney later in court making an issue about us questioning him without his Miranda rights." Floyd was quick to add. "We dropped him at the city jail and we'll talk to him first thing in the morning. But, for now Harry and I need a good night's sleep."

"Yes," said the rarely sympathetic Lieutenant McGee. "Get some shuteye, and don't come in too early in the morning. He'll wait for you."

***

"We just got back and I'm on my way home. It was a long trip and we are both worn out," Harry told Jessica on the phone.

"Would you like me to come over and fix some dinner for you?"

"No Jess, all I want is to flop onto my bed."

"Maybe I'll come over and flop with you."

"Jess I'm even too bushed for that, but give me a rain check for tomorrow night."

***

The small interrogation room consisted of a scarred metal table and three metal chairs, two on one side of the table and one on the other. They were all bolted to the floor. The lone chair sat lower than the other two, so the person being interrogated had to look up to the detectives. It gave the good guys a psychological edge.

As soon as the three got seated, before a word was spoken, Floyd read him his constitutional rights under Miranda. "Eddie, do you understand those rights?" Banks just nodded his head. "No Eddie, that's not good enough. You have to say, "Yes, I understand them" or "No, I don't". You've heard them enough times that you could recite them to me."

Banks looked at Floyd without saying a word for almost a minute, and then suddenly said, "Yes, I understand them."

"Okay Eddie, now there's one more mountain to climb. You've seen this form many times, the one where you have to state that Miranda has been explained to you and that you understand them. The same form you've signed many times." Banks hastily scribbled his name and the date.

"Last week when you were picked up by the police you were driving a stolen car. Why was that?"

"Because that's what I do Detective Washington, you know that. I steal cars."

"Where did you find that one, the white Toyota?"

"It was in a parking garage where I shop for most of my cars."

"Was that in Miami or some other place, maybe a parking garage in another state? And what about the woman who was with the car?"

"I don't know nothin' about no woman. Maybe I did pick up the car out of state, but don't try to hang no rap on me about a woman."

"You know Eddie, like the last time. You kidnapped and raped that woman when you stole her car down in south Florida."

"Hey, I did my time for that… but if you're gonna' talk shit to me about another one… I'm telling you I didn't kill no woman… and I'm not saying another fuckin' word."

***

The following day the same three were back in the interrogation room. Banks still hadn't said anything in response to the questions put to him. He wouldn't even acknowledge a simple "good morning Eddie," or "how are you feeling today?" not even, "would like some coffee?" He just sat mute, until Harry spread the crime scene photos out on the table. He looked at them, showed no interest. So Harry gathered them up, put them away, except one. Banks glanced at it, then looked away. Within a few seconds he looked again. It was the photo of Shirley Duncan still in her shallow grave, on her back after the medical examiner had turned her over, her eyes open, looking straight at him. It was the same pose that had affected Harry so deeply. Banks looked at it, then quickly turned away. He repeated that several times. He started to rub his arms while looking, then he started to scratch his arms. Within minutes, he could not look away and his scratching drew blood. All this time, he rocked back and forth in the chair, moaning softly. There was not another sound in the room.

He was ready. It was that psychological moment that only occurs once during an interrogation, if at all, when a suspect wants to tell, has to tell. Eddie Banks was ready to tell them what he did to Shirley Duncan. Just then the door opened, someone stuck his head in to say that the coffee was ready. Banks snapped out of his trance… He never said another word about Shirley Duncan.

***

Eddie Banks was denied bond and remanded to the county jail. When his trial came up several months later, the public defender pled Banks not guilty, and Banks chose not to take the stand to testify in his own behalf. There were no witnesses for the defense and the jury agreed that the state proved its case beyond a reasonable doubt. Eddie Banks was sentenced to life in prison, without the possibility of parole.

Alan Traker had been in the courtroom throughout the trial. As soon as the judge left the bench, he approached Harry and Floyd. He was crying and telling them how much he appreciated their efforts putting that no good bastard in prison and hoped he'd rot. "I just wanted to personally thank you both so very, very much. I know that Shirley is looking down and thanking you also." Alan Traker was overcome with emotion and could no longer talk. He simply walked away and left the courthouse.

Harry solemnly said, "Makes it all worthwhile, doesn't it partner?" Floyd slowly nodded his head.

CHAPTER

21

It was quite a party. The men had never before been around an assortment of such gorgeous women and girls in one place, at one time. They'd had attractive women in the past, more attractive than most of their wives. The big difference in these women was that they were here to fulfill all of the men's most private sexual desires. At home they settled for boring sex… insert tab A into slot B… sometimes good sex, but all of the exciting and stimulating visual aspects men crave are mostly gone after years of marriage. What the men were experiencing with these women was something many of them had not experienced for many years or ever.

Because of meticulous planning prior to the party, if one of the men wanted an Asian woman of a certain age, she was there for him. The other women and girls were there waiting: three Caucasians, two Hispanics, a Middle Easterner and a beauty from an island in the South Pacific. It was not only the nationalities they desired, but also the range in age.

As requested the women and girls paired off and put on a show for the men; showing them how two women made love; not just a stilted, mechanical performance, but a tender love as deeply committed as any lesbian couple. It was beyond the comprehension of the men looking on. Finally, a few of the men selected two women each for a ménage au trio, as the others watched.

One of the women; a Hispanic girl could not force herself to meet the requirements. She held back, spreading her legs when forced to, but giving nothing else. One of the men was left out and had to share another with a friend.

When the orgy was over, it was six in the morning, Mr. Collins reported to Olga who waited outside of the main room, out of sight but close enough should there be any problems. After all the men had gone, he told her of the reluctance of the girl causing two of the men to double up. She said that Mr. Zherkov would be in touch later in the day. Mr. Zherkov, she assured him would take appropriate action to see that it would never happen again.

Zherkov and Collins met for dinner that evening. Zherkov was apologetic. "This woman will be punished severely. I'd like to make this up to you. I invite you and your disappointed friend to an evening with two other women, as my guests."

Both men left the restaurant, Collins feeling better about the situation. Boris Zherkov in a quiet rage went back to his suite in the compound to settle down. Should he administer corporal punishment to the offending girl to be witnessed by the entire assembly of women? Or should she be confined to the cage in the corner of the large room where they would all see her, without her daily dose of heroin for several days? Which torment would more likely ensure a change in her attitude the next time she was sent to give the most pleasure to a man or woman?

"Olga," Boris said into his phone. "Have Awa to join me for dinner. And, the girl we got the complaint about… the one from Chile… lock her in her room without her daily treatment. I'll decide what to do with her later."

"Before you decide," replied Olga. "Remember that the last one you beat with a belt became useless to our clients."

***

At seven o'clock that evening an anxious Boris Zherkov awaited the soft knock on his door. This time instead of calling out for his visitor to come in, he got up from his recliner, and opened the door himself. There stood Awa Senghor who just by her presence changed his dark mood to sudden delight. "Come in

Awa. Sit by the fire. You look lovely in that white dress. I'm hoping to see some more white against your dark brown skin."

"Thank you Boris, you are very kind. And yes, I have your favorite white lacy things, very shear in the right places for you."

"Here is a glass of the red wine that you liked the last time. I have ordered filet mignon with all the trimmings. Olga tells me you like yours medium well. While we sip the wine before dinner, tell me, is everyone is treating you well? You have everything you need? If not, I'll see that it is corrected."

"Yes Boris, everyone has been very kind to me. Of course, that includes you."

Dinner was served and was prepared just right for them both. As they were eating, Boris could not give his full attention to Awa. "You are aware of the problem with the girl from Chile. You see Awa, fear and pain are the only ways to keep them all obeying. When I get a complaint from a client, who was not happy with the performance expected of the woman, then I must discipline her, a punishment so fearful that it is a lesson to all the women. You've seen one of the girls punished, witnessed by all the rest. We have a reputation to maintain that the services we deliver are guaranteed to satisfy and will not be matched or exceeded by anyone else." Boris stopped talking and poured himself another glass of wine. Awa still had enough in her glass. He was obviously troubled about what to do with that girl.

"Why is he telling me all of this?" Awa thought to herself. *"Does he want my opinion, and if so, how can I help that poor girl?"* "Boris," she said, "instead of beating her, or withholding her daily dose of the heavenly liquid, why not show her what she did wrong and let her correct it next time?"

"No Awa, I've learned years ago that the only way to rule is with an iron fist. Show no mercy or compassion", Boris said slowly, with a venomous look in his eyes; a look that Awa had not seen before. Evil that shook the marrow in her bones.

"But, let's not talk of that now," he said. "After dinner we'll go for a drive, I'll give the driver the night off. No bodyguards, just the two of us. We'll drive out to the lake, a place where I spend a good deal of my time. Within thirty minutes of leaving the compound Awa saw the water that reminded her of the waterfront in Dakar, where she had lived and worked. There were several immediate differences; there was no surf, the water was calm where it merged with the dry land; no fishing boats of any size, no creaking, rusted freighters and tankers. It lacked all the activity and noise of a commercial port. As they drove further out on the quay, there was a variety of sleek pleasure boats, from small open speed boats to large ocean going yachts. Boris drove on and stopped beside the largest and most impressive yacht in the entire marina.

"There she is, *'The Czarina.'* She'll take you anywhere in the world, even to Senegal."

CHAPTER

22

The squad room was relatively quiet for a weekday at ten in the morning. The usual chatter, occasional laughter, a sudden outburst of profanity caused by the two fingered typing of a computer illiterate, older detective, almost finished with a lengthy report, when the screen went black. The continuous back and forth banter…

"Listen up!" Lieutenant McGee shouted from his office doorway. "There's been a shooting at the Kennedy High School in the 2nd Precinct. "First unconfirmed reports of several fatalities and several more wounded. The Emergency Response Team is on the way to back up the 2nd Precinct cops. No information yet on the shooter. All of you who can break away, head that way. Harris and Foster take the lead, those of you whose assistance is needed, do what you can. The rest of you clear out. It'll be a cluster fuck, as it is, with too many there adding to the confusion."

And confusion it was: police, fire rescue, ambulances, school teachers and officials, news media, hundreds of panicked parents descended on the school, and the general public gathered for blocks around, adding to the chaos.

Harry and Floyd entered the mobile command post and found the on-scene commander with a phone in each ear and dozens of first responder officials talking to him at once. When the detectives got his attention they learned that there were three fatalities, each high school students, two were victims, and the third was the shooter, who had killed himself. Four other students had non-life threatening wounds. The rest of the students and teachers had been evacuated from the school.

Harris and Foster, with the assistance of six other homicide detectives including Lincoln and Washington, remained at the school to sort out the details, get witness statements, supervise the crime scene techs with the collection of evidence, the taking of photos and measurements, plus all the other functions that are needed at a crime scene.

All of the victims were seniors at the school and were known to each other. The motive appeared to be jealousy on the part of the shooter. The female victim had left him and began dating the male victim. The shooting occurred in a hallway as classes were changing. The two dead victims were walking down the hallway holding hands and without a word to anyone, the shooter opened fire. The other wounded students were not intended gunshot victims, but rather were in the wrong place at the wrong time. Walter Mathews, white/male age 17, was a good student and had never come to the attention of the police for any reason. He came to school that day armed with a fully loaded 9mm handgun. He was the last victim.

By the end of the second day the other detectives were pulled off the school shooting to handle the never-ending mayhem and violence occurring in different parts of the city. Harris and Foster spent the day putting together a comprehensive report, then submitting it to Lieutenant McGee.

***

When Harry got home later that day, he found Jessica sitting in her car in front of his building. "I heard about the shootings at the high school yesterday, and knew that you were involved with the investigation. What a tragedy, three lives gone and for what? In our day it would have resulted with the two boys in a fist fight."

"I've handled every manner of violence that one person can

inflict on another." Harry said in a low voice. "But, when it involves kids, and these were kids, it really gets to me. These seventeen year olds didn't have a chance to grow up, to live life. It's really depressing."

"I knew that you would be down about it, so I brought over some groceries to make dinner for both of us. And, after dinner, I thought maybe we could discuss it. If you've had enough already, maybe we'll just relax and be together. That will make you feel better."

Jessica put together a quick and tasty meal of thick bone-in pan-fried pork chops, potatoes Anna, and fresh ears of corn. Harry didn't have much to say during dinner but, soon afterwards with his usual after-dinner coffee, he startled Jessica by suddenly exclaiming, "What the hell has gotten into people lately? You turn on the TV news or pick up the morning paper and there's another senseless tragedy somewhere. Some kid with a loaded gun goes to school and starts shooting. A man with a gun and a grudge against his boss or co-workers shows up at work and starts blasting. Then it's a shopping center, or a movie theater and any other unlikely place. The result is carnage and most of the time the dead are innocent victims."

Harry got quiet and just stared at nothing at all. Jessica didn't know what to say, but knew that Harry wasn't through.

After a few minutes he turned to her, his eyes watery and said, "As tragic as those things are, I've learned to rely on my psychological defense mechanisms and remain detached and professional while investigating. The domestic homicides and street corner killings are just another day at the office. But, what I can't get over, what I can't deal with are heinous crimes against innocent children. Some deranged lunatic who snatches a seven-year-old child off the street as he or she walks to school, or some madman enters a home through an open window in the middle of the night and kidnaps the sleeping child from its bed. When we find that child, dead or alive, we learn that it had endured unimaginable horrors. Sometimes that child is never found. Is he or she dead?

Or, is that poor innocent child still being subjected to the worst kind of depravity?" Harry could not contain his tears.

Jessica went over to the couch where Harry was sitting, put her arms around him and gently rocked him. "Harry, come inside and lie on the bed while I hold you. Let go Harry, let it all out. You have years of hurt in you, get rid of it." In the bed neither spoke another word, and within five minutes Harry slipped into a deep sleep.

CHAPTER

23

For three days the young Chilean woman sat cramped in the small cage. It had been rolled into the center of the large gymnasium floor where all the other women sat in the bleachers to witness her punishment. She was given a minimum of water and a bowl of tasteless gruel each day to sustain her. The lone item with her was a bucket to relive herself in sight of all the others. But the worst of her torment was the lack of the needed daily dose of heroin. As the withdrawal pains worsened, her crying and the pleading only got louder. By the third day the pain was so excruciating that her begging and screaming was heard outside the confines of the gymnasium.

Boris Zherkov walked across the floor and stood before the cage. "I have in my hand a full syringe of the golden liquid that you need so desperately. I can unlock the cage and end your pain and misery. I will empty the syringe into your arm, and then let you go to your room for a shower and change of clothes. You may then eat a good meal in the dining room. Is that what you want?"

"Oh yes," she said. "I'm begging you Mr. Zherkov, I'll do anything you want me to do."

"The next time I send you on an assignment, you will please the client whether it is a man or woman, or maybe more than one at the same time. You will not act like a robot as you did the last time. You will comply with their every wish, satisfy any sexual fantasy, and convince them by your attitude and actions that you are the lover of their dreams."

"Yes, yes I will, I swear it on my mother's grave."

Boris let this filthy, haggard creature, still crying and doubled over in pain, out of her confinement and injected her with the heroin. Olga helped the woman to her room and stayed with her while she made herself presentable. By the time they were seated in the dining room, the drug had taken effect. Olga cautioned her to eat modestly and slowly to avoid getting sick since this was her first real meal in three days.

Meanwhile this harsh lesson was not lost on all the others.

Awa had been in the bleachers along with the others. She was sickened by this cruelty. She thought, *"I am lucky and fortunate that Boris Zherkov has taken an interest in me or that poor woman could very well have been me. How much longer will Mr. Zherkov treat me in this special way? When will he get tired of just looking at my naked body, and force me to have sex with him? Worse than that, he might send me out on assignments. Is there anything I can do to save myself and the others? Think, Awa."*

CHAPTER

24

"Olga, you have been very valuable to me and to this origination since you've been here," a pleased Boris Zherkov said to her. They were sitting in his luxurious penthouse downtown, away from the compound, just the two of them. "I trust you as much as I trust my closest associates. Had it not been for you and your writing skills, in addition to you being fluent in so many languages, we might have had to shut down this business long ago."

Boris Zherkov was aware that along with the money that each of his kidnap victims sent home each month, the families would expect a letter or note assuring them that they made the right decision. Each woman wrote that she was glad to be able to send money that the family needed so desperately, that she was treated well and that she was happy. Olga dictated the letters, and had each woman write in her own language and in her own handwriting. Olga then reviewed the letters for content. Of those few languages that she did not understand, there was always a staff member who did. Those letters were then sent to the Zherkov Enterprises' office in the city where the woman was "working" to be post marked from that city.

It was rare for one of Zherkov's "harem" to have more than one or two assignments in a day's time. Whereas, it was not unusual for some ghetto pimps to force his prostitutes to service a dozen or more different men a day. Those women lived cramped together in rat-and-roach infested hovels. They rarely ate a decent meal.

***

Boris Zherkov traveled around the world to visit those of his offices that handled his other interests--- illegal guns and drugs. He always arrived unannounced to check on his employees, and review the books. Those who were found to be skimming or cheating were dealt with the old KGB way. When he returned to his suite in the compound, he had Olga to bring one of the girls or women to relax him after an arduous, globe spiraling journey. It was obligatory for her to achieve his total sexual pleasure.

Awa was summoned to Boris' suite once or twice a week to have dinner with him. His only demand was to admire her in different stages of undress until she was standing before him naked. Olga had warned her that this infatuation of his just ogling her would soon end. Awa thought of nothing else but finding a way, an opportunity to escape before he got tired of just looking at her, and demanded sex with him, or sent her out on assignments like all the others.

CHAPTER

25

"Three months had gone by and Zherkov had not gone to check on his other offices. He enjoyed the dinners with Awa, and her company for those several hours. *But it's time for me to pay them another visit while the other offices are not expecting me,* thought Boris. He left that morning and was gone for three weeks.

When he returned, the news that met him was not good.

"A United States Congressman! She refused a United States Congressman." Boris shouted in Olga's face. "Tell me again what happened and don't spare me the details."

"It was that young woman from India, the one who has caused problems for us since being here. First she threw a fit because she was forced to wear western clothing. She only wanted to wear her sari. Then she demanded to go to a Hindu temple to pray. She also demanded a special diet void of meat; she was afraid that all the meat was beef which is prohibitive to Hindus."

"Why then Olga, if you knew of all these problems, why would you send her to service such an important person as a United States Congressman?"

"We received the request in the afternoon for that same night. At the time she was the only one available. The majority of girls had the flu, or some other illness, with high fevers. Others had a stomach bug that's been going around. The rest had their periods. This was all going on when you were away."

"Maybe I'll call him to offer my apologies. I'll tell him I've voided his invoice. I'll send him two compliant beauties with my compliments."

"I haven't told you the worst part," Olga said. "When she refused him he tried to force her. That's when she scratched his face so badly that he bled. I was waiting in the hotel lobby as I always do. The first I knew of what happened is when she came down and told me. I went back up to his room, and that's when I saw his bloody face. He was so angry he wouldn't talk to me. He slammed the door."

***

The following day every girl and woman was ordered into the gymnasium. The Indian woman was led in to the middle of the floor stripped naked, screaming and crying, pulled by a chain attached to an iron collar around her neck. Boris appeared shortly and stood next to her. He addressed the women in the bleachers. "This woman was sent out on assignment to service a very important client. Once in his hotel room she refused him. He tried to convince her that she was there to satisfy his every sexual desire, and pulled her down onto the bed with him. She resisted and scratched his face until she drew blood. There are various violations here that bring different punishments. What this woman did calls for the death penalty."

Boris Zherkov then pulled a handgun and shot her in the center of her forehead. She collapsed to the floor, dead. From the bleachers, came gasps, screams, crying and then silence.

The gymnasium emptied quickly as staff members immediately cleaned the blood from the floor. The faint odor of cordite lingered. Zherkov returned to his suite and called Olga, plus three male staff members, to report there. "I want you to take her body to the yacht and cruise out to deep water, attach one of the heavy anchors to the end of the chain, and then drop her overboard. Olga, I want you to go along to make sure my orders are followed to the letter, then report back to me."

Boris Zherkov made the important call to the congressman's office. He was told the congressman would be out for a few days due to a minor accident. A short time later, Olga returned and reported to her boss that the mission had been carried out.

"Olga this whole situation has left me very angry and that's not good for business when dealing with clients. I need to get rid of this anger and relax. I want you to take Awa downtown to the spa and get her feeling and looking good. Then go to the better dress shops and get her a tight- fitting dress that will show off her beauty, and purchase the lingerie I like.

***

The next morning after breakfast Olga and Awa were in the back seat of Boris' limousine as Victor, one of the trusted body guards, drove them downtown. After their first stop at the spa, Victor drove the two women several blocks to begin shopping. He told Olga that he would be across the street at the café and would watch for them when they came out.

The last time Olga took her dress shopping, Awa noticed a French flag flying on a building two doors down from the dress shop. She had found out from Olga that it was the French consulate. Awa had made up her mind… it was her only way out. There were several policemen on the streets that she had seen before, but the only languages she knew was French and the tribal language of Senegal. She had learned French in school when Senegal was a French colony. If she tried to ask them for help, they would not understand her. But, if she could get to the consulate Awa hoped and prayed they would understand her and help her.

Just as they were about to enter a dress shop, Awa broke away from Olga and ran for the consulate. She banged on the locked doors, screaming for someone to help her. Two French soldiers opened the doors, and Awa almost collapsed with relief. By then Olga was trying to pull her away and Victor was running from across the street. Awa was screaming in French to the soldiers that she had been kidnapped and was being held prisoner. The soldiers pushed Olga away, taking Awa inside, and closing and locking the doors. She was led to an office where two men and a woman sat behind desks. They gave her a glass of water and waited for her to calm down. Then she told them her story.

The French Consul General made a phone call to Police Headquarters asking to speak with the police chief. A major answered and when the Consul General identified herself, she was put through to the chief. Once she told the chief of Awa's situation, he assured the Consul that detectives would be there shortly.

CHAPTER

26

"Lincoln, Washington, come into my office," Lieutenant McGee shouted across the squad room. "You two have had your fun playing on the lake, but instead of enjoying yourselves, you had to but into Coast Guard business because someone dragged a body from the lake… It's time to get back to work. I just had a call from the chief's office. Some hysterical woman came to the French Consulate off the street claiming to have been kidnapped and held prisoner. The Consul General herself called and spoke with the chief who wants detectives over there right away. It seems this frightened woman has a bizarre story that we need to hear."

***

"It all started in Senegal when I lost my job at the fish packing plant," Awa, now calm, related her incredible tale to Harry and Floyd, as the Consul General Marie Dubarre translated. "Two men offered me a job as a model in New York City, making a lot more money that I could ever make in Senegal, money that my family needed. They told me of the glamorous life-style top models live. They would pay the airfare and provide a passport, a visa, and spending money that I could pay back in small amounts.

When the plane landed a car was waiting, and on the ride from the airport I was drugged. I woke up locked in a small windowless room where two men came in three times a day with food. They also stuck in my arm a needle, which I later learned was heroin. About a week later a woman named Olga came into my room and told me that I was not in New York City and that there was no modeling job. She said I would work as a prostitute along with other women and teen age girls. I was moved to a larger, nicer room where the door was not locked and I was free to move about this big compound with the others. We all ate our meals in a nice dining room.

"How many women and girls are being held prisoner in this compound?" Harry asked Awa.

"I really don't know, but I would guess about twenty-five." This caused Harry and Floyd to briefly look at each other. Harry nodded, and Awa went on.

"I was brought to an office where I met Boris Zherkov, a very scary Russian, the man in charge. He told me that I could never leave, that I had no money, and no passport. He said I was a heroin addict, and without money I could not get the heroin that I would need. It would be very painful without it."

'We cater to a high class clientele and some very important people.' "He bragged to me." 'When we send you out on assignment, you will satisfy their sexual fantasies, whatever they are. If you fail to make the client happy you will be punished severely.'

"I've seen some of these punishments. They are horrible." Awa said. "I remember one poor woman that Mr. Zherkov put in a cage naked in the middle of the gymnasium floor for three days with hardly any food or water. She didn't get her daily ration of heroin. By the third day she was crying, screaming and begging for one more chance to please a client. The rest of us were ordered into the gymnasium to see what would happen to any of us, should we not completely satisfy the client. Mr. Zherkov released this broken woman from the cage and gave her a dose of heroin. He then told Olga to get her cleaned up and get her some food. But, the worst was a poor Indian woman who Boris Zherkov shot in the head and killed her.

Again Harry and Floyd looked at each other; "Harry, the body of the woman the fishing trawler turned over to the Coast Guard a few days ago." Floyd said, at the same moment Harry was thinking it. "She could have been Indian, and she was shot in the forehead."

"Where is this place, this compound?" Harry asked. "Can you take us there?"

"No, I don't know where it is."

"How long was the drive to downtown? Can you remember anything that you saw on the way?" Floyd asked.

"We drove about twenty or thirty minutes from the compound to the downtown spa," she said. "I do remember a very large cross standing all by itself in an open field."

"Yes, we know the one; it's as tall as a two story building, about ten miles north of here. How far is that cross from the compound?" Harry asked, trying to get a fix on the compound.

"I'm not sure, but it took about ten minutes."

"Don't worry about Awa, detectives. She will stay here at the Consulate." Ms. Dubarre announced. "She will be under the protection of the French Government. We will have a doctor come in to see her about the heroin addiction. We shall do whatever is necessary to ease her withdrawals. In the meantime, detectives, please rescue those poor women from the hell they are living in, and have that horrible monster brought to justice."

***

A short time later in Lieutenant McGee's office, Harry and Floyd briefed him on the entire situation. "I'll notify the commander of the Coast Guard station and advise him that the body of the woman the trawler fished out of the lake; the one who was shot in the head occurred within our jurisdiction." McGee told Harry and Floyd. "I'll make arrangements to have her body transferred to our morgue."

"Another thing Lieu," Harry asked. "Will you arrange with our Air Unit to have one of their helicopters available to assist us in locating that compound? It would be more likely to find it from the air than from the ground, based on the times and distances to downtown that the victim estimated, plus that giant cross gives a direction from downtown. She also sketched out what the compound looks like."

CHAPTER

27

"What do you mean she got away from you?" Boris Zherkov screamed in Olga's face. "And at the French Consulate two soldiers brought her in after one of them pried her from your grip? Where was Victor?"

"He was waiting across the street in a café, waiting for us. When he saw her run, he ran across the street to help, but he wasn't quick enough." Olga dropped to her knees. "They took her inside and locked the doors. That's the last we saw of her. Please Boris I've always been loyal to you. Have mercy."

Boris was in a rage. "You stupid! Stupid! Do you know what you have done? She will tell them about this place and what we do here. They will call the police. Then it's just a matter of time until they are knocking at our door. Get out of my sight! Now! I will deal with you and Victor later, but first I must calm down so I can think."

***

From the air Harry and Floyd observed the open field with the giant cross. The pilot flew the helicopter in each azimuth to a distance of fifty miles out. As they flew about thirty miles out in a northwesterly direction, Floyd said "Look over to the right Harry; that looks more like the compound than anything else we've seen so far."

"It does," Harry answered. "But, let's fly the remaining azimuths so we don't overlook an area that looks more like it. Before we send the troops in to the wrong place we had better be sure. When we've seen everything from up here, let's go back to the Consulate, get the victim and let her see from the air the place we think is the compound. If she thinks that's it, we'll take her back to the office, get with McGee and come up with a plan."

***

Later at the Consulate, Harry and Floyd met with the Consul Ms. Dubarre, the Vice Consul, Mr. Louis Verdome and Awa Senghor. "Madam Dubarre," Harry said. "We would like to have Awa to accompany us in the helicopter to confirm that what we saw from the air is indeed the compound. We would like Mr. Verdome come also to interpret."

The Consul replied immediately, "A good idea, Louis will go with you. Let me ask Awa"

After a few words in French, Awa answered, "Oui."

***

A short time later, at the homicide office with Awa and Louis, Harry made introductions. Lieutenant McGee said, "I'll alert the Special Operations Section to have their SWAT people geared up, ready to go as soon as you give me a confirmed location of the compound."

Floyd spoke up, "If they stand by in the field with the large cross, they will be a lot closer when they are green-lighted."

"Okay," said Harry, "Let's get back to the heliport."

CHAPTER

28

In Zherkov's suite, the telephone rang, it was the private line. "Boris, this is Ed Knowles can I speak freely?"

"Of course you can. What can I do for the Chairman of the Public Safety Committee?"

"It's not what you can do for me, it's what I can do for you. Twice now we've done business and both times were extremely satisfactory. My wife and I have been truly happy for the first time in years, and for that I feel obligated to return the favor. I have confidential information that the police are about to raid your compound and arrest you."

Boris Zherkov knew what was coming and did not want to be there when it did. He gathered up computers, documents and other incriminating items that would fit into his car. He had plenty of money and could replace his clothing and other personal items. He had heard a helicopter pass overhead. That must be the start of it. He had to get out fast. He remembered from his tenure with the KGB; airports, train terminals, bus stations and all roads leading out of the city would be monitored. He thought his office high above downtown would be safe temporarily until he could disappear somewhere in the city. He left the compound and devised a plan on the way.

***

As soon as he got to his downtown office he called the compound, "Olga, I want you to take Ivan and Victor with you to the boat right away. You need to get away from the city" *I should have killed the three of them, but I needed them for my plan to work. The police will think I am aboard the boat. That will give me time to find a place to hide out.*

***

The police helicopter took off with the four on board, headed for the large cross. Harry told the pilot to head in the direction where earlier they thought the compound was spotted. On the way, Awa told Louis, "The compound has a six foot wall around it, there's one gate. This gate always had one or two men with guns." As they flew over Awa said to Louis. "Down there, that's the compound!"

Harry called Lieutenant McGee. "Lieu we've got a conformation on the area that was in question this morning. We'll meet you and the emergency response team at that cross."

The field was swarming with police personnel. As they landed Floyd said to Harry, "It looks like the entire Special Operations Section is already here."

Lieutenant McGee was talking with Major Holland, the on-scene commander. Harry and Floyd briefed them with the intelligence they had concerning the compound. "We checked the permit office at City Hall. This compound is listed as a non-profit shelter for stranded foreign women, run by a Russian philanthropist, Boris Zherkov."

The Major then addressed his troops. "We will assault the compound with speed... SWAT will force the gate... neutralize any armed resistance... The rest of SOS personnel will surround the compound and scale the wall with ladders if necessary... You might also encounter armed people who might resist... your orders are the same. There are approximately twenty-five to thirty females within the compound... All are innocent victims that we are here to rescue. Most of them don't speak English, so use your body language. We'll have translators, chaplains and psychologists standing by at the command post... All males within the compound are to be considered armed and dangerous... The compound is approximately thirty miles northwest of here... As soon as we arrive you have the green light... Let's get started."

As the assault began, the helicopter landed in a field adjacent to the compound. Awa told Louis that Boris Zherkov has an office in one of the buildings downtown. "But I have not been there. He has a yacht," she added, "the biggest one in the marina, and I have seen it. Its name is *The Czarina.*" Louis translated this information to the detectives.

Harry got on his radio and called the dispatcher.

"Homicide 134 to radio."

Dispatcher: "Go ahead Homicide 134"

"Homicide134: Notify the Coast Guard and advise them to be on the lookout for a yacht, '*The Czarina*' on Lake Rockford. On board is one Boris Zherkov, a Russian national wanted for murder and numerous other felonies. This person is armed and dangerous. There might be other armed persons on board. Notify us if contact is made. Also be advised that an arrest warrant has been issued for Boris Zherkov."

Dispatcher: "Copy that."

Harry approached Lieutenant McGee, "Lieu, Floyd and I would like our chopper to fly us out to the CG cutter so we'll be there to make the physical arrest."

"Okay Harry, I'll clear it with the boss. If he approves it and the Coast Guard has no objections, then its okay with me.

After several phone calls, Lieutenant McGee informed Harry and Floyd that the Chief of Detectives had approved their request, and the skipper of the cutter would welcome their presence.

***

The assault on the compound was successful. All the men inside put their weapons down and their hands up. The women were hysterical and confused, as soft-spoken female police officers gently led them out of their prison, to the command post where they were met by people who would try to help them out of their nightmare. The female victims would have to give written statements at some point, but not until their medical issues were addressed. Eight men, all Russian nationals were handcuffed and transported to the city jail where they were booked on numerous felony charges. Several teams of crime scene techs arrived to photograph the entire compound, and collect any physical and forensic evidence.

Boris Zherkov was not among the male prisoners. After an intensive search of the entire compound, he was not found. This confirmed the conclusion that he had left the compound before police arrived, and was now on his yacht, somewhere out on Lake Rockford.

The action over, the excitement diminished, the girls and women, including Awa Senghor, were safely processed at the command post. Arrangements were made and they were soon taken to a detox center for treatment of their heroin addiction.

CHAPTER

29

The Coast Guard cutter, with Harry and Floyd on board, and two helicopters were searching the vast emptiness of Lake Rockford for *The Czarina.* In less than two hours one of the helicopters came upon a large vessel and dropped down low enough to identify it. The commanding officer on board the cutter was notified and given the co-ordinates specifying the boats location. Within thirty minutes the cutter overtook it. "Attention Czarina." The first officer called over a loud speaker. "This is the United States Coast Guard. We are fifty meters to your stern. We intend to board you."

There was no reply from *The Czarina.*

The first officer called again. "We are coming along side to your starboard. Any attempt of armed resistance will be met with deadly force." Armed CG sailors and officers, including the two detectives, boarded *The Czarina.* Olga, Victor and Ivan surrendered meekly. Harry and Floyd did all they could to contain themselves. "Which one of you is Boris Zherkov?" Harry asked. All three said he was not on the boat. "Well, where the hell is he?"

Floyd handed a copy of the arrest warrant to the Coast Guard Commander and told him, "This man, Boris Zherkov, who is named in the warrant, is not aboard this boat according to these three. Will your men assist me and my partner in searching the entire boat? The CG commander complied, but asked "What about these other three?"

"They are his accomplices and are now under arrest. We will take them with us once we return to your station."

Their search of the boat did not turn up Boris Zherkov. "We will tow the yacht back to our station," the CG skipper told the detectives. "Then you can take charge of your prisoners."

***

When the cutter arrived at the Coast Guard station with their prisoners, Harry and Floyd called for a paddy wagon and a car. Harry thanked the Coast Guard personnel for their cooperation. The two vehicles headed for police headquarters, where the prisoners were each placed in a separate holding cell, until they could be transferred to the city jail.

***

The following day, Olga was brought back to police headquarters and led to an interrogation room where Harry and Floyd were waiting. "Olga Aslof," Harry said looking at her… "You are facing very serious charges… conspiracy to murder, kidnapping, false imprisonment, illegal drugs and running a prostitution ring involving minors, among other lesser charges. What we want from you is information concerning Boris Zherkov's whereabouts. If you cooperate with us and your information leads to his capture, then you testify in court against that same Boris Zherkov, we will talk to the District Attorney on your behalf. We can't speak for the DA, but there is a good chance your cooperation might lessen your sentence considerably."

"I would, but I am so afraid of Boris. You don't know what he can do to a person."

Floyd spoke up. "There is no reason to fear Boris Zherkov any longer. If he doesn't get the needle, he will spend the rest of his miserable life in prison. Based on your sentence, you will be in a women's prison which is several hundred miles away from where he would be. The only time you will see him is in the court room from the witness stand. He will be at the defendant's table in chains.

"But first, we have to find him." Harry said to Olga. "All modes of transportation out of the city have been alerted for Boris Zherkov and we are to be notified should they find him."

"He has five offices around the world. His main office is downtown in this city, in the penthouse of a very tall building. I know where it is, I've been there."

"What are the other four cities? Harry asked. Olga did not hesitate. "Paris, London, New York and Lisbon"

Olga spent the next two days telling the detectives everything she knew about Boris the man, Zherkov Enterprises with the four other offices around the globe, dealing in illegal drugs and illegal guns, how he managed to kidnap so many girls and women around the world, and what life was like in the compound. She also provided a client list for sex with women and teenage girls, the clients included a U.S. congressman, a state senator, the city public safety director, a bank president and many other important people. She told them there were also women on that list.

"One thing that was different. He had an infatuation with Awa Senghor, the woman from Senegal, Africa. She's the same woman who broke away from me and was taken into the French Consulate. He didn't send her out on assignments with clients, he did not have sex with her himself. All he wanted was to watch her undress and then to look at her naked. He had me take her to special spas and buy her expensive clothes."

The next morning Harry got on the phone with an INS agent. He explained the situation with the girls and women now being treated at a detox facility. "Yes Agent Moore, technically they are illegal foreign aliens. But due to their circumstances they should be treated as innocent kidnap victims. They have no passports, no visas, no identification and no money."

"But they are still illegal aliens, Detective Lincoln and we have standard procedures for deportation."

"Listen Moore, is there no one there with some common sense? Let me talk to a supervisor." Harry said raising his voice.

After a pause another voice came on the phone. "I am a

supervisor Detective Lincoln; my name is Wilkes. Agent Moore explained this unusual situation and I'm sure we can bend the rules. I'll see to it that we cut through the red tape. Let me know when they will be able to travel."

"As soon as their heroin habit is cured, they should be returned to their native countries, courtesy of the United States Government." Harry stated, "I'll let you know when."

Harry's next call was to the State Department to advise them of the situation. "Agent Wilkes at INS has been made aware also, he told the agent from State."

At the same time, Floyd made calls to the FBI to make them aware of the situation. He then called the DEA about the illegal drugs at Zherkov Enterprises in the four cities. He also placed a call to the ATF informing them of the illegal guns at Zherkov Enterprises in those same cities.

CHAPTER

30

Boris ordered Olga, Ivan and Victor to take *The Czarina* out as a decoy to buy himself some time. He was not on board *The Czarina.* Instead he made his way to the skid-row section of the city where he got himself a room at a run down, fleabag rooming house. He checked in under the name George Williams, paid in cash from a large roll of bills, and went up to his assigned room. "The bathroom is down at the end of the hall." The desk clerk yelled after him.

The desk clerk thought about it and suspected that something wasn't right about Mr. George Williams. He mentioned it to Officer Brent, the cop who walked the beat and always stopped in to chat and use the restroom. "I'm tellin' ya Brent, somethin' smells with that guy Williams. He checks in about an hour ago wearin' a thousand-dollar suit with five hundred dollar shoes and a hundred-dollar haircut. He pulls out a wad of bills and pays for a week in advance. I ain't seen that much money on one guy 'cept in the movies. He didn't have no kind a luggage 'cept two briefcase lookin' things. He had a funny accent and wasn't very friendly."

Harry answered. "Homicide, Lincoln. Yes, my partner and I are the detectives looking for that Russian fugitive. You say The Savoy Hotel in the third precinct? Yes, I know where it is. Yes, I also know it's not The Ritz Carlton." Officer Brent relayed what the desk clerk had told him about the man. "He just doesn't fit; you know, like 'the square peg in the round hole'. I thought about the lookout you put out on the Russian."

"You did the right thing Brent," Harry told him. "Stick around the lobby. Don't let him leave, but be careful, he's armed and very dangerous. We'll get the SWAT team headed your way, and we're leaving downtown right now.

***

They were all in place and ready. All the civilians were evacuated from the third floor. SWAT lined the third floor hallway on either side of the door marked 3B. 3rd precinct cops outside on the ground in the rear and side alleys of the hotel. Harry and Floyd stood-by at the end of the hallway near the stairs. On the pre-arranged signal door 3B was taken down with a battering ram and a flash-bang grenade was thrown into the room. Boris Zherkov had been sitting on the bed. Before he realized what all the noise was about, he was face down on the floor handcuffed. Harry and Floyd entered the room and advised the SWAT commander that he and his partner would take the Russian off his hands and transport him to the homicide office to process him in. Have your man retrieve his cuffs, I'll use mine.

On the way through the hotel lobby they saw Officer Brent. "We're grateful to you for alertness and quick action," Floyd told him. "Because of that a very bad man is off the street and will hurt no one else. We'll be sure to send an atta-boy letter to you commanding officer." And, to the desk clerk, Floyd said, "Don't be surprised if you get a letter from the chief of police."

At the homicide office, Boris was placed in a holding cell, a solitary cell in the basement away from everyone else. Harry had Olga brought in. She identified the man as Boris Zherkov. Floyd returned Olga to the women's section of the jail, then went to the squad room to start what would be a voluminous report.

Harry Lincoln was finally alone with Boris Zherkov. "Okay Mr. KGB man, you're a real tough guy with a bunch of helpless and defenseless girls and women. You're lucky that a lot of people saw you leave that hotel without a mark on you, because nothing would give me greater pleasure than to strip you naked and beat you unconscious with a thick leather belt."

"Please Mr. Detective, would you please loosen these handcuffs on me?" Boris asked. "They are cutting off the circulation in my hands and starting to hurt me very much."

"Let me adjust them for you," Harry squeezed them as tightly as he could. Zherkov cried out and begged him to please loosen them. "Okay tough guy, let's see how tough you are when it's you on the receiving end of excruciating pain. Those cuffs will stay just the way they are until morning."

Boris Zherkov started to beg and plead, and then he began to scream, and within a few minutes he started to cry. Harry looked at him without pity, without mercy. "Is that how those girls and women begged, pleaded, screamed and cried, Mr. Tough Guy?... Have a good night." Harry turned his back and walked out of the cell.

The next morning Floyd went down to the holding cells to bring Zherkov up to an interrogation room for questioning. He found him on the floor, unconscious. Upon a quick examination he found the handcuffs still on. His hands had turned purple, grotesquely swollen to twice their normal size. He tried but could not unlock the cuffs with his key. They had cut through the skin and were embedded in the flesh down to the bone. He notified Harry and then Lieutenant McGee who in turn called fire rescue. As the firefighters worked with their metal cutting equipment, Zherkov stirred and began to beg and cry. The handcuffs were finally cut off but cutting them off caused more damage to his hands. Zherkov was sent to the hospital under heavy police guard. His ankles were secured to the hospital bed while the doctors treated him.

***

When the three were back in McGee's office, the lieutenant closed the door and said, "Harry, you've got to get rid of your venom, that hatefulness that causes you to become a vigilante. We are police officers, not vigilantes who render street justice to perpetrators because they committed horribly heinous crimes against innocent defenseless victims." Harry sat and said nothing. Floyd just listened and thought of what Liz Kovak had told him. "I don't know how far this episode will go, and who's to complain? But you know internal affairs. We all know that piece of shit deserved it and more, but we can't do it. So Harry next time think about it before we all get fired, and control your temper… like me." That forced a few chuckles.

Lieutenant McGee changed the tone. "You both did an outstanding job on this case, the same as others that you've worked as partners. 'The Presidents'… I like it."

***

Later, sitting in Mike's Tavern enjoying a burger and a brew Floyd said, "You know Harry, that woman from Senegal, Awa Senghor. She is the most beautiful woman, that I've ever seen in person."

Epilogue

The doctors saved Boris Zherkov's hands, but they were so damaged, nearly useless. He could hardly eat or dress himself. There was no department inquiry into the cause of the injuries suffered by Boris Zherkov. Harry Lincoln had administered some street justice for the female victims. The buzz around the department was about the pay back by Harry Lincoln. No one cared… not even Internal Affairs!

Each of the female victims went through the detoxification treatment. Their heroin addictions cured, they were sent back to their homelands, escorted by caring and courteous U.S. State Department personnel.

Boris Zherkov was found guilty on all counts. He was sentenced to the death penalty. Ivan Bluvich was found guilty, sentenced to thirty years. Victor Romanoff was found guilty and sentenced to twenty-five years. Olga Aslof, due to her cooperation and testimony, was allowed to enter a plea, she received a five-year sentence, with three to serve, and five years of supervised probation when released from prison. The other men arrested at the compound were sentenced to not less than twenty years each.

Harry and Jessica rented a boat with a cabin and galley, spending a weekend on Lake Rockford. They spent most of the time below in their oversized bunk, coming up on deck only to enjoy the fresh air, the water and the magnificent sunsets, while sipping some vintage French wine.

And Floyd…

Dear Ms. Senghor,

I am Floyd Washington, one of the detectives that you met at the French Consulate during that dark time in our city. I have some vacation time coming and am planning a trip to Senegal. I will be staying at the Imperial Hotel in downtown Dakar. I would like to invite you and your family for dinner with me, as my guests. If you are interested in my invitation, please write to me, Detective Floyd Washington, in care of Zealand Police Headquarters, Homicide Squad, Zealand, VA 21308, USA. When I receive your letter I will let you know when I am going to be in Dakar.

With sincere respect and admiration,

Floyd Washington

P.S. Madam Dubarre translated this letter into French for me at the consulate.

The Steel Swastika

Prologue

The front door of the synagogue was wide open. "*Odd,*" the man thought, "*I am always the first one in to open the shul early on the weekend, for Shabbat.*" He was responsible to see that everything is in order for the holy services. The man entered and walked down the center aisle between the pews. The sacred Torahs were strewn about, the holy scriptures desecrated.

Suddenly, he stopped. Stunned. He could not believe what he was seeing.

The Rabbi, his back pressed against the wall. He did not respond when the man called out to him. The Rabbi was bloody, not moving.

"No, no! My GOD no!" The man ran out into the middle of the busy street screaming, babbling. "Help him, please help him. Nooooo!!" Passers-by asked what was wrong as they hurriedly led him back onto the sidewalk. Someone called 911.

Two NYPD patrol cars responded quickly. The cops calmed the man down, reducing his hysteria to a level where he was able to tell them what he had seen inside. "I can't believe it; I can't believe it!"

The distraught man led the four police officers inside where they halted, captured by what they saw behind the altar -- the Rabbi, large nails driven through the palm of each outstretched hand, large nails through the instep of each foot. He was nailed to the wall. A rope around his neck tied to an overhead beam held his head facing upward. It appeared as though the Rabbi had been crucified.

Pinned to the front of his shirt was a note: "*This will happen to all you Christ killin' Jew bastards!*" It was signed, not with the name identifying the person who wrote it, it was signed with a symbol – the Nazi swastika.

One of the responding police officers called for a superior officer, then roped off the entrance to the synagogue.

Because all such calls are monitored at central communications, NYPD homicide detectives, the medical examiner, and crime scene techs, were dispatched to the scene. A resurgence of neo-Nazi activity had plagued New York City in recent months. What made this different were, the note pinned to the victim and the significant way in which he was murdered.

The New York Times reported it on its front page; so did other national and inter-national news reports, print and electronic. Big bold red headlines screaming across the entire front page of the New York Post proclaimed: NEO-NAZIS CRUCIFY RABBI IN BROOKLYN SYNAGOGUE!

The synagogue had deteriorated since it was built in the early 1900's. Some years later it was dwarfed as five-story apartment buildings arose on either side in this working-class neighborhood of Brooklyn, New York. Now this storefront place of worship was hardly noticeable as people walked by. It was an Orthodox Synagogue, the original congregation comprised mostly elderly Jewish men and women mainly from Eastern Europe. The majority came to the United States to escape the Russian pogroms. Years later many of the subsequent generation of European Jews, became aware of what was happening in Germany and in neighboring countries where Nazis ruled or influenced government. They fled Europe before Hitler could send them to their deaths. Millions more Jews in many countries in Europe were not so fortunate.

CHAPTER

1

On this mild and sunny Virginia day, two Zealand PD homicide detectives descended the concrete steps of the criminal courts building. "One more murdering bastard off the streets," proclaimed Harry Lincoln as he 'high-fived' his partner Floyd Washington. The two detectives were leaving the District Attorney's office after submitting their latest case file to the DA for prosecution. Assistant District Attorney Martin Kline thanked them and assured them that a conviction would be a 'slam-dunk.'

"It's been a long tough case," Floyd remarked. "Sometimes it caused me to lose my appetite and keep me awake at night. I know it was the same for you Harry. Let's head over to Mike's Tavern, have lunch, and enjoy it without thinking about anything else except what we are eating."

Harry thought for a moment and spoke slowly as if he were talking to himself, "As vile as this last guy was, I think that Russian barbarian last year was worse," referring to billionaire sex-slaver Boris Zherkov, now sitting on death row.

***

Back at the squad room, their digestive systems once again back to normal, Homicide Lieutenant James McGee was pleased with the final briefing from Lincoln and Washington on the homicide case just turned over to the district attorney. They added the 'slam-dunk' comment by ADA Kline. "You did a good job on a very high-profile case," McGee told them. "The chief and chief of detectives asked me to pass on a couple of 'atta-boys' to you both." McGee's smile then faded, and his usual scowl appeared. "Pleasantries over, back to the real world. An elderly man was brought into the ER at Zealand Memorial in critical condition. He was beaten badly. A 5th precinct uniform is waiting for you with the particulars. Keep the 'atta-boys' coming, can't have 'The Presidents' get an 'aw-shit'."

***

They found the responding officer in the police detention area down the corridor from the ER. "The victim had just come out of the little synagogue on 10th Street near Maple Drive in midtown. He walked the short distance to where the alley separates the apartment buildings. That's where he was grabbed and dragged into the alley." The officer referring from his notebook. "They beat and kicked him until he no longer screamed nor moved. Several people on the street heard the screams and hurried to the alley in time to see three men running away towards the opposite end of the alley. The victim was on the ground bleeding. He was not moving. One of the witnesses called 911."

The cop handed several sheets of notebook paper to Washington. "Here, I got the names and addresses of the witnesses, and a vague description of the perps. I don't have an ID on the victim. All the other stats are on these sheets." The cop left thinking, *"I'm glad to be just a beat cop answering calls, handling wrecks and writing traffic tickets. I'd hate to work past my eight-hour watch and have to figure all that shit out."*

***

"Ah, my two favorite detectives," exclaimed Dr. David Deutch, Chief Physician of the ER, as he shook hands with Lincoln and Washington. "I suppose you are here concerning the elderly gentleman brought in about an hour ago?"

"Yes doc," said Harry, "What can you tell us about his condition?"

"His injuries are severe. When he arrived he was unresponsive. The trauma team was able to bring him around and stabilize him. He's up in the operating room now. Because of the extent of the trauma he suffered, the nature of the injuries and his advanced age I cannot give you a prognosis at this time. As of right now, he is critical." Dr. Deutch paused, then added, "When you find out who he is and if he has any family, please let us know."

"Yes, we are about to look into that now," Floyd told him. "We'll be in touch."

***

"Morris Silverman," said Rabbi Aaron Rothstein identifying the victim, as he sat in the front pew of the old synagogue with the detectives. "Why would someone want to hurt a mild-mannered eighty-six-year-old man?"

"That's why we are here, rabbi. We think robbery might have been the motive. His pockets were empty, no wallet, no money, no watch or rings. What can you tell us about him?"

"He is a member of our congregation. He also comes in several times a week when we are not having services to help with chores, you know, 'house cleaning'. We are cleaning out the shul of things that have collected over the years and no longer have any need for." The rabbi paused, then continued. "It's dirty work. So, Morris keeps an old pair of overalls here to change into. When he got dressed and left earlier today, he forgot to take his wallet and those other items you mentioned. I have them inside, I'll get them for you."

Harry asked, "Do you know of any problems he might have had with anyone, any threats or enemies? We also will need his address."

"As far as I know there was nothing like that, but I'll ask around. His address is here in his wallet," the rabbi said as he handed the wallet to Floyd. "Morris lives with his daughter and her family." Floyd wrote out a receipt for the wallet, watch, wedding ring, two credit cards plus forty-three dollars in bills.

"I'm very worried about Morris. I would like to know how he is doing."

Floyd responded, "Mr. Silverman was in the operating room when we left the hospital to come here. He is in critical condition; the outcome is unknown at this time."

Harry handed the rabbi the cards with their contact information, asking him to call if he had any additional information about anyone who could have attacked Mr. Silverman. "As you make inquiries of the congregation, and around the neighborhood, please call us with what you learn."

As they were leaving Floyd told the rabbi that they would go by the address and notify Mr. Silverman's daughter of what happened to her father, and where he is. The recovered items would be turned over to her.

CHAPTER

2

After they parked the car, the trio went directly into the main building to speak with Hans Schultz the club president. "Hans you were right! Zealand does have Jew churches an' we found a crummy little one," said the biggest of the three. "We watched it for a time an' when some old Jew came out we followed him. We snatched him into an alley an' beat an' stomped the shit out the little Jew bastard until he stopped hollerin', an' didn't move no more. The ol' kike didn't even put up a fight. Some people come an' looked down the alley, so we took off."

"They never seen our faces," bragged one of them, "it was worth the four-hour drive to get to kick the kike." Causing the four to have a good laugh.

***

Nestled in the Appalachian Mountains of West Virginia lay seventy-eight acres of abandoned farmland. It had been auctioned off in the late 1960's to an individual for a fraction of its worth. The original farmhouse, and the barn along with almost a dozen out buildings built after the first world war were still standing. The new owner, Herman Schultz Jr. did not work the land. Instead, he used the location to form a social club for members only. Under the veneer of respectability, it was really an ominous secret society. They were aligned philosophically with dozens of other similar white supremacist groups across the U.S. The big difference was that this group was prone to extreme violence.

Its membership, numbered close to one hundred, consisted exclusively of white Christian males, some with wives, some with girlfriends, some with both. The men ranged in age from the late teens to the sixties, a few at seventy or eighty plus years. They were mostly working class, although there were professionals and politicians. The electricians among them updated the electric system with new wiring replacing old wires having insulation that had deteriorated, causing dangerous short circuits. The plumbers modernized by replacing all the old pipes with brass and copper pipes and installed indoor bathrooms with hot and cold running water. The carpenters renovated and added sturdy lumber to shore up the old sagging buildings.

***

Herman's father, Herman Schultz Sr. and his wife left Germany in the mid 1920's because of bad economic times there. They emigrated to the United States. They were processed through Ellis Island, and took up residence in New York City. When the U.S. stock market crashed in 1929, precipitating the economic depression, he was worse off than when he was in Germany. He was disillusioned and became very bitter. There was no steady work. He and his wife avoided starvation by getting whatever nutrition available in bread and soup lines. They lived in a rundown one-room cold water flat, with a communal bathroom at the end of the hall. They lived a meager existence on part time work, cleaning streets, and whatever other menial type work when they could get it. Herman Schultz Jr. was born, a mistake of his parent's careless sex in 1930, adding to their burden and increasing the new father's bitterness.

***

Schultz Sr. kept up with the political situation in Germany through newspapers and the radio. National Socialism was gaining momentum in the 'old country,' as he referred to it, indicating he still felt more a part of Germany than his new country. A new charismatic leader of the National Socialist party emerged. In 1933 Adolf Hitler and his Nazis took control of Germany.

That same year Franklin D. Roosevelt was elected to his first term as President of the United States of America. His top priority was to pull the country out of the economic depression. Within a few years, through Roosevelt's "New Deal" programs the Great Depression ended, and the country went back to work. Slowly, the people in the U.S. got their lives back.

Still a German citizen, Schultz Sr. cared more about his Fatherland then the country he lived in. The fact that he now had a steady fulltime, well-paying job, living in a nice five room apartment and his small family ate three good meals a day, his loyalties never the- less, remained with the old country. Hitler and the Nazis, as well as most German citizens blamed the Treaty of Versailles ending World War I for all of Germany's ills and misfortunes. But the National Socialists took out their venom on the Jews and communists. Both, the Nazis said were behind a worldwide Jewish-Zionist plot to turn Germany into a communist state with the Jews in charge.

From 1933 the Jews of Germany were persecuted. They lost their livelihoods. They were no longer allowed to practice medicine, law or any other profession. Those with businesses were first boycotted and then destroyed. They were assaulted and beaten in the streets by anyone who blamed the Jews for their own failures. The police stood off at a distance and did not intervene. Not much later, all the Jews were rounded up and forced into concentration camps.

Schultz Sr. idolized 'Der Fuhrer,' the German words for 'The Leader', Adolf Hitler. The senior Schultz attended huge German-American Bund rallies in New York City's Madison Square Garden. Twenty-two thousand of them, some with brown shirt, storm trooper-like uniforms, Nazi swastika armbands, singing

German patriotic songs, straight right arm "Sieg Heil" salutes. Addressing the crowd from the stage, each speaker's fanatic anti-Semitic rhetoric had the audience in a frenzy. Schultz was on his feet. He hated the Jews as viciously as any Nazi did in Germany.

Herman Schultz Jr. grew up in this household, hearing his father rant of his hatred of the Jews. In September 1939, when young Herman Jr. was nine years old, Germany invaded Poland starting World War II. By that time Jr., like Sr. was a fervent anti-Semite. Schultz encouraged his son, and some of his friends to wait outside after school for the two Jewish boys in his class and beat them up. The father told his son and his friends that when Germany won the war, Hitler was coming to the U.S. to finish the job on the Jews. "When that happens, we'll catch you and cut your eyes out," jeered the young bullies to the Jewish boys.

In the ensuing years, Herman Jr. completed high school, met a girl through the Bund and they married. More time passed before they had their only child, a son they named Hans. Herman Jr. worked a variety of inconsequential jobs until he was in his late-thirties when, with the aid of Herman Sr. was able to acquire the abandoned farm.

***

The old farm was home to young Hans. He attended a small country school within a thirty-minute drive from the farm. When Hans was midway through elementary school his grandfather Herman Schultz Sr. died from cancer. Hans recalled how Grandpapa Herman talked about the Jews, and how and why he hated them. As time went on, Hans now going to the small high school adjacent to the elementary school, his father continued the anti-Semitic indoctrination. Along with his hatred of the Jews, Herman Jr. included; "the niggers, spics, slopes, rag headed camel jockeys, faggots and the fuckin' liberals."

After high school, Hans stayed at the farm to help his father, Herman Jr. run the 'club.' Several years passed until Herman Jr.

became too old and frail to function handing over the leadership to his son. Hans Schultz, the third generation bigoted anti-Semite, was tired of all the ranting and raving achieving no evident objectives. His goal was to increase the violence from coast to coast throughout the country.

"Enough talk," Hans shouted to the crowd of members at a large gathering. "I want action like the last few times. We're going to make the Jew liberal press sit up and take notice. 'There is a new order!'" Hans mimicking his Nazi forefathers of the 1930's.

CHAPTER

3

Morris Silverman died on the operating room table despite that the doctors feverishly attempted to save him. The multiple injuries sustained by this elderly patient were too severe. Upgraded from aggravated assault, Detectives Lincoln and Washington now had a homicide to investigate.

"Harry let's round up those witnesses who talked to the officer," Floyd said. "Maybe they saw more than just three guys running."

***

"I was just coming out of the cleaners when I heard screaming. It was coming from the alley across the street. By the time I got there, three guys were at the opposite end of the alley running away. I saw them from their backs. I never saw their faces. I went to the man on the ground, he wasn't moving. Several other people came and were looking at him. I called 911."

"Other than their faces," Harry asked this witness from the list provided by the police officer at the hospital, "could you tell if they were teenagers or grown men, what were they wearing or whatever else you can tell us that might help to identify them? Could you tell if they were white or black?"

"They were men all right, pretty big too. I think they were white. That's about all I can tell you about them because my attention was on this poor guy just lying there bleeding." He then asked, "How is he?"

"He died at the hospital." Floyd handed him their cards asking him to call if he thought of anything else. "As we learn more you might have to come and give a written statement." Floyd thanked him as they left to find the other witnesses. As they were located and interviewed, no additional information was learned.

The next day Harry and Floyd knocked on doors most of the day and part of the evening. Canvassing a crime scene was basic homicide investigation 101. The task of speaking with the occupants of the apartments facing the alley on both sides was time consuming. Most who had witnessed the incident from their windows said the same thing. They heard the yelling, saw the assault of the man on the ground, and three men running. They all agreed the attackers were white. They each said they could not identify them. However, they did say there was some sort of design on the backs of their jackets. The detectives gave their cards to all, requesting they call should they think of anything else.

After briefing Lieutenant McGee on the day's events, the detectives were at their desks entering the interviews into the case file. Harry said "We all know that a graphic design on the back of a jacket is a common sight. Violent motorcycle gangs like the 'Hell's Angels' the 'Outlaws' and the 'Banditos' to name a few, wear their colors on their jackets. But so do a lot of social clubs each display an emblem identifying who they are."

""You're right Harry," said Floyd clearing off his desk. "However, most are not criminal nor violent."

***

Driving home, Harry stopped to pick up a take-out dinner of fried chicken and salad. Once inside his very private loft, he quickly removed his suit and the annoying tie, changing into a pair of sweats. While eating his dinner, he watched the local news. There was very little of the Silverman homicide. The national and international news followed, which he tried to watch, workload permitting, on a daily basis.

With the TV now off, and the kitchen cleaned up, Harry settled into his comfortable recliner, when the phone rang. It was Floyd. "Harry, I've been thinking about those designs on the jackets of the three perps. Let's not focus too much on them and get sidetracked with a lot of effort that might go nowhere."

"You're probably right Floyd, that same thought has been rumbling around in my head also. I'll see you in the morning."

He would spend the rest of the evening reading the book he had started the night before, *The Story of Danny Dunn,* by the Australian author Bryce Courtenay. In one phase of Danny Dunn's life, he was an Australian soldier during world war ll. Captured by the Japanese, he spent almost two years in a POW camp enduring cruel, brutal treatment from sadistic prison guards. He had been repeatedly beaten with rifle butts and truncheons, leaving a permanent spinal injury, the loss of an eye and his face disfigured. The meager rations of rice and gruel left him almost skeletal upon his liberation. While reading, Harry tried to imagine himself in that situation. Were he to survive the POW camp, would he react as did Danny Dun, after the war. It was an interesting question, food for thought.

It was after midnight when heavy eyelids forced him to put the book down and go to bed. The alarm went off much too soon, the green numbers read 6:00 am. Harry got out of bed and once in the shower slowly came awake. The tepid water felt good and relaxing. He knew that within the hour, as soon as he got to the squad room, the serenity he felt would be interrupted by some violent tragedy that would become his world for a while. He thought, *"well Harry you wanted to be a homicide detective."*

CHAPTER

4

The old barn had been renovated into a large assembly room with theater-like seating. Dur Fuhrer, Hans Schultz called for a meeting of the members. "As you all know, several days ago three of our troopers went to Zealand and beat an old yid to death. It was reported on page six of the daily newspaper there. It was not even the lead story on their local TV news, it was only reported after the first commercial break. It hasn't been mentioned in the news since."

Hans paused as he looked around silent room.

"As you also know, me and some of the boys went up to Jew York City and found us a ratty little Jew church where we met the rabbi and made him famous. We nailed his kike ass to the wall right there in front by the altar."

The room came alive with some hooting and hollering.

"It was front page headlines in every newspaper up there. It was front page news in most papers around the whole U.S. All the networks televised it their top story. It's almost two weeks now and they are still talking about it."

After a few minutes when they all quieted down Hans made his point.

"So, when we go on these assignments and operations, we want to make some noise, do something special. Get the attention of the public and let the press spread the word. We don't want to be identified. But we want them all to know that these incidents will continue until all the undesirables are driven under rocks like the vermin they are."

With that the entire room jumped up, stood at ridged attention, clicked their heels together and gave a stiff-armed salute with a resounding, "Sieg Heil!"

"But above all, this compound, our headquarters is to be top secret. Those who live here and the rest of you who live elsewhere, this location will remain anonymous to the outside world. We are fortunate here in the mountains of West Virginia to be ignored as a private social club. So, get with your group leaders and let's make some noise!" As the meeting broke up and the members filed out, Schultz watched and felt confident that his following would remain loyal, keeping all activities secret.

"Sheriff Hayes," said Schultz, "could I have a private word with you?"

Blanton County Sheriff Luke Hayes presided over all law enforcement duties in this small rural slice of West Virginia. The Sheriff and his three deputies were valuable assets, their loyalty unquestioned. It was no different with the county manager and the two council members, as well as the rest of Blanton County's business and professional leaders.

"Luke, we are the best kept secret since the 'Manhattan Project' of World War II. I attribute that to you and your men," Hans beamed.

"Hans you can depend on us. No outsiders gonna' be snoopin' round here." The sheriff paused, then followed with "…ya know Hans speakin' a World War II, 'ol Adolf had it right about the Jews. Maybe things might have been different today. But that dumb bastard fucked up when he double-crossed his Russian buddy Stalin and caused his army to fight a war on two fronts. Adolf's big damn ego did him in."

***

Later, in his private office Hans Schultz sat in one of the comfortable club chairs talking with Otto Shafer sitting in the other. "Otto you've been with me since I took over this organization. You are my most loyal and trusted lieutenant. I've been thinking about expanding and increasing our efforts."

Hans was staring through the window behind his friend and seemed to be talking to himself. "There are many brotherhoods like ours, groups across the country that think like us."

He now looked directly at Otto. "They have different names, some names derogatory, shouted over and over by the liberal Jewish press meant to demonize us all: White Supremacists, Neo-Nazis, Skinheads, Ku Klux Klan, among others not so popularly known. What if we all were to merge into one vast brotherhood from coast to coast? Together we would give them something to shout about. Think of what we could accomplish."

"I like it," beamed his number one yes man. "But how in the hell are you gonna' do that?"

"Just watch me Otto," said a smug Hans Schultz. "Just watch me."

CHAPTER

5

"Lincoln, Washington in my office," bellowed Lieutenant McGee across the squad room. As the three settled in around his desk the lieutenant asked for an update on the Silverman homicide.

"We don't have a hell-of-a-lot more than what was initially reported. Three large white males, ages 20's to 30's wearing matching jackets with the same design on the back. We've ruled out robbery as a motive," Floyd read from a small notebook.

"Mr. Silverman had just left his synagogue a half block from the alley where the assault took place," added Harry. "Floyd and I have been thinking about the homicide in New York City that's been all over the news. The rabbi found inside nailed to the synagogue wall over the altar. We wondered if there might be some connection, or was it just a weird coincidence?"

"You know what I think of coincidences. Check it out and see where it goes. Let me know," said McGee signaling the end of the meeting. "But first go by the Zealand ER on a vicious aggravated battery. Meet a uniform there for the details, then go up to the burn unit. That's where your two victims are.

***

The officer waiting in the hospital's police detention area gave them the slimmest of details. "I received a call of an unknown disturbance at the Homestead Apartments in the 3rd Precinct, one of those run-down neighborhoods that is being gentrified. As I got out of the car I heard the screams. I followed the sounds to an open apartment door and went in. The source of the screaming was coming from two men, one on a bed the other lying on the floor. They both looked like they had been burned. Several large empty cooking pots were on the floor. Everything was wet. I called for an ambulance."

Then he added, "Sergeant Evans called for a crime scene unit. When the techs arrived, they took photos and measurements. They also collected the pots and some other items."

***

The Zealand Hospital Burn Unit was the largest in the state. "They are both heavily sedated and unable to talk," the doctor informed Harry and Floyd. "They have extensive third degree burns primarily in the pelvic and rectal areas. Their faces were also badly burned. It appears that the cause was liquid, probably boiling water. They also sustained injuries about the head and face. The trauma made clear that they were beaten. It will be several days before you can speak with them. If you want to look in on them for a couple of minutes, the nurse will give you lab coats and masks. Keep your distance from their beds. In their present condition they are very susceptible to infection."

***

"My God Harry, what little was visible, not covered by the dressings was hideous," Floyd said in the car heading back to the apartments.

"Yeah partner, third degree burns on the human body are tough to look at. Probably the most painful injury there is," Harry agreed. "Let's talk with the neighbor who called 911, then knock on some doors to try to find out who else saw or heard anything."

***

The apartment belonging to the victims had a sign on the door. 'Crime scene. Do not enter!' Crime scene tape crossed the door in several places.

They knocked on the door across the hall. Ms. Elsie Green the neighbor explained to the two detectives what caused her to call the police. The seventy-two-year-old woman lived in her apartment for over twenty-five years. "My husband died near five years ago, and I've been staying by myself since," she said. "These apartments, just like the neighborhood been black until those two young white men moved in a while ago. Nice polite boys never heard much out of them."

"Did they have any company? Did you notice anyone visit them?" Floyd asked.

"Not until late last night when I heard all the commotion, the screaming and hollering. I had just gone to bed. I got up and looked out of my front door peep hole and saw some white men running down the hallway. I went to my window and saw them get in a pickup truck and leave in a hurry. The screaming was still going on from the boy's apartment, so I called 911."

"Ms. Green could you describe the men you saw? How many where there?" Harry asked.

"It all was so fast all I could tell they was big white men, but older than teen-agers. Then when I saw them getting in the truck, there were four of them, but it was too dark to tell anything else."

"How about the pickup truck Ms. Green?" What can you tell us about it?"

"Well I can't say what kind it was, but it seemed like it was very big and it had two wheels on each side of the back. In the dark it looked like some kind of maroon. Oh, and it made a loud noise when it drove off."

CHAPTER

6

"We hit the jackpot Mr. Schultz, it was awesome. Those two fuckin' faggots won't be doin' none of that queer shit for a long time, if ever again." The four men had returned from Zealand and were in the main office reporting to Hans Schultz.

"Just start at the beginning and tell me what happened," instructed the boss.

"Well we drove around the city until we found that queer joint you told us about. We went in and saw that it was filled with only men, well they were not really men, they were faggots. Not a woman in the place. Slow music was playin' an' they was dancin' with each other. Two of them was doin' a lot of kissin' while they was dancin'. After a while they left an' we followed them to these apartments where they lived. We parked and saw them go in a ground floor apartment. We sat in the truck for some time watchin' people comin' an' goin' an' the only white people we saw was those two faggots, the rest was niggers. It got late an' things slowed down so we got out of the truck an' looked around."

Another of the foursome interrupted, adding: "In the back was a small porch with a slidin' glass door leadin' into the apartment. The dumb fucks left it unlocked an' made it easy for us."

The first of the thugs continued. "We went in real quiet an' stood in the livin' room an' listened. The place was all dark. The only light was comin' from down a hall which turned out to be the bedroom. We heard some noises from there, ya know like when ya gettin' it on. Talkin' shit an' moanin', an' like that."

A third goon of the quartet insisted in telling the next part. "We bust in an' there they was both nakid on the bed. One of them on his knees an' elbows, his ass stickin' up in the air. The other one behind him mounted like a bull on a cow, packin' that ass with a good dose a' AIDS. I pulled the bull off the cow and he started to scream and holler an' I told him to shut up. He kept on, so I hit him in his nose with my brass knucks, which flattened it bloody all over his face. He stopped. I told him if he made any more noise I would hit him again. He did. So I hit him in his jaw and mouth, breakin' his jaw and removin' some teeth. He was cryin', no longer screamin'. The others were doing the same to the cow."

The first one and apparent leader of the foursome wolf pack followed up. "There was two large pots on the stove, one filled with soup the other boilin' some kinda noodles. Both burners still on. Two other big empty pots was hangin' on ceillin' hooks. We filled them with water an' put em' on the stove, the burners turned up to high. They both started to holler again, and each received a hard kick in the balls. After that they couldn't talk. When all four pots were bollin' the water and soup was poured over their dicks and balls, and into their asses. Some boilin' water was poured on their faces so they wouldn't be pretty boys no more. We hung a sign around one of their necks, *'Say goodbye to the rest of the faggots an all the other trash who want to take over our country.'* We drew a Nazi swastika at the bottom like you told us. The screamin' and hollerin' started again an' that's when we got the hell out of there. No one saw us."

"Good job boys," beamed Hans Schultz. "Mission accomplished. Let's see how much coverage this gets in the newspapers and on TV. It might not be as much like when we crucified that Jew rabbi in New York, but the press eats this shit up. Sells a lot of newspapers and ups the TV ratings. That's what they call their bottom line."

CHAPTER

7

They sat near the rear of the restaurant dining room at a window table. The view was picturesque and peaceful, a mountain stream flowing over rocks in continuous motion through the rustic foliage and trees. The table was set with a crisp white linen table cloth and napkins with four place settings of fine china, sterling silver cutlery and sparkling crystal glasses.

Floyd had invited Harry and Jessica for dinner at this popular upscale restaurant to celebrate his engagement to his girlfriend, Awa Senghor. The four had been double dating for several months and became as close as family. Floyd and Awa had made the decision in the last few days and wanted to make it official to their best friends with a nice dinner.

Each time Harry saw Awa it was a bitter-sweet memory. A year and a half ago, he and Floyd had broken up the sex slavery ring operated by Boris Zherkov a billionaire Russian gangster. His henchmen searched depressed areas of countries around the world for poverty stricken young women, although only exceptionally attractive young women. The promise of better lives, lured the women to his base in Zealand, Virginia where they were held captive. They were forcibly given large doses of heroin until they were hopeless addicts. These young women were required to sexually service the very rich and powerful of the city, and to satisfy every perversion, fantasy and fetish. Any complaint would cause the offending woman to suffer harsh physical punishment. But the main control was withholding their daily dose of heroin which they each desperately needed.

Awa Senghor, one of these unfortunate young women was recruited from Dakar, Senegal on the west coast of Africa. However, after the usual indoctrination including her forced heroin addiction, Awa had not been sent to service any clients. Zherkov kept her for his own pleasure, which strangely enough did not involve any type of physical sexual activity. He had gotten plenty of that from any of the women under his control. The pleasure from Awa was visual, as he liked to look at her dressed and undressed. Her wardrobe was chosen by Zherkov, from form-fitting dresses, skirts and tops to sexy, intimate lingerie. When they were alone, Awa had to pose for him in various ways modeling these items of clothing. He also required her to be completely naked standing, sitting, lying down or simply walking around the apartment. He looked at her, but never touched her.

Lincoln and Washington were assigned as the lead detectives. This brutal enterprise was broken up, Zherkov and his gang arrested, the women rescued. During the rescue mission Floyd could not take his eyes off Awa Senghor. He considered her the most beautiful woman he had ever seen. The women were admitted to a drug rehab center to end their addiction. After several months the U.S. State Department made arrangements to return them to their countries of origin.

"Harry, I can't get Awa Senghor, the woman from Senegal out of my mind," Floyd repeated in the following weeks. "That smooth dark ebony skin, her outstanding figure and her face with those beautiful features. The elegance of her close-cropped hair completed the picture. I dream about her all the time. In addition to her beauty, she carries herself with an air of royalty."

"Listen partner, do something about it. Take some of that vacation time you've been saving and pay her a visit." Harry was glad for Floyd's interest; he had grieved over his wife's death long enough. It was time for another woman in his life.

Floyd did take the trip and the week-long visit. It was enjoyable for both him and Awa. However, they had trouble communicating. Awa spoke only French (the main language of

Senegal, plus the local Senegalese dialect) and Floyd spoke only English. Fortunately, a family member spoke both interpreting each for the other. They both agreed to study the other's language. They exchanged letters and shortly after, Awa obtained her passport and required visa. Floyd sent her travel money for the trip to Zealand and rented a small studio apartment for her in his complex. She got a job at the French Consulate in downtown Zealand where the Council General, a sympathetic woman who was instrumental in Awa's rescue, had not forgotten her.

Harry stood up from the table holding his wine glass. "I guess this is where I'm supposed to make a toast to the future bride and groom. I'm happy for both of you. I'm glad it's gotten this far. Now I won't have to hear about 'the beautiful girl from Senegal' for eight hours every working day. So, Jessica and I salute you both, wishing you the same happiness in the coming years that you are feeling right now. Let's drink up!" Harry sat down adding, "Just one more thing. I had better be the best man and Jessica the maid of honor."

***

The following morning word of the engagement had gotten around the squad room. Most of the homicide detectives remembered Awa when she and dozens of other women were rescued from captivity. They knew that Washington had returned her to the U.S., and that they were dating. There were acknowledgments from colleagues, mostly from the female detectives. "Congratulations Floyd," said one of the women. "I know you will make each other happy. After what you both have been through, it's time for happiness." And another, "Good for you Floyd, glad you found the right one. You both will be better off once you get married."

Getting married was one of those things that had been going around in Floyd's head for the past several days. The words that seemed to sum up the entire relationship with Awa were --the opening lines from the Charles Dickens' classic novel, A Tale of Two Cities. *"It was the best of times, it was the worst of times, ..."*

The cloud that Floyd was floating on had suddenly returned to earth when from across the squad room, "Lincoln, Washington called Lieutenant McGee, the hospital just called, one of your burn victims is able to talk."

***

Two bloodshot eyes, flattened nostrils and a toothless mouth were evidence of a person visible through the mass of bandages encasing the head and face of the man struggling to talk. In spite of the massive trauma he suffered, he was determined to tell the detectives what had happened. They leaned down as close as they could and listened intently.

"I first noticed them at the club, we all did. There were four of them, large white men real redneck looking. They kept staring at us until we felt so uncomfortable that we left. They must have followed us home and broke in, because the next thing they attacked us. They poured scalding water and boiling soup over us both and beat us in our faces. All the while they were calling us queers and faggots, saying they were going to rid this country of our kind also the Jews and blacks, although they used the 'N' word."

He started to moan and said that Richard was not able to talk yet. "It's really hurting me to talk so I've got to stop. Will you please ask the nurse to bring me some more pain medicine on your way out?"

On the elevator after a brief stop at the nurse's station Harry asked, "Did you get all of that?"

"I think I did," said Floyd, "I give him a lot of credit for his ability to talk that much knowing the pain he must be in."

The identity of the victims was entered into the case file. George Moffit wm 32 and Richard Hendricks wm 28. Both local from the Zealand area. "The crude hand-written sign Harry, the one with the Nazi swastika left in their apartment," asked Floyd. "Wasn't that similar to the one hanging from the rabbi in New York City?"

"It sure seems like it. Let's contact the NYPD and ask them to fax us a copy." Within a short time, they had their answer. The crude signs were similar, the wording different, but the message was the same.

"Let's buzz the National Crime Information Center," said Harry. "Let's see if they have picked up any chatter concerning hate crimes with those type of signs left with the victims. One in New York City, the other here in Zealand. Could be something starting in more than one place."

CHAPTER

8

Hans Schultz sat alone at the bar drinking a beer while observing the scene around him. Country music blared from the juke box, competing with the shouted arguments laced with curses and threats from the all-white, mostly male crowd. The air was heavy with cigarette smoke causing the ceiling lights to fog. The law of the Commonwealth of Virginia made smoking in public places illegal. That law and some others were ignored by the patrons of this timeless bar. The old wooden floor warped and splintered with age was wet in spots from spewn dark tobacco juice.

Hans Schultz made the four-hour drive to this economically depressed section of Zealand. This area of the city remained lower working-class whites despite most businesses leaving and some abandoned homes. Hans remembered this bar. He parked among the many pickup trucks of every description, most older models, lined up on both sides of the narrow street. More than a dozen motorcycles were parked on the sidewalk near the door.

As Hans nursed his third beer, his attention was drawn to a group of men seated around a table in the corner. One of them seemed to be doing most of the talking, gesturing with his arms and hands. Occasionally hitting the table hard with his fists as the others listened quietly, nodding their heads in agreement. Within a short time, this man walked to the bar next to where Hans was sitting, put his empty bottle down and ordered another beer. On the side of the man's neck between his jawbone and shirt collar, Hans noticed an inch square tattoo of a Nazi swastika.

"I give you and your friends a lot of credit," Hans said to the man standing next to him.

"Oh yea, why's that?" The man answered looking at Hans suspiciously.

"Because when times got rough around here you didn't run away like a lot of those gutless bastards who lived here," Hans said loudly, looking the man straight in the eye. "You stayed put and didn't let the niggers and spics take over your neighborhood."

"Are you a cop? Or some kind of newspaper guy?" The man pointed his finger in Hans' face. "Maybe you're some fuckin' bleedin' heart liberal wanting to stir up some shit?"

"No, no, and no! My name is Hans Schultz. I live in the mountains of West Virginia about two hundred miles from here. I'm the president, the leader of a whites only club several hundred strong. We want to rid our country of the Jews, the niggers, the spics, the slopes, the rag headed sand jockeys, the fuckin' faggots, and the bleedin' heart liberals. We are ready, willing and able to do whatever it takes. I think we might be able to help each other."

"Okay, I'm gonna take a chance that you're legit, and what you told me is true. If I find out different, that you are bullshitin' me an' got something up your sleeve, you're liable to end up with a nine millimeter slug in each knee cap. My name is Doug Springdale. I live about four blocks from here. I'm a construction worker building that new bridge a few miles upriver."

He then said very cautiously, "I know four other people in four different cities that could be interested, but before I start naming names, I gotta be sure of you."

Hans thought he had hit the jackpot. "Listen Doug, when you get a couple of days off, why don't you drive over and visit my place and check us out? Here's my number."

***

Within a week the man from the bar contacted Schultz. Directions were given, and arrangements made for a visit. Two days later, Doug Springdale along with three other men arrived. They were met warmly by Hans Schultz. "One thing Doug, before we get down to business. I must ask that you and your men submit to a pat down search, just so we can be assured that no one is wearing a wire." The four were clean. No offense was taken. Otto Shafer joined the group, and after introductions were made, Springdale and his men toured the Schultz compound.

Later in the main building, this small group was served lunch privately permitting them to discuss things important to them. No one else was admitted. By the end of the day, everyone was comfortable with each other. That's when Hans decided to drop the bomb and cement the relationship.

In the confines of the hushed room, Hans Schultz looked intently at Springdale and said in a slow clear voice, "You heard about the Jew Rabbi crucified on the altar of the Jew church up in Jew York City? And you heard about the two faggots scalded with boiling water, and their faces broken up so bad that their mamas would not know them? And about the old kike beaten and stomped to death in an alley after leaving his Jew church? Those last two happened in Zealand." Hans paused and said with a measure of pride,

"All three was us!"

Doug Springdale and his entourage momentarily sat quiet. Springdale spoke up, the arrogance in his voice replaced with a respectful tone, "Mr. Schultz, I'll give you those four names and how to get in touch with them."

***

Several days later, the three sat in his private office where Hans Schultz had summoned Sheriff Hayes and Otto Shafer. "In the last few days I've made contact with those four groups Springdale gave us," Schultz informed them. "They are pretty much scattered about the country: New Orleans, Louisiana – Boise, Idaho – Montgomery, Alabama – and Denver, Colorado. The Jew press calls them white supremacists, hate groups like: neo-Nazis, KKK, skinheads and some other handles.

"I spoke with the leaders of the groups in each of those cities. We all agreed that we should combine forces because we want the same thing -- to give our country back to the God-fearing Christian white man. We are going to meet somewhere soon to make our plans. The Boise and Montgomery guys said they will get in touch with some groups they know from other cities."

CHAPTER

9

"Detective radio 199 calling Homicide 134, 136..."

136: "Go ahead 199"

199: "At Zealand Memorial ER, signal 50 (person shot) on an officer. Perp is also a 50."

136: "Copy that"

After squeezing their way through the crowd of cops at the entrance of the ER, Harry and Floyd were met by Dr. David Deutch. "It appears as though the officer was hit with three rounds. One in the chest, what you guys call 'center mass', another in the upper left arm at the shoulder, the third in the left thigh. The round in the chest would probably have been fatal but for his vest. The other two bullets passed through, missing any vital areas before exiting. The trauma team is currently prepping him for the OR. The development of the bullet proof vest is the second best thing invented behind the convince of 'paying-at-the-pump'." This broke the tension, bringing smiles to the faces of the three. Dr. Deutch added, "he'll be fine. He is a very lucky man."

"How about the other guy doc," asked Harry. "The one who shot the officer?"

"He came in DOA. It looked like he was hit four times center mass. We tried to bring him back, but it was too late. He was gone," said Dr. Deutch.

***

Initial reports indicated an attempted assassination. The

sudden, unprovoked shooting of a police officer while walking his beat as dusk settled over the city. Evening watch Officer E. R. Mosley was halfway through his shift when a man walked up to him without a word, pulled out a gun and starting shooting. On his way down Mosley returned fire hitting the man four times, killing him. Several people on the street plus others from an adjacent building witnessed the shootings.

Police Officer E. R. Mosley is a seven-year veteran of the Zealand Police Department.

"We had just walked past each other. I kind of waved at him and said,

"How're you doing officer?"

"He nodded his head and said," 'fine sir, and you?'

"I didn't take more than a couple of dozen steps when I heard the gun shots. When I turned around I saw the cop and another guy, both on the ground." This witness called 911.

Harry and Floyd spent the next couple of days interviewing and taking written statements from witnesses to the shooting.

"I am retired and in poor health I pass time looking out my second story window. I always see that cop walking down the street. Everyone around here knows him and chats with him. He's popular with folks in the neighborhood. The day it happened, it was just starting to get dark. But still plenty of light for me to see this big white guy walk right up in front of Officer Mosley and just shoot him. On the way down Mosley was able to draw his weapon to get off a few rounds. I grabbed my cell phone from my pocket and called 911."

The woman, still somewhat shaken, told the two detectives, "I own the florist shop a few doors down the street from where this happened. I heard some noises, but it never dawned on me that it was gun shots. People were yelling and screaming. I came outside and saw people running towards a police officer down on the sidewalk next to another person also on the ground. I could hear sirens in the distance and then from everywhere came police cars, followed by fire trucks and ambulances. Someone in the crowd said that Officer Mosley and the other man had shot each other. I was relieved to learn that the officer was going to be alright. Most days he would come into the shop to say hello and ask how I'm doing, stay for a few minutes looking at the flowers and plants. Several weeks ago, he came in and wanted to get his wife a dozen red roses for their anniversary. I told him there was no charge because I appreciated him looking out for me. He thanked me but insisted on paying for them. I made out the bill which covered my cost, not the selling price for the flowers. Why did that man shoot him? Was it because Officer Mosley is black?"

"We don't know that yet," answered Floyd. "But we are going to find out."

***

Was the motive strictly a hate crime because Eugene Mosley is black?

Was it because Mosley is a police officer?

Was it because Officer E. R. Mosley is a black police officer?

Had there been prior contact between the two that resulted in a grudge shooting?

Those questions were being asked by law enforcement, by the media and by the general public. The unknown white male carried no identification, all his pockets were empty. His prints were sent to the FBI fingerprint data base. The gun used had been reported stolen from a car break-in two months prior.

***

Later in the day Lincoln, Washington and Lieutenant McGee were in the latter's office, the door closed. The three were in a brain storming session. "The motives for some of these recent crimes has not been determined," said Lieutenant McGee. "Let's look at the last three cases you two are working. Hate crimes would fit in all three."

McGee continued, "Brown and Ellis caught a case three nights ago where a black couple pulled into their driveway and were shot and killed as they got out of the car. A neighbor across the street heard the gun shots. By the time he looked out he saw a light-colored pickup truck speed away. A sign, similar to the one found attached to the rabbi in New York, and the one found at the scene where the gay couple were scalded, was around the man's neck with racial warnings and a Nazi swastika. And the small mosque that burned down last night had a swastika spray-painted on the van parked in the driveway. Murphy and Beecher said the fire department's arson investigators determined it was arson. There were no witnesses."

The three sat quietly for several minutes, each with his own thoughts until Lieutenant McGee broke the silence. "It appears that all these cases are probably hate crimes. You two follow up with NCIC and any other sources to learn if there's been a recent uptick in hate crimes anywhere, specifically crimes marked in any way with crude Nazi swastikas."

McGee continued, his tone of voice changed. "Until Officer Mosley was shot the media coverage had been routine, no front page or number one TV news stories. But when they get wind of those swastikas stuck on the victims, news people will start digging. Then there's the mosque fire, and the police shooting… all hell is going to break loose."

***

On his way home Harry contacted Mule, a very special confidential informant, for a meeting. As Harry waited in the parking lot of the bowling alley he observed the familiar car coming from the opposite direction and then pulling up alongside. "Hello Mule, thanks for coming on such short notice." Harry said greeting his very confidential, CI. "We've had a series of hate crimes in the city including the black police officer the other day. Not all were black. There was an elderly Jewish man and a couple of gay men. The connection is a crude sign – a Nazi swastika symbol -- found on some of the victims. Another related crime we believe, is that small mosque that burned last night. All we've got to go on is large white men from 20's to 40's, and a couple of pickup trucks, one a maroon with duel wheels on the rear, with loud pipes. Sounds like a bunch of rednecks."

"I'll put the word out to my people," said Mule as he made some notes.

"One other thing… "There was an incident up in New York City where a Jewish rabbi was found nailed to the wall at the altar in his synagogue. The same type of sign, a fuckin' swastika was found hanging from his neck. So, it appears that incidents might be more wide spread beyond just here in Zealand. Thanks Mule, you know I always appreciate what you do for us. And I'll be looking out for your son as always."

Harry had assured Mule that if he saw or heard of Mule's seventeen-year-old son with the local thugs or gang members, Harry would notify him.

***

Harry's next call was to Ham, his other dependable confidential informant. "I'm glad I caught you. You have a minute to talk?"

"For you Detective Lincoln, I got more than a minute. Wat-cha got? Wanna meet the same place?" Shouted Ham over loud rap music in the background.

"No need to meet this time Ham," as Harry repeated the same information he had just given to Mule. Keep your ear to the ground. Let me know if you hear anything. Thanks man… later."

CHAPTER

10

They came from different parts of the country gathering at the Schultz compound in the rural mountains of Blanton County, West Virginia. "Welcome to you all," announced Hans Schultz to the seven visitors and their entourages, sitting in the main building. "I want to thank each of you for coming to this meeting, some of you traveling far from home. You all have probably heard word- of- mouth what this is all about, piquing your interest enough to take the time plus the expense to get the details right from the horse's mouth." Hans paused momentarily. "Please no comments about the other end of the horse." Evoking laughter in spite of themselves as they sat warily, waiting for those details.

"We are fast losing our country! Those of us in this room along with millions of white folks are going to lose our God-fearing Christian country. The Jews, those Zionist bastards will take it like they took over in Palestine. The niggers and the spics will get more violent as they rob and shoot us, then rape our wives. And if that's not bad enough, those barbarian Islamists will cut our heads off or put us in cages and burn us alive."

The quiet room started to breath, heads nodded and there were soft mutterings to each other.

"Your daughters will not be safe from the rapists," continued Schultz, "your sons will not be safe from the faggots. What must we do about it?" After a few moments he answered his own question.

"We must declare war!"

"Yes, declare war. You've been invited here because you feel as we do. You have been doing the same in your towns as we have been doing here. I salute each of you for that. But all that activity is viewed by the cops as local problems. We want to change that. We want it to be a national problem. But first we have to organize, ya know so the right hand knows what the left hand is doing. We must set goals. We have to all agree on what is it that we want to do? We will form an organization that brings us all together to act as one. We have developed a mechanism to do just that."

Hans paused and picked up a bottle of water from the table next to him and drank, waiting for any comments or questions. When there were none, he continued. "We have already started the war going to Jew York City and crucified that kike rabbi in his ratty little church. It's been all over the news so I'm pretty sure you all have heard about it. In the past week or so we've gone to Zealand in Virginia and fucked up some of those sub-humans. The Jew press calls them hate crimes."

The room came alive as Schultz talked. Clapping, whistling with a chorus of hooting and hollering. "The kicker was the signs we left with some of the ones that we did in, each sign with a big Nazi swastika." By this time the room full of white supremacists, the Aryan brotherhood, neo-Nazis, skinheads, Ku Klux Klansmen and other redneck types were standing, strutting, dancing and hi-fiving. "By your response, I assume that you are all with us," shouted Hans Schultz as the seven group leaders came up to shake his hand.

After the noisy demonstration subsided, and order was restored Hans addressed the invited guests. "Our little group here in West Virginia has now expanded to seven cities across the country. We are now an organization of significant size that should expand as the word gets out. It's up to all of us to spread the word. We need to expand, not only into other major cities, but also into small cities and towns. Strength in numbers, and plenty of white men who feel as we do will join us."

There was more clapping and hi-fiving. Hans waited until he again had their attention, then continued. "We'll use this compound for our headquarters. It's out of the way and protected from prying eyes and ears." He then displayed duplicate copies of the Nazi signs they had used explaining how they were left hanging around the necks of those people they had fucked up. "A couple of times we were not able to leave these signs, but when you can it's very important to do so. We torched one of those rag head mosques at night when no one was around, so we spray painted the Nazi swastika on their van parked in the driveway. The pigs knew it was the same as our signs."

***

They broke for lunch consisting of a variety of sandwiches, donuts and other pastries with soft drinks and coffee, prepared for them by a kitchen staff omitting beer or other alcoholic drinks. Those would be available after business was concluded.

***

"Now that your hunger is satisfied is not the time to take a nap," quipped Hans with a bit of humor. "We have some more business to cover before the party begins this evening." Having their full attention now, Hans got serious again.

"Our organization must have structure. Each chapter will have leaders determined by its members. Those leaders will choose their lieutenants. My lieutenant is the man sitting to my right, Mr. Otto Shafer. A strong chain-of-command is vital. Vigorous discipline must be instilled. Any violation will have severe consequences. Every member will be sworn to a strict code-of-silence. Understanding that if arrested during or after conducting a mission, he will not cooperate with the law. He will remain mum. If he talks and rats out his brothers to get a reduced sentence or for any other reason, benefitting him personally, he is signing his death warrant. The Aryan brotherhood has a strong presence in every state and federal prison in the country."

Hans went on to stress that each chapter will operate separately and independently. "However, we all need to stay in touch with intelligence and operational matters. I don't trust corresponding via the telephone, email, or social media. We have to stay connected so let's do it the old-fashioned way -- The U.S. Post Office and keep that to a minimum. Anything of a confidential or critical nature will be in person, face-to-face. If it's a matter for us here at headquarters, I will be willing to travel to your location. When your presence is required here such as meetings, your travel expense is your responsibility, we will provide meals and lodging."

Hans Shultz thought that was enough talk for one session. He did not want to burden them with information overload. He was familiar with their intellectual level. He thought it best to end now, giving them time to digest all that was said. "Before we break for the day, I want all of you to think about what was said today." Hans was tired of talking and didn't want to get into any discussions this late in the day. "At tomorrow's meeting feel free to bring up any issue that you have a problem with, or any concerns with what's being proposed. All of your questions will be answered."

"One more thing, the Nazi Swastika will be our symbol, our calling card, our signature. It will be left each time we rid our country of some sub-human vermin. We had new signs printed so that each will be uniform, there are enough to take with you. The Nazi swastika is prominently displayed along with the name of our new organization… 'The Steel Swastika'!"

The room exploded! One of the men from the Boise, Idaho contingent stood up at ramrod attention, clicked the heels of his hobnail boots and gave the straight arm salute shouting 'Sieg Heil.' He started to march as others jumped from their seats, fell in behind him emulating the large beefy man with the shaved head. Within moments every man, his arm stretched forward, was goose stepping in single file, chanting in uniform cadence. As the column snaked around the room the chant began growing louder and louder…

"the steel swastika!"

"The Steel Swastika!!"

"THE STEEL SWASTIKA!!!"

CHAPTER

11

As he lay next to Awa, Floyd said, "It's what I want more than anything. I want us to be married and raise a family. But there are things you need to understand. Being a police officer has its downsides, the obvious such as the danger, low pay, and odd hours are only a part of it. These things apply to all who wear the badge. A homicide detective has issues that compound the effect on family life." Floyd paused for a few moments searching for the right words to explain honestly, compassionately and delicately.

"Any major police department is a twenty-four-hour day, seven days a week operation, broken down into eight-hour watches or shifts. The work week is not Monday through Friday with the weekends off. When assigned to a homicide where the person or persons responsible are unknown, that eight-hour shift goes out the window." Floyd wanted to explain as plainly as he could due to Awa's limited English. "There are many things to be done that can't wait until the next day. When you finally get home, you are exhausted, it's a cold dinner, a few hours' sleep, a quick shower, a change of clothes, then back to work. That continues until the case is solved or there are no more leads to follow. The impacts on the spouse could be many such as, the cancelled dinners or outings with family or friends. A normal social life sacrificed. For a couple with children there are often the missed dance recitals, little league games, school plays or choral concerts."

Floyd waited for some response from Awa. She remained quiet.

"When Harry meets a woman that he is interested in and starts to date, he tells her by the second or third date that he is not interested in marriage. He is decent man and doesn't want to waste her time with him if marriage is what she wants. He says he is a homicide detective first. Marriage, family, neither exist for him at any time in his future."

Awa had not uttered a word. Floyd continued, hoping she would understand.

"I am different Awa; I want you to be my wife. But I want also to continue as a homicide detective. I felt that I had to tell you all the things that might come up some time in the future. I have to be honest with you even if it causes you to change your mind, and I lose you."

Then holding his breath, Floyd asked, "Please Awa let's get married."

Awa spoke for the first time. "Oui cheri we will get married."

***

Upon arrival at the squad room Harry and Floyd detour en route to their desks to the back of the room. The coffee is fresh, and the donuts have just been delivered. This jolt of caffeine, they believe will fortify them for the unknown events of the day. Coffee in one hand and a plain donut in the other, Floyd heads for his desk. Harry followed with the same balancing act, his morning treat was filled with strawberry jam.

"Lincoln, Washington," called Lieutenant McGee from across the room. "Grab your coffee and come in here." As soon as they were seated McGee asked about their hate crime inquiries. "I realize it's only been a few days, but we need to jump on it."

"We've only received a smattering of response so far," said Floyd. "Just the usual, nothing outstanding and no mention of those Nazi signs."

"Okay, but when and if you get a hit, I want to know about it right away. In the meantime, what about Officer Mosley? Was he part of this surge in hate crimes? Or did the timing of his shooting just fall into the midst of the others?" Don't tell me about a coincidence. You know what I think of coincidences."

Harry responded. "Lieu, there was not one of those Nazi signs found on the dead shooter. He did match the general description of the perps in some of the other hate crime cases. Big beefy white rednecks."

"Stay with it," the lieutenant ordered. "The Mosley shooting along with the hate crime cases have top priority. Deputy Chief Watkins wants to be kept in the loop on this. I'll report to him daily. He'll brief Chief Lansing." McGee paused and as he continued his tone of voice changed. "Every detective in the squad is carrying a maximum load. The recent retirement of our oldest homicide detective plus the two that were promoted have left us critically understaffed. Unfortunately, the beat goes on. It's about to get worse for the two of you."

Gone was McGee's normal booming voice as he spoke his next words just above a whisper. "Head on over to Zealand Memorial ER and meet with Sergeant Scott of the 2nd precinct in Dr. Deutch's office. They'll brief you on the details of a kidnapping/sexual assault/aggravated battery. The victim, a fifteen -year old girl is in the ICU."

***

"It's a wonder she is still alive," Dr. Deutch told them in his office with the door closed. "Her physical injuries are severe. Likely, so are her emotional and psychological injuries. She's heavily sedated. Her parents are with her now. You won't be able to talk to her until tomorrow or the day after, if then."

"Here's a copy of the initial incident report," Sergeant Scott said handing Floyd the single sheet. "There's not much on it except the time and place of occurrence, although there's a couple of people's names on there you can talk with."

***

At the nurse's station of the ICU, Harry and Floyd identified themselves before inquiring as to the condition of Latasha Shields. "Excuse me detectives," said a woman from behind the counter. "I am Dr. Dianne Marlow, Latasha Shields' attending physician. How can I help you?"

"Harry Lincoln and Floyd Washington," answered Harry introducing himself and his partner. "We will be investigating this case and thought we'd come here to learn whatever we could from her parents. We understand from Dr. Deutch in the ER that she's in bad shape and heavily sedated."

"Yes, I'll show you to her room. I'll ask Mr. Shields to step out. Mrs. Shields would be of no use to you at this point. She just sits at her daughter's bedside holding her hand. She has not stopped crying. I would ask that you not go into the room for the next couple of days until Latasha is fully awake and able to speak with you. It appears to have been a very brutal attack."

"Mr. Shields," said Dr. Marlow, "Detectives Lincoln and Washington will be investigating Latasha's case. They would like to have a word with you."

"We are very sorry about your daughter," Floyd said softly, "We'd like for you to tell us, if anything, what you might know about it."

"All I can tell you is when we first saw her in the emergency room, she was crying hysterically and kept saying through her sobs… 'Daddy they hurt me, Daddy they hurt me so bad.' That's all she said. Then she fell asleep because they had just given her something before taking her to the operating room. She's been out the whole time here in this room." He became overcome with emotion and could no longer talk, tears streaming down his cheeks.

"Detective Lincoln and I will look in on her each day until she feels well enough to talk to us. In the meantime, here's our cards. You call either one of us day or night. I give you my word that we will not stop until we find whoever did this to your daughter."

Dr. Marlow walked with them towards the elevators. She stopped and said, "This might not be the time or place for it, but are your names really Lincoln and Washington? I seem to recall reading a newspaper article some time ago about 'The Presidents' but I had to ask."

"That's us," confessed Harry Lincoln, grinning.

CHAPTER

12

Harry and Floyd were briefing Lieutenant McGee on the latest developments. "We've gotten quite a few responses to our hate crimes inquires. It looks like these crimes are becoming organized, identifying themselves, 'The Steel Swastika' which was printed on the signs along with the Nazi swastika. The first report of those signs was at a Jewish Synagogue in New York City. Then a few showed up here in Zealand connected with hate crimes and seems to be expanding nationwide."

Floyd explaining further. "And Lieu, we got an ID on the perp in the Officer Mosley shooting. The FBI identified him from their fingerprint data base...

...Charles Kirkwood, w/m 37 yeas-old. 431 Nixon Avenue, Zealand, VA.

He's got an extensive rap sheet: Assault, burglary, larceny, several DUI's, and numerous traffic offences. Kirkwood served seven years of a ten-year sentence for assault on a police officer. He got out a month ago. We are giving it to the media, along with his mug shot. The motive has yet to be determined: The three most probable motives might be a hate crime connected to these other hate crimes; or a police officer assassination; or maybe a grudge murder from a past arrest. This one we are looking into... It could be any of these or some we have not yet considered. So far it's a crap shoot."

At this point, Harry jumped in, explaining to McGee. "In the Latasha Shields case, we spoke with a man who had been walking his dog in Stone Ridge Park, where the assault took place. He said the dog bolted from the path they were on and bounded with a bark into a heavily wooded area of the park. He called, and the well-trained dog returned, stood before him barking, then ran back into the woods. the dog's owner called a second time and the dog again reacted in the same way, barking the whole time."

Harry looked sheepishly at McGee, knowing it sounded like a scene from an old *'Lassie Come Home'* movie. "He said he followed the dog about fifty feet into the woods where he found the girl on the ground, on her back unconscious. She was naked and bloody, her torn clothing scattered about. Near her there was a bicycle, which has been identified as hers. He called 911."

Harry took a long swig of water from plastic bottle. Floyd resumed the briefing. "We spoke with a man and a woman who were walking together on the path prior to the man with the dog." Floyd paused for a minute and then continued reading from their statements…

…'We saw four or five teenagers, although they could have been young men in their early twenties, come out of the woods, hollering and high-fiving as they ran down the path going from us. They were black males, wearing 'rapper' type clothing with red 'do-rags' on their heads and red bandannas around their necks.'

"So, Harry and I are thinking that this is not connected to those escalating hate crimes with the Nazi swastika signs. The perps observed in those cases were all white men older than teenagers. The victim in this case is black and so are the suspects. The get-ups and the prominent color red says some faction of the 'Bloods.' This appears to be gang related activity, possibly some sort of initiation rites."

"Tomorrow is Latasha Shields' third day in the ICU," Harry informed Lieutenant McGee. "Dr. Marlow said she would be well enough for us to speak with her. We realize that everyone in the squad is overloaded with their own cases. If it's okay with you, we'd like to bring Adams with us if she can spare an hour or so. In a sexually violent gang rape like this one, we all know that a fifteen-year-old female victim would feel more comfortable speaking freely about the details to a female detective than to one of us. And as you also know, we need all the details."

A few minutes later, Floyd was at his desk entering the latest information on their multiple cases, bringing the files up to date. Harry motioned that he was going out for a few minutes. He left the headquarters building and found an empty bench in the small park across the street. He speed-dialed Mule and Ham, giving each the information on the Latasha Shields case. Confidential Informants are the life blood of the detective. For nearly a decade, Mule and Ham, both street-wise, well connected and highly dependable CI's have been the fuel driving the success of Homicide Detective Harry Lincoln.

***

Dr. Marlow escorted the three detectives into the room where Mr. and Mrs. Shields were at their daughter's bedside. They had been there the entire three days and nights, either together or one at a time, the other going home to clean up, eat a bite and get a few hours of sleep. Introductions were made all around as Dr. Marlow took note of the numbers and other information displayed on the various monitors to which her patient was tethered. "Latasha how are you feeling this morning?" The doctor asked.

"Better," she answered slowly just above a whisper. Her extensive injuries included her face swollen and bruised, one eye completely closed, and a cracked voice box in her throat.

"All your vital signs are good, and your injuries are slowly starting to improve." Dr. Marlow assured her, as well as an anxious Mr. and Mrs. Shields. "Latasha, these three police detectives would like to talk with you and ask you some questions. "Are you up for that?"

Latasha hesitated as she looked around the room. She didn't say anything; her one good eye said it for her.

Detective Nancy Adams had seen that look before. "Latasha,

how about my two partners take your mom and dad down to the cafeteria for a cup of coffee? Dr. Marlow has other patients to look in on, so that will leave just the two of us here in the room where we can talk, girl to girl."

Latasha nodded, this time without any hesitation.

After the others left, the two looked at each other for several moments in the quiet of the room. Until Detective Nancy Adams said in a soft, soothing voice. "I'm not going to tell you that I know how you must feel -- because I don't know. It has never happened to me. However, I will tell you that I've investigated too many of these crimes. The animals that commit sexual assaults are vicious, depraved cowards. There is not a true man among them. And then to beat you so badly is beyond depravity."

Adams paused momentarily, then continued. "Detectives Lincoln and Washington will be investigating your case. They are two of the best. They will find who did this to you. Although you will have to help. Tell them everything you know. In the next few days, when you are feeling better, they will be talking with you, asking questions. I know it will be embarrassing. Be honest with them as you will be with me. We have been doing this for a long time. We have heard it all. I will take your initial statement, and they will follow it up."

Tears were running down Latasha's cheeks as she sobbed, "They hurt me so bad!"

"Latasha you said 'they'. Was there more than one?"

"Yes. And I recognized one of them even though they had their faces covered with red bandannas. They were holding me down on the ground tearing my clothes off. I was trying to fight them when my hand grabbed one of the masks. I pulled it off his face. He is a senior at my school. He's on the football team." Latasha paused, and took a breath.

"His name is Jarrad Jergens. They call him J.J."

"How many others Latasha?"

"I think there were four others besides Jergens."

The injured victim was having a difficult time talking. Adams didn't want to push her. She was able to tell just enough to establish basically what had happened and vaguely how it happened. A more detailed and lengthy statement would be taken in a few days as her ability to speak improved.

Harry and Floyd returned to the room along with Mr. and Mrs. Shields. Adams stood up and said, "we've been here long enough. You need to get some rest. We'll be back when Dr. Marlow says you feel better and can talk without any pain." Harry and Floyd sensed that Adams was anxious about something and wanted to speak privately with them.

The three detectives were silent in the crowded corridor and in the elevator. But once in the parking lot walking to their car, she smiled and almost shouted, "Harry, Floyd, there were five attackers and she's identified one of them. His name is Jarrad Jergens, goes by J.J." Adams then told them the short story.

She went on. "Then after we snatch J.J., he'll start naming names, resulting in the four other tough guys getting picked off, one by one." Detective Nancy Adams engaging in a bit of cop humor, gets in a dig with straight face as she continues. "I suppose 'The Presidents' can handle all that without the additional assistance again of a woman detective?"

"Nancy, we know you are overloaded, up to your gorgeous ass with your own cases." Harry said with a smile. "I speak for Floyd and myself to thank you for coming with us. But we didn't expect you to hit a home run. And another thing, if we are the Presidents, you surely are the First Lady."

Some laughter, a few high fives, and a couple of hugs when Floyd said, "hey it's lunch time, let's go to Mikes and get a hamburger. The presidents treat for the gracious first lady."

***

In the next several days Detective Adams was able to take a complete and detailed written statement from Latasha Shields. Starting with the time and date of occurrence Latasha said, "I was on my way home from school, riding my bike on the path through Stone Ridge Park when some guys came out of the woods and grabbed me…" On the strength of the entire statement as probable cause, Lincoln and Washington obtained an arrest warrant for Jarrad Jergens. During the first interview, Jergens admitted his part in the sexual assault. He said he raped the victim along with the others, naming them all. He did it, he said as a requirement of the initiation for membership into the Bloods gang.

"I raped her, but that's all I did," pleaded Jergens. "The two older members, Brown and Johnson were the ones who beat her so bad."

Lincoln and Washington then obtained additional arrest warrants naming the other four attackers. Deputy Chief Watkins ordered those warrants handed over to the gang unit and fugitive squad for the arrests. "I want Lincoln and Washington free to concentrate on this latest rash of Nazi hate crimes."

CHAPTER

13

A voice from across the squad room shouted. "Lincoln, pick up on line three. A guy says he wants to speak with someone about the Officer Mosley shooting."

"This is Detective Lincoln. How can I help you?"

"Actually, I'll be helping you. But not on the phone. Is there some place we can meet?"

Harry replied, "There is a small diner two blocks from Zealand Memorial Hospital. Would that be convenient for you?"

"Yes, my name is Tony Royston, I'm a forty-year-old white guy. I'm wearing a blue plaid shirt and a blue baseball cap. I'm driving an older model white Honda."

"My partner and I will be there shortly, in a Ford 'Crown Vic,' black."

***

Sitting in the rear booth of the diner, Royston told Harry and Floyd. "The guy they showed on TV, Charles Kirkwood the one who shot the cop, I know him. We were special guests of the Commonwealth of Virginia for several years. We both were doin' time for different things. We managed to stay away from the prison gangs. We spent a lot of yard time hangin' out talking to each other.

We weren't buddies because of an ugly incident between us one day on the freeway. He told me that during that incident this Zealand cop beat him with a club, broke his collar bone and also fractured his knee cap. He said the pain is still in his shoulder and neck, and he's walked with a limp ever since. He would say over and over that one day when he gets out, will be payback time. That cop was officer Mosley!"

Harry thought of Deputy Chief Watkins' order, but if listening to this guy's story might establish the motive for the Mosley shooting, it would be worth their time. "Sounds interesting," Harry prodded, "tell us about it."

"I was driving with my mother and nine-year-old daughter on Interstate 81coming home from a kid's birthday party, a friend of my daughters from school. All of a sudden in my rearview mirror I see this huge pickup truck ridin' my ass. It was so close all I could see was the big bumper with the bars like on the cop cars, and part of the grill. I'm in the center lane doin' about 70, keeping up with the traffic, so I slow down thinkin' maybe he'll go around me. He does, and when he gets alongside I see it's one of those monster pickups, with oversized tires and the body jacked way up. He's motionin' for me to pull over, but there's a tractor-trailer in the right lane so I keep goin' in the center lane. He pulls a little ahead of me and angles into my lane trying to force me over. That's when I hit his truck and we both stop…

…It's no more than a fender-bender, but now we're blockin' two of the three lanes of the freeway. He gets out of the truck and looks at the damage, which is not much more than when someone opens their door and puts a ding in your car. Someone musta called 911, because traffic is startin' to back up really bad. I get out of my car and see him walkin' towards me holdin' a tire iron hollerin' an' cussin' an' threatenin'. He's pissed because he says I cut him off 'back there' and he almost wrecked. I don't know what he's talkin' about and tell him that. I said if I did that I was sorry, and I didn't mean anything by it. But he's so mad he doesn't want to hear it.

We are just about to get physical, when we hear a siren. A state police car pulls up and a trooper gets out. He gets between us and tells the guy to drop the tire iron. He doesn't. Instead he hits the trooper in the head knockin' him down and out cold. I go to grab the guy but am pushed out of the way by a Zealand cop who musta' got there right after the state trooper. The guy tries to hit the cop like he did the trooper, but the cop was faster and hit him on the shoulder with his baton, breakin' his collar bone. The guy still has a little fight left, when the cop hits him again, this time on the knee cap, putting him down screaming in agony...

...More cops and troopers show up, and a couple of ambulances are called. They take the trooper and the guy to Zealand Memorial. The one I keep referin' to as the guy is none other than Charles Kirkwood who was arrested for aggravated assault and aggravated battery on a police officer...

...The cops check me out and find I'm wanted on a burglary warrant. They put cuffs on an' let me talk to my mother before putting me in the cop car. All I have on me is seven bucks, an I give that to my mother. She tells me that there's not much food in the house, but not to worry, that they'll get by. Before they take me away I tell the cops that my mother don't drive, and ask if they could get her and my daughter home."

Harry spoke up, "I remember when that happened back then. Why are you telling us all those details Tony, where are you going with this?"

"Because Detective Lincoln, you might have a good memory but like the man used to say on the radio somethin' like; 'And now you know the rest of the story...' The first time my mother visited me in prison she told me what happened after they took me away. She said that it was officer Mosley who volunteered to drive them home. She told me that on the way to the house he asked her about food and money. Before they got there, he pulled into the Publix supermarket and stopped in front. She said he took out his badge case and pulled out a fifty-dollar bill. He told her he keeps it there for emergencies. He gives it to her and says for her and her granddaughter to go in and get whatever food they need that the fifty will cover. He tells her that he'll be right there when they come out."

Harry and Floyd see that Tony is getting emotional, and they give him time to collect himself.

Tony asked. "What is it you guys say? 'To protect and serve.' Officer Mosley served that day, he went above and beyond serving. During those years in the joint, I never forgot that."

***

With Tony Royston's written statement, the Officer Eugene Mosley shooting was cleared, and classified as a personal grudge. This allowed the motive of the case to be removed from the recent hate crime's file now known as the 'Steel Swastika' cases.

CHAPTER

14

In the large conference room adjacent to the Zealand Police Chief's office, a high-level meeting was already in progress. The subject of the meeting was, "The Steel Swastika." The participants seated around the table represented various law enforcement agencies: The Zealand Police Department, The Ridgewood County Sheriff's Office, The Ridgewood County District Attorney's Office, The Federal Bureau of Investigation, and The New York City Police Department.

Fred Roman, Special Agent in Charge of the Zealand FBI field office said, "The first of these Nazi swastika signs appeared in New York City at the scene of a vicious hate crime. Shortly after, those same signs were left at hate crimes here in Zealand. Within the last week we've gotten reports of hate crimes with the same kind of signs from several different locations across the country. They were signed, 'The Steel Swastika' along with the Nazi emblem." It appears that these groups now have a name and are organizing nationwide."

NYPD Detective Lieutenant Harry O'Riley spoke next. "On the crucifixion of the rabbi in the Brooklyn synagogue, a witness saw a black pickup truck occupied by two white males leave the scene in a hurry. The witness thought it had a D.C. plate, but none of them got the number. We later found an abandoned pickup matching that description on the Brooklyn side near the approach to the Brooklyn Bridge. We ran the plate and found that it had been stolen two days earlier from the Georgetown area in Washington. It had been wiped clean of prints."

"Since the incident in New York City," said Zealand P.D.'s chief of detectives Deputy Chief Watkins, "we've had several hate crimes where those signs were attached. An on-duty black police officer in uniform was shot on the street by an unidentified white male, who was shot and killed by that officer... He was able to get off several rounds as he went down. Although no Nazi sign was found, we suspected it might be connected. After the shooter was identified we learned the motive was a grudge shooting motivated by a previous arrest. It was not part of these recent hate crimes."

Zealand Police Chief Lansing addressed FBI Special agent Roman. "Based on what we know at this point, this group representing itself, 'The Steel Swastika' is likely responsible for the recent hate crimes. Several states are now involved in addition to New York and Virginia, including Idaho, Alabama and Texas that were reported yesterday."

"It looks like we have cross jurisdictions," said Ridgewood County D.A. Dick Donahue. (Dick Donahue had won the recent election over Robert Carlisle and was now the new Ridgewood County District Attorney). "What will the bureau's position be on prosecution," He asked Special Agent Roman. State or federal?"

Roman answered. "That decision will have to be made in Washington. Until then let's take it on a case by case basis, but my guess is it will also be on a state by state basis. And we might have to form some sort of multi-jurisdictional task force probably headquartered here in Zealand."

***

Lieutenant McGee returned from the meeting and waited until watch change to brief both the day and evening watch detectives. "So, the incident in New York City was the first claimed by this neo-Nazi group. Then that same group, connected by those signs commit a few hate crimes here in Zealand. As of yesterday, three more cities have reported those Nazi signs found at the scenes of hate crimes. But now we know they have a name, "The Steel

Swastika' that was on the signs in the latest incidents. It now appears that they have organized and gone national." McGee paused for a minute and then continued. "Don't be surprised to be bumping into and falling over investigators from different agencies: the state, the sheriff's office, the D.A.'s office and the feds."

CHAPTER 15

It was a beautiful sunny Saturday morning, the day of thirteen-year-old Aaron Horowitz's Bar Mitzvah. People filed into the Temple and claimed their seats, a proud Mr. and Mrs. Horowitz in the front row, aisle seats. Aaron and Rabbi Feldman stood at the altar, the cantor off to one side. Aaron had recited the ancient Hof Torah in Hebrew, and was about to give his English, "Today I am a man…" speech. Those first words did not leave his lips when four men with guns burst through the front doors shooting. After the first moment of silent shock… pandemonium!

People screaming, running, trying to hide behind anything that could shield them. Some of the fortunate ones were able to flee out the side doors and rear doors. Others were not as fortunate. The shooting continued for less than a minute, nevertheless long enough that many people were shot. Some died instantly, notably Aaron Horowitz and Rabbi Feldman. The cantor furtively slipped back into the office and called 911.

The first responding patrol car arrived within two minutes. The gunmen already gone.

"Inside, inside they're all shot, all dead," screamed a hysterical woman to that first officer as he jumped out of the patrol car. "All shot… All dead," crying as she sat on the front steps holding her bloody arm. The officer immediately stepped through the front door and was shocked as he viewed the carnage. He grabbed his radio…

"2204 to Radio: Multiple gunshot victims on call, some dead, some wounded. Start fire rescue, a superior officer and homicide, and all the ambulances in service," he radioed.

"Radio to 2204: Copy that."

As more patrol cars arrived, information about the gunmen was vital. "There were four of them," a wounded man lying on the sidewalk told one of the cops. "They ran out the front door, jumped in a grey SUV that was parked right out front, and took off fast."

"What did they look like, and what were they wearing? Did you see the tag, or notice the number? When they left, which way did they go?" The cop needed to get as much as he could, as soon as he could.

"They were young white guys. I think the SUV was a Ford and I'm not sure, but it might be a Virginia tag. It turned right and headed south on the Concourse." The man was holding his side, moaned and took a deep breath. "Officer, I've been shot twice and I'm hurting bad."

The cop knelt down beside him, squeezed his other hand and gently and said, "An ambulance will be here in a minute or two… the medics will give you a shot of morphine for your pain. You'll be at the hospital as fast as they can get you there. You've been a great help." The cop got up and keyed his radio, relaying the information to the dispatcher, who then broadcast it city wide…

"Radio to all units on all channels: Standby for a lookout on multiple gunshot victims from the Jewish Temple in the Second Precinct. Cars be on the lookout for a grey SUV, possibly a Ford, traveling south from the 3200 block of the Grand Concourse, occupied by four young white males. This vehicle possibly bearing Virginia tags, number unknown. Occupants armed and very dangerous, wanted for multiple homicides and aggravated assaults. Use extreme caution."

***

It was bedlam. The Temple, this place of worship was at this time more like 'Hell on Earth.' The previous hysterical screaming was now replaced by crying, wailing, moaning and shouting. The shouting mostly from the fire rescue EMT's, and those from the many ambulances. A triage was set up on the front lawn of the Temple, coordinated by two doctors, guests at the Bar Mitzvah who were luckily not hit by the barrage of bullets.

It was a catastrophe of major proportions, the worst mass slaughter in Zealand's history. Thirteen dead, twenty-three wounded, with some of the wounded in critical condition. A grim total of thirty-six innocent people shot. The Steel Swastika signs were scattered on the floor and some of the pews inside of the Temple. Several were taped on the outside of the front doors as well.

They kept arriving, those top tier people not usually present at homicide crime scenes: Zealand's Police Chief Lansing, and Chief of Detectives Watkins… Ridgewood County Sheriff Bert Logan… Ridgewood County DA Dick Donahue with one of his ADA's… Ridgewood County's Chief medical examiner and two investigators. The head of the crime scene unit, who hardly ever leaves his desk was there supervising his techs. Chief Lansing instructed the 2nd precinct commander to, "Get all of those patrol cars back on the streets to look for that SUV. Leave just a few here for crowd control." The chief radioed the traffic captain to send some motorcycle units for traffic control, the rest to look for the SUV.

A large black SUV pulled into the circular drive beyond the yellow crime scene tape. The mayor and three aides stepped out. Chief Lansing walked down to meet him. They talked for several minutes, the assembled media close enough to snap photos and get video. His honor said he didn't have the facts yet to answer their questions, but promised that whoever committed this horrendous barbarity would be brought to justice… etc. etc. Within ten minutes he got back into his vehicle and left.

Chief Lansing, Deputy Chief Watkins and Lieutenant McGee stepped away from the hub of the activity for a private conference. "Lieutenant," the Chief asked addressing Lieutenant McGee, "what are your plans for investigating this slaughter?"

"Well Chief, we've been dealing with this new menace now for the past two or three weeks," McGee said. "We know what they are, they've made that quite clear. But we don't know who they are. I'm giving the lead to Detectives Lincoln and Washington. They are the best I've got, and they are already investigating several of these cases. They will have the support of the entire homicide squad."

The chief nodded in approval. "They will have the support of the entire Zealand Police Department. Notify Deputy Chief Watkins of whatever you might need. And keep him advised on a daily basis."

***

The stolen SUV was located later that day, double parked in front of an apartment building on Sumner Avenue and 168th Street. It had been abandoned, wiped clean of fingerprints.

CHAPTER

16

"Hans Schultz, beaming, sitting in his office with Otto Shafer, Sheriff Hayes and the four Temple gunmen, boasted, "We really got their attention this time boys. It was the top story on the national TV news, seen all over the country. Maybe even in some countries around the world, Israel for sure." He refilled the four glasses and said, "drink up boys, you sure deserve it. If this was the army I'd be pinning medals on you."

Schultz had to say it again. "The largest and most important Jew church in the city of Zealand, Virginia. The carnage you boys left has them all in shock. Afterwards, they were all there, everyone who was anyone. Even the mayor showed up to say how sorry he was and gave a little speech. '… Those neo-Nazi cowards will be caught and swiftly be brought to justice'… bla bla bla, all that horse shit. He just wanted to get his face on TV, and the Jew vote in the next election." Hans got up signaling that the meeting was over. "Okay boys, I want you to go home, and lay low for a while. Again, great job."

Hans, alone with Shafer and Hayes said to them, "We got word that two days ago, three cities put the Steel Swastika on the map. A sign was left with each of three dead bodies: a nigger, a spic, and a rag head. Yesterday two more cities did the same, this time: a Jew, and a faggot. It looks like our nation-wide movement has started."

"I spoke with our satellite city commander in Atlanta. Every year they have a large 'Gay Pride Parade,' hundreds of marches, thousands of spectators. The route is straight down Peachtree street, the main drag, ending at Woodruff Park in the heart of downtown. The parade will be this Saturday."

Hans finished his third cup of coffee. "Snipers with military equipment will be placed along the route on the roofs of the low buildings, and on the third and fourth floor windows of the taller buildings. Those snipers will be spaced evenly along Peachtree Street. A mission coordinator will be in the park to radio the riflemen that the front of the parade has reached the termination point. He will then give the order for all to open fire. They will have been instructed that their targets are the queers in the parade, not the spectators...

...All of them are military trained and will be wearing latex surgical gloves before they touch their weapon and ammunition, all stolen, therefore the immediate users will be unidentifiable. They will be making dry runs throughout the week. Each sniper will know their positions, the best way to enter and exit the buildings. After the attack, they will leave the weapons, the ejected cartridges and unused ammunition. More important, our signs will be left there also. When they leave the buildings, the shooters will get lost in the panicking crowds."

Most important, it will be on national TV."

Sheriff Luke Hayes had been nodding his approval while Hans was talking. "I think it's a good plan, very well thought out. I just hope they don't get a case of 'Murphy's Law.' You know the one that states, 'everything that can go wrong, will go wrong.' The thing that concerns me the most, regardless of where the operations take place. Here in Zealand, New York City, Atlanta or any city that now operates under the banner of 'the Steel Swastika' is the prospect of someone getting caught, either in the act or after the fact."

The sheriff continued. "We all know that the cardinal rule, the number one priority is, the 'Code of Silence.' It's drilled into their heads time after time. We also know it is very tempting, if caught, to cut a deal, to expose the 'SS' and get a reduced sentence, maybe forty-years down to five or ten. Although they are all told the punishment that awaits them in prison, any prison state or federal, it only takes one rat to expose our entire organization."

"I agree with Luke," Otto Shafer said. "It's not just the boys there in Zealand that we pretty much have control of. Now with our recent expansion, we must rely on all the satellite commanders to maintain control of each of theirs. I think it would be wise to call for a meeting, bring all the commanders in."

***

The Zealand meeting was held on the same day as the Gay Pride parade in Atlanta. Steel Swastika leaders of nine cities were in attendance, Hans Schultz presiding. The purpose of the meeting they were told, was the conduct of their men, should they be caught by police during or after an operation. Just as it was getting started, a door to the big room opened and a man entered hollering, "turn on the TV!"

'Breaking News' in red letters across the large screen.

"Downtown Atlanta is in chaos. We are getting reports of multiple shootings at the Gay Pride parade. Our team covering the parade is at the scene and ready with some sketchy details. What can you tell us Bob?"

A reporter was standing in the street, crowds of people running, sirens screaming. Atlanta, Georgia printed at the bottom of the screen.

"Well Jane, mass hysteria here on Peachtree street, the parade route for the annual Gay Pride parade. Reports of gunshots from some of the buildings lining the route along Peachtree from Baker Street to Woodruff Park." The camera panned the chaotic scene as police, fire rescue, and ambulances descended on Peachtree Street.

"There are people on the ground, but we don't know if they were shot or trampled in the crush to escape the shootings. It appears likely that participants in the parade were the intended targets. At this time, we don't know if there were any or how many fatalities. I'll stay on it and report back with more details."

The TV was turned off and the room became jubilant with 'Sieg Heils', straight-armed Nazi salutes, and high fives all around. Hans Schultz was beaming. "The Steel Swastika will be the number one story on all the network TV news shows, and headlines in every paper."

CHAPTER

17

For more than three weeks there was only the usual routine activity---domestic homicides, street corner shootings, drive-by shootings, stabbings, witness statements and the usual paper work. The homicide detectives were able to catch their breath again. They felt lucky to have the off days that they had coming to them. It also gave those assigned to the SS cases time to continue their investigations… although without much success.

As Harry and Floyd had just left the office, to get some breakfast, the dreaded call exploded over the police radio on all frequencies. *"Any car near Tremont and Walton Avenues, in the 7th precinct Signal 63/50/4!"* They looked at each other and Floyd repeated, mostly to himself "Officer needs help / Person shot / Ambulance on the way."

So many police units responded on their radios, some were jamming others. When there was a pause in the radio traffic Harry was able to transmit, *"Homicide 134 and 136 en route."* Converging on that intersection from marked patrol cars to the police helicopter, as well as mounted and foot beat cops who were in the area.

A police officer lay on the sidewalk, blood spilling from multiple gunshot wounds from the back of his head down to between his shoulders. Under him was a cardboard sign with the words… 'The Steel Swastika' and the Nazi emblem. Fire Rescue was trying to stabilize him, but the wounded cop was unresponsive. He was quickly loaded into an ambulance, patrol cars and motorcycle units escorting, other units blocking intersections, racing to Zealand Memorial Hospital.

The ER doctors tried to revive him. They could not. Police Officer Eugene Niles was pronounced dead in the trauma room.

On the blood-soaked sidewalk in front of the butcher shop, Detectives Lincoln and Washington watched silently as a crime scene tech placed the bloody cardboard sign into an evidence bag.

***

For years this neighborhood had been home to mostly middle-class Jewish people. In the last decade the demographics had changed. Now the area was a mixture of Jewish, Black and Puerto Rican residents. A produce store on the corner of Tremont and Walton sat next to a Kosher butcher owned and operated by an orthodox Jew and his wife. Harry and Floyd and other detectives were looking for witnesses, anyone who might have seen what had happened; more than that they were looking for anyone who saw who shot the police officer? There were a number of pedestrians on the street, but when the shooting started everyone ducked for cover, trying to find a place to hide.

The detectives queried the produce man. "I was in the back of the store uncrating lettuce when I heard what sounded like shooting. I wasn't counting but it seemed like a half dozen or so shots. I heard a commotion on the street; people running, screaming. Then I saw the cop down on the sidewalk. I called 911."

Harry and Floyd went next door to the butcher shop and talked with Max and Ester Goldman. "I was sitting at the front window waiting for my nephew to come so he could deliver some orders," Mrs. Goldman, crying told the detectives, "That was when Officer Niles walked past and waived, he always waves. Then two men ran up behind him and shot him," she said.

Floyd asked gently, "Mrs. Goldman, can you tell us what these two men looked like?"

"They were both big, fat and bald, with full beards."

"Could you tell about how old they were? Were they white or black?"

"Two white men and I would guess somewhere in their thirties."

Harry asked, "Mrs. Goldman, did they leave on foot or did you see them get into a vehicle?"

They ran around the corner of Walton Avenue. The next minute I heard a loud motor and saw a big grey pickup truck, the kind with very large tires, come out from Walton Avenue, going very fast. It turned onto Tremont and went towards Jerome Avenue."

"I heard the shots and immediately heard my wife scream." Mr. Goldman added. "When I looked, I saw people were running and screaming. That's when I saw Officer Niles down on the sidewalk. I ran outside to see if I could help him. But there was a lot of blood and he wasn't moving. I yelled for someone to call an ambulance. Mr. Sturgis next door said he had already."

Lieutenant McGee arrived and told the other detectives on the scene that Lincoln and Washington would take the lead, the other detectives to assist in canvassing the area to find witnesses. McGee asked the patrol lieutenant to have the intersection blocked off to all vehicle and pedestrian traffic.

The word spread that Niles didn't make it; he was DOA at the hospital.

The crime scene unit started to process the entire area under the direction of Lincoln and Washington.

Several hours later, in Lieutenant McGee's office, Harry and Floyd briefed him on their progress. "Lieu, so far the best witness we have is Mrs. Goldman from the butcher shop," said Harry. "She and Mr. Goldman are now giving their written statements, along with Mr. Sturgis from next door at the produce store. None of the other people who were near the scene, we've spoken with, could add to what Mrs. Goldman witnessed. They all ran in a panic. Hopefully some of those who we haven't spoken with will give us a call."

McGee said, "Maybe they can add to what we've gotten from Mrs. Goldman. In addition, there are teams of detectives conducting a more thorough canvass in the neighborhood, mainly on

Tremont and Walton, two blocks in each direction from the intersection. Someone might have been looking out of their window at the time."

After a moment, Harry and Floyd looked at each other as an angry Lieutenant James McGee fumed. "The Nazi bastards crawled out of their sewer here in Zealand again. Because of that blood-soaked sign, we don't have to guess the motive. A uniformed cop shot down on a busy street in broad daylight, is something we don't ever take lightly. It always has top priority. But now there's an additional dimension. We must stop them before more innocent people are killed. So, you two stay with it."

They sat at their desks as Floyd composed a case file, entering all they knew at this time, Harry stared out of the window at nothing in particular, deep in thought. "Floyd do you remember back in the '70's and '80's when a militant black gang, calling themselves the Black Liberation Army, went from city to city assassinating white policeman on the street, most often in broad daylight. I'm thinking this might be the opposite, a Neo-Nazi group of white supremacists that gunned down Niles. Did they kill him simply because he was a cop? or because he was a black cop?"

Floyd answered, "From the descriptions given by Mrs. Goldman, they certainly fit the stereotype of the white supremacist. The MO is similar to the BLA, so the answer to your question would determine their motive. Do they just hate cops? Or is it a racial thing?"

***

They met at the usual place, a parking lot away from the neighborhood. It wouldn't do for one of the homeboys to see Ham talking to the cops. "What have you heard about the black cop in the 7th who was shot on the sidewalk in the middle of the day?" Harry asked as he and Floyd sat with Ham in the detective car.

"The word is a couple of Klan dudes without their hoods or sheets. I'll ask around and if I hear anything you want to know I'll give you a shout." Ham had always been true to his word in the past. The word circulated on the street that the cops were looking for two fat scruffy-looking white cop killers. They were driving a grey pickup truck with huge tires and loud mufflers. A full description was put out nationwide on the National Crime Information Center.

***

Harry and Floyd went back to the scene to canvass again hoping to find a witness they might have missed the first time. Besides knocking on doors, they stopped people on the street. Those who did hear gunshots could not supplement Mrs. Goldman's information.

Later, back at the office, their supplemental report completed, entered into the file… it was quitting time. "You got some big plans for tonight partner?" Harry inquired.

"If that means partying, the answer is no," Floyd said. "On the way home, I'll stop and pick up a pizza and settle down with Gunga-Din; a good story by Rudyard Kipling with a powerful message."

Harry did not go home right away. He called a number he'd called many times in the past. "Officer Eugene Niles was gunned down in the street up in the 7th. I need your help again Mule. So far all we have is two fat, scruffy white males, bald headed with beards. They fit the stereotype of the neo-Nazi white supremacist, driving a grey pickup with large over-size tires and loud mufflers. At this point, we don't know their motive. Do they hate cops? They hate blacks? Or both?"

Mule and Ham were two of Harry's best confidential informants, the difference was the nature of Mule's special relationship with Harry. Several years ago, when Harry was about to get his gold detective shield, Harry's father, Homicide Detective Ben Lincoln, introduced the two. Mule insisted their connection be kept from everyone: friends, partners, wives and girlfriends. This agreement had paid off for Harry in clearing cases, just like it had for his father previously. Both CI's, Ham and Mule are black and were Harry's eyes and ears.

Ham picked up the talk, the rumblings from the street as he "hung out" with the boys on the corner.

Mule was known as a "fixer" in several neighborhoods. He would settle disputes and kept the thugs in line, when he could, without the police or any other city official's involvement. He was respected and feared by all who knew him. The last time a police officer, a black female was killed in the line of duty, it was Mule and his associates who found the two murderers. The only thing Mule asked in return, besides remaining anonymous, was if Harry saw his teen-age son about to do something that he shouldn't, to bring him home so Mule could kick his ass.

The next call he made was to his current girlfriend. "Jessica, if you're not busy tonight I feel like one of Ralph's steaks."

"Yes Harry, I'd love to. I'll meet you there. Seven o'clock."

The combination of the twelve-ounce rib-eye cooked just right, and Jessica across the table, was enough to temporarily purge his mind of the killers, two pieces of shit not worth two dead flies.

Later, when they arrived at the loft, the first stop was the shower and the relaxing warm water, but not too relaxing with Jessica bathing him like a baby. And Harry being a fair guy believed that one good turn deserved another. After drying off, their skin pink from the hot water, they lay side by side in Harry's king size bed listening to Ravel's Bolero, one of the sexiest, most sensual pieces of music ever composed. Jessica caressed him lightly with her soft fingers, and between her loving touch and Ravel, Harry was inspired. She was so inviting, he loved looking at her and wanted all of her. He started caressing and kissing her all over until they were head to toe. Harry was not a sprinter, but a marathon man taking her with him. When they ultimately reached the finish line, they untangled until their heartbeats were back to normal. Jessica took a cool shower this time and when dried off, got dressed. When she left, Harry fell into a deep sleep.

CHAPTER

18

The preliminary casualty count from the massacre in Atlanta was released to the media: twenty-three dead from gunshots, thirteen others dead, trampled in the crush of the escaping crowd. Numerous gunshot victims being treated at hospitals, as well as various injuries from broken bones to cuts and bruises. A number of the wounded and injured receiving treatment are in critical condition, which may increase the final fatality count.

The Atlanta Gay Pride parade and Zealand Bar-Mitzvah statistics, plus recent hate crimes reported in eleven other cities and towns across the country prompted the second high-level meeting in Virginia's largest city. This multi-jurisdictional taskforce, which had been suggested at the previous meeting was formed with additional cities and states, plus at the federal level both the FBI and the Department of Homeland Security.

ZPD Chief Lansing stood and rapped his knuckles on the table until the buzz of individual conversations stopped, and the room became quiet. "Good morning, I am Zealand Police Chief Robert Lansing. As the unofficial host for this meeting of our new multi-jurisdictional taskforce, I'd like to welcome you all. At some other time, we'll have to appoint a few members to conduct these meetings in an orderly fashion, using some type of parliamentary procedure. Until then, I'll act today as moderator. As we all know, many parts of the world, and a few places in our country have been ravaged and terrorized by Islamic extremists, known as ISIS and also as ISIL. However, our task is at the other end of the spectrum -- the neo-Nazi, white supremacists group calling itself,

'The Steel Swastika.' Their horrific hate crimes committed across the country by this extremely dangerous gang must be stopped as soon as possible. Our mission is to lead the charge. Let us now have your comments and your input. Raise your hand if you want the floor. As you stand, please introduce yourself."

A hand immediately raised. "I'm Atlanta Police Deputy Chief James Hogin. Our investigation into the gay pride parade homicides revealed that the Steel Swastika bunch was responsible. We found four locations along the parade route where gunmen were staked out -- two from the roofs of the lower buildings, the other two from the windows in the taller buildings. These locations were discovered due to witnesses observing muzzle flashes, plus the trajectory of the bullets. We determined it was the SS gang because at each site they left their calling card. At these sites we also found the military sniper rifles with scopes and bi-pods that were used. Also recovered were unused ammunition, and ejected brass. All these items were taken in burglaries from gun stores around the Atlanta metro area during the last three weeks.

Everything at these sites was processed by our crime scene unit. No forensic evidence was found, everything was wiped clean. Because of the mass panic, the shooters were able to slip away without anyone noticing. Four of the critically wounded have since died in the hospital, bringing the number of fatalities as of now to twenty-seven shot, and thirteen trampled. Our investigation is continuing."

Deputy Chief Watkins nodded to Harry, who then stood. "I'm Zealand Police Homicide Detective Harry Lincoln. "We all know that these recent hate crimes started in New York City with the crucifixion murder of a rabbi. Shortly after, Zealand was the location of six hate crimes. Those Nazi signs were left at five of the scenes, a swastika was spray-painted on a van at number six. The questions are: Why Zealand, Virginia?' Are they headquartered here? Who are they?

Several times when witnesses saw the perpetrators, their descriptions were vaguely similar; the stereotype neo-Nazi, white supremacist. None of these witnesses can identify them. We now know that that group has expanded and has been committing hate crimes across the country. My partner Floyd Washington and I have been put on special assignment to identify them. If Zealand shows up in your investigations, please contact us."

FBI Special Agent Roman stood and introduced himself. "The FBI will set up a special unit in conjunction with the National Crime Information Center. This unit will be the clearing house intended to monitor anything connected with The Steel Swastika. The crimes being committed fall under dual jurisdiction, state and federal. The Attorney General's position is that local law enforcement investigates these crimes, and that county district attorneys to prosecute. Defendants may also be tried at a later time under federal statutes. The resources of the FBI and Department of Homeland Security will be available to assist you."

***

Each of the other new members got up and gave a brief summary of Steel Swastika crimes in their jurisdictions. Then Chief Lansing stood. "I want to be sure that all of you know that one of our Black police officers was shot and killed while walking a beat in uniform... on a busy street ...in broad daylight. Two men walked up behind him and fired. They fit the general description Detective Lincoln gave today. A Steel Swastika sign was found beneath the body of the murdered officer. Be sure to alert all police officers in your departments."

The meeting was adjourned.

CHAPTER

19

Floyd Washington knew too well about racial hatred, bigotry, and injustice. Growing up in a small town in south central Florida, he saw it every day. Florida along with its border states of Georgia, Alabama, and the rest of the southeastern states were racially segregated by law. The law, then commonly known as the Jim Crow law. Blacks, or their official designation of the time, 'Colored' were treated less than second class citizens.

Floyd's father worked on a local farm picking cotton in the hot Florida sun during the day. Evenings, he was a janitor for several small businesses. On many occasions Floyd, as a small boy saw his father talk with some of his employers. He had to remove his cap, address them all as 'Boss.' As Floyd grew into his teenage years, he became more and more aware of Jim Crow. In his daily life almost everything around him was designated either 'White' or 'Colored,' even the emergency rooms at the hospital. If a black man or black woman should use or do anything marked for whites, the punishment was usually jail time, preceded by rough treatment by the arresting "law officers." He saw rioting in major American cities, property damage in the hundreds of millions of dollars from fires. Later as a young man, Floyd witnessed civil rights laws passed, dismantling the racial segregation allowed by Jim Crow laws, replaced by social integration.

***

Now off duty, sitting in his newly acquired Zealand, Virginia townhouse, Floyd thought about those years, and how far he'd come. His mind wandered back in time way before Jim Crow, to the warring tribes of West Africa. A village would be attacked by warriors from another village, and people kidnapped. They were taken to the coast and sold to British, French, Dutch and later American slave ship captains. Chained and packed into the ships holds in inhumane conditions, these unfortunates endured the month(s)-long voyage to the new world. Those who survived were then sold to plantation owners, and forced to work, subject to severe punishment, including death. This harsh life for the many thousands of African slaves, their children, and their children's children continued until the end of the civil war, when slavery was abolished.

Floyd also thought about another gross injustice committed upon the indigenous people of North America, the Native Americans, who were known as Indians. The coming of the Europeans to North America was the beginning of the end for those Indians. In the years that followed, The United States of America was formed. Violent wars were fought between the United States government and the Native Americans. In the end, the many Indian tribes were defeated. They had to surrender their lands and forced to live on reservations chosen for them.

And to a lesser extent, Floyd thought of the indignities suffered by Japanese-Americans. After the Japanese surprise attack on Pearl Harbor, the U.S. Government reacted with what could be called mass hysteria. The concern was the fear of espionage. Because of that fear, many American citizens of Japanese descent, and their families living on the west coast, were interned into concentration camps.

He had always been interested in history, both American and world events. From the beginning of mankind to the present, he was saddened by the evil cruelty that some had inflicted upon others. Floyd thought that the twentieth- century was at the top of the heap. Dictators such as Hitler, Stalin, Mao and Pol Pot defined evil cruelty. There were other twentieth-century villains who didn't get as much notoriety. Hitler and the Nazis caused him to think of the Holocaust where six million Jews were murdered for the crime of being Jewish.

Which brought Floyd back to the present, and the neo-Nazi gang, 'The Steel Swastika' who hated all minorities, and were committing terrible crimes. He thought himself fortunate to be a part of the task force whose mission it was to find them, stop them, and bring them to justice.

***

The following morning Floyd was the first of the day-watch detectives to arrive at the squad room. Harry came in with most of the others. He was surprised to see Floyd already on the computer. "Good morning partner, you're in early."

"Yeah Harry, just thought I'd do a little homework before McGee sends us running."

"What did you do last night?"

"I finished my Rudyard Kipling book, Gunga Din."

"After that, don't tell me you watched one of those dumb cop shows on TV."

"No Harry, I just relaxed and did some thinking."

"About what?"

"About stuff."

CHAPTER

20

They elected to celebrate their first wedding anniversary with a romantic dinner for two, at an upscale restaurant atop one of the tall buildings overlooking 'The Point' in downtown Pittsburg. The well-known point in this western Pennsylvania city is at the confluence of the Allegheny and Monongahela rivers, together forming a third... the Ohio river.

Bernard Johnson, a twenty-eight-year-old architect was the only black architect in this medium size firm of eleven architects. His wife, the former Sandra Modell was an independent interior decorator. Sandra Modell-Johnson was white. They took a lot of good-natured kidding from close friends at various get-togethers as the imbibing progressed. The mostly off-key strains of "Ebony and Ivory" were serenaded to the handsome couple.

There were times before they got married, when friends, and some family members had serious discussions with Bernard and Sandra about the racial issue and the bumpy road ahead. "It will be very subtle... The looks, the whispers, the coldness, the exclusion, from both the white and black communities."

From Sandra's sister, "Think about when you have children. A bi-racial child in school will be taunted and bullied by classmates. Children can be very cruel, causing deep psychological scars that last a lifetime."

Despite all that, one year into their marriage, neither experienced any problems concerning those warnings. However, there was no child yet.

Bernard then paid their bill, leaving a generous tip, and drove the short distance home. He pulled into his assigned parking spot of the building's underground garage. As they got out of the car, they were suddenly accosted by three men who grabbed them both. Before Sandra was able to scream, she heard gunshots and saw Bernard fall to the ground. Then a jolting pain and a flash of bright light. She slipped into darkness. She remembered nothing after that.

***

Sandra opened her eyes slowly, it was dark, quiet, the only light shone down from the moon. She touched her aching head and face.

"Why am I lying in the grass? Is that blood that I've wiped from my head and nose? My God I'm naked," Despite the darkness, saw her tattered clothes scattered on the grass.

And despite her fear about what might have happened, she began to realize, *"Those men in the garage, they shot Bernard. Oh my God, is he okay?"* As her head cleared further, she realized she had been kidnapped, beaten and raped.

She gathered up her clothing and dressed, covering herself as best as she could. Her entire body hurting, Sandra starting walking, soon seeing that she was in an industrial area. She walked a few blocks toward one of the buildings that was lit, and active with workers. Some men on the loading platform saw her. They helped her inside and called 911.

At the hospital Sandra Johnson told the detectives what happened. Later, as they were working the crime scene, the sign was found… *"This is what happens to white bitch whore trash who spread their legs for filthy stinking niggers."* The Steel Swastika was at the bottom.

Bernard Johnson had already been found in the parking garage, dead from two gunshots to the base of his skull. The sign was hung around his neck… *"This is what happens to filthy stinking niggers who mess around with white women."* The Steel Swastika was at the bottom.

The Pittsburg PD detectives sent copies of the entire case file to the Task Force Headquarters in Zealand. Included was the surviving victim's statement which stated in part... *"All I can remember about the three men before I was knocked unconscious was they were white and seemed to be out of place in this building of expensive condos. I would not be able to identify them."*

***

Another case file was received at the Task Force from the small town of Granby, Colorado west of Denver. A small informal outdoor wedding of a lesbian couple in this picturesque Rocky Mountain town was in progress. It was suddenly interrupted by a large silver pickup truck that appeared on the dirt road adjacent to wedding site. Automatic gunfire from the truck killed the couple and the preacher, and four of the nine guests. Of the remaining five, only one was not hit. He called 911.

Later at the crime scene, several of the neo-Nazi signs were recovered. No further information was given on the shooters, nor the truck's license plates.

***

A week later at Zealand Police Headquarters, Detectives Lincoln and Washington were wading through the growing Steel Swastika case files from around the country. Another disturbing file marked for their attention came in from Miami.

The victims in this case were an elderly Jewish couple. Ninety-three-year-old Aaron Moskowitz, and ninety-two-year-old Rebecca Moskowitz had a history, not experienced by most. They had lived through the horrors of Hell, and survived. As teenagers, they had met seventy-four years ago, while both were forced into an overcrowded railroad cattle car. The year was 1942, during the Second World War. The forty-five-car freight train with over ten thousand people left the railway terminal in Prague, Czechoslovakia. Men, women, children, babies, the elderly, all with the yellow cloth Star-of-David sown onto the front of their clothing. The train was heading east. It's destination… the Auschwitz concentration camp!

"The final solution to the Jewish question" was being carried out, not only at Auschwitz, but also at other Nazi death camps. When the train arrived, most of the Jews went directly to their deaths in the gas chambers. Aaron Moskowitz and Rebecca Cohen were spared because they were young, heathy, and strong. For the next three years they worked, staying alive while enduring and witnessing unimagined cruelty. During that nightmare, they got to know each other. In 1945 the Red Army of the Soviet Union liberated the camp. The two friends, along with thousands of others made their way west to a refugee center. After the war, with the aid and help of various refugee and relief agencies, they were able to immigrate to the United States. They ultimately settled in Miami, Florida living common-law as Mr. and Mrs. Aaron Moskowitz.

Over the years they had raised a family, a large family. Children, grandchildren, and great grandchildren. However, Aaron and Rebecca had never been formerly or legally married. After so many years, their family planned a simple ceremony in a small synagogue. A license was obtained, and the marriage was conducted by a rabbi in order to be legitimate in the eyes of God, and the State of Florida. Later, the four generations celebrated with the two elder Moskowitz's in a private dining room at a restaurant.

After the party, the newlyweds, Mr. and Mrs. Aaron Moskowitz were driven home by a family member. Home was a one-bedroom cottage in a fifty-five years or older community. Once there they changed into their night-clothes and robes, then turned on the TV.

They were suddenly startled when glass shattered, and two objects came through the front windows. Several neighbors heard and felt the explosion and called 911. When the first fire truck arrived, the cottage was fully involved in huge flames and thick smoke.

After the smoldering ruins cooled down, the fire battalion chief entered and gave the all-clear sign. Then the medical examiner and a pair of detectives also went inside. They found the burned bodies of Aaron and Rebecca Moskowitz.

Attached to the mail box at the end of the driveway was the neo-Nazi calling card. Printed on it… *"These two old Jews escaped the SS ovens at Auschwitz but did not escape the flames of The Steel Swastika… Heil Hitler!"* At the bottom the Nazi symbol.

CHAPTER 21

In the office of the West Virginia compound. Hans Schultz, Otto Shafer and Sheriff Luke Hayes reviewed the latest actions. Hans gloated, "They were just perfect. Each one carried out with precision. But if I'm to be recognized as Der Fuhrer of the new 'Fourth Reich' I want to do something so spectacular, that The Steel Swastika will be known all over the world."

Hans then told them of a plan that he was formulating in his mind.

"When Hitler invaded Poland to start World War Two, the Nazi SS formed special units that would follow the regular German army as they overran all the Eastern European countries including the Soviet Union. These SS killing units, known as. 'the Einsatzgruppen' would then round up all the Jews from the cities, towns and villages in these countries. These Jewish pigs were then forced to dig huge trenches they fell into after being shot by the SS of the Einsatzgruppen. Thousands of mass graves, containing the bodies of hundreds of thousands of Jews were discovered and exhumed after the war."

Shafer and Sheriff Hayes looked at each other, both wondering why the history lesson. Hans read the perplexed look on their faces. "I'd like for us to do something similar, of course on a much smaller scale. The tactics would be somewhat different, but the outcome the same. Have our Einsatzgruppen units all over the country executing not only Jews, but all the other sub-human swine, those enemies of White Christian America." Hans stopped talking for a minute, giving the two men time to absorb what he intended, then continued. "Otto, I want us both to take a trip to Zealand, meet with some of our people there. I want us to test the feasibility of forming these units and conducting such an operation."

***

Sixteen elderly Jewish men and women gathered early this Saturday morning at the Zealand First Baptist Church, as they did each Saturday. After coffee and freshly baked pastries, they boarded the twenty-passenger church mini-bus driven by a church volunteer. This was a gracious gesture by the church to assist some of its neighbors, transporting them to their place of worship, on their Sabbath. The destination, a small, very old synagogue built in 1877. The forty-minute drive across Zealand, to just outside of the city limits, in unincorporated Ridgewood County stood the ancient structure. It was located alone in an abandoned field, nearby some woods.

***

Arnold Hurst, the Zealand satellite commander was asked by Hans if there was a way to conduct an operation as he had described. The following day Hurst met again with Hans. "Yes, every Saturday a church bus takes a bunch of old kikes to some Jew church in the middle of nowhere." And then told the details as he had learned from his sources.

"Okay," said Hans. "Select a half dozen of your best and most trusted men for this Saturday. In the meantime, the three of us will do the planning, going over all the details. We'll need about twenty-five shovels, and...and... tell your men to bring their hunting rifles."

***

The bus stopped at the front door of the synagogue. The passengers had just settled into the pews of the old structure, when men with guns burst in shouting anti-Semitic obscenities. Everyone including the rabbi, the cantor, and three additional worshipers were ordered outside. The driver was pulled off the bus. All were forced to walk across the field to the edge of the woods. They were then lined up side-by-side facing the woods, each given a shovel, ordered to start digging.

Hans sputtered in his despicable way, "These broken-down old yids can't dig a ditch. But I want each one of them to at least turn over one full shovel of dirt. When that's done, I'll give the order to fire."

And fire they did… leaving twenty-two dead bodies on the dirt, with a shovel near each body.

***

Because they were the Task Force coordinators, Detectives Lincoln and Washington were called to the scene by Ridgewood County Sheriff Bert Logan.

The sheriff said, "A man and his wife came here to attend services. They were in shock, but he was able to call 911. This is what we found when we got here," pointing to the twenty-two bloodied, bullet riddled victims. Crime scene tape surrounded the area, keeping a thirty-foot 'Do Not Enter' buffer. The detectives stood silently, just looking.

The rage building in both.

"Harry, Floyd," said Sheriff Logan. "Walk with me back to the synagogue, I want to show you something." Attached to the front door was the familiar The Steel Swastika sign. On it was a hand-written message. *"This is the work of the reborn SS Einsatzgruppen that will eliminate the Crist killin Jews and all the other sub human swine from our country."*

CHAPTER 22

Homicide detectives everywhere understand that occasionally crimes are committed that can only be described as barbaric, uncivilized, cruel, and outrageous. They are high profile, and the demands on the detective causes him or her to work twelve, fourteen-hour shifts, day and night. The normal eight-hour shifts no longer apply, until these brutal crimes are stopped. Their physical and mental endurances are sometimes strained to the limit…

He was in a deep sleep, dreaming. He always dreamed but when he woke in the morning, he never could remember the dream. In this dream a phone was ringing. It woke him, and in the next instant, opening his eyes, he saw on the bedside table, his cell phone lit up. It wasn't a dream. On that same table the green digital numbers on the clock read 3:22 a.m. He picked up the phone. "Yes?"

"Detective Lincoln, this is Harper in communications. An officer has been shot. You and Detective Washington are needed in the ER at Zealand Memorial right away, on the orders of Lieutenant McGee."

"Have you called Washington yet?"

"No sir, that's my next call."

"Tell him I'll meet him there."

***

They met at the hospital entrance and had to bull their way

through a sea of uniforms to reach the ER. Lieutenant McGee was already there. "Lincoln, Washington," he called standing near one of the trauma rooms. "Officer Clyde Willis, 5th precinct was hit three times. One in the shoulder, one in the upper arm, and one grazed the back of his head. They just took him up to the OR, the doc says he's going to be okay."

McGee paused for a moment, checking his emotions. "One of the mutts who shot him is in the trauma room next door. Willis was able to return fire, hitting him twice, one in each leg. The other mutt ran, but Willis thinks he might have hit him also."

"Has anyone talked to him?" asked Harry. "Has he been advised?"

"No, I've left that for you two. There're two uniforms from the 5th in there as the docs work on him. They've been told not to say a word to him." McGee's expression changed as he looked at Harry and Floyd. "One of those neo-Nazi signs was found on ground next to Willis' patrol car." McGee knew the questions the detectives were about to ask. He held up his hand. "Let's walk down the corridor to the detention area and get the details from the 5th precinct morning watch commander."

Lieutenant Brady said, "Detectives Lincoln, Washington. Your boss told me that you guys are going to handle this. I feel much better."

"Good to see you Lieu," said Harry, who had worked under his command when he was in uniform. "We just got here. We learned that Willis is going to be okay. Tell us what the hell happened."

"Officer Willis is assigned to car 1505, one of the beat cars in midtown. About 3:00 o'clock this morning, give or take, you'll have to get the exact time, he's in his patrol car parked on the left side of one-way 8th Street at Spring. In his side view mirror, he sees two men walking up the sidewalk towards the rear of his car. They come up to the driver's side window, which is open, as if to ask directions. Instead, they called him a nigger cop, and both started shooting."

Brady stopped talking for a few seconds, blinked his eyes once or twice, and cleared his throat. "Willis told me that he had sensed that something wasn't right, so he un-holstered his gun and held it in his lap. As soon as they fired their guns, he came up with his, and shot back immediately. One went down, the other took off running. Willis thinks he hit the one that ran. He said they were two white males, mid-30's to mid-40's, couple of red necks."

"Thanks Lieutenant. We'll get a statement from Willis as soon as he's up to it." McGee, Lincoln and Washington walked back to the ER to check on the wounded shooter.

Lieutenant McGee's cell phone rang. Harry and Floyd heard McGee say into the phone, "Have them seal it off and start the crime scene techs, also notify the medical examiner. Detectives Lincoln, Washington and I will be there shortly."

And to Harry and Floyd he said, "That was the communications sergeant. The body of a white male was found under a parked car at 5th and Spring. That's three blocks from the attack on Officer Willis. The cops there figure it's the other shooter." As they were leaving the hospital, heading for their cars, McGee said, "I'm glad that commo sergeant called my phone instead of putting it on the air. The media would have picked it up on their scanners... they would be swarming the place."

***

The scene was buzzing with activity: blue lights, uniforms, and loud chatter from police radios. Also, some curious neighbors, standing across the street from the grey parked car.

"He's under that car, the grey one over there," said the sector sergeant pointing. "1502 got a call about a drunk passed out under a car. We've been all over this area looking for the guy who fled after he shot Officer Willis.

Three patrol cars showed up to check it out. They shined flashlights under the car, called out to him and prodded him with night sticks. They got no response. Two night sticks had blood on them. We backed off and made the necessary notifications: homicide, medical examiner, and crime scene techs."

They walked over and looked under the car with flashlights, and saw a body not moving. "Do you know who called it in?" Floyd asked.

"That elderly gentleman over there, sitting at the top of that townhouse steps."

The medical examiner arrived and met with Lieutenant McGee. Harry and Floyd walked across the street to talk with the witness on the townhouse steps. "Hello, I'm Detective Washington. This is my partner Detective Lincoln."

Smiling, the man said, "You got to be kidding. Show me some ID, Mr. President."

Harry and Floyd displayed their badges and photo ID's to the man, whose eyes widened as he read their names. "Okay," said Floyd. "Now that we've introduced ourselves, who are we talking with?"

"Well I'll be damned, I didn't mean to be disrespectful, but I thought this was some kind of gag. I can't wait to tell my breakfast gang that I met with two presidents this morning." By this time all three were smiling. "Anyway, my name is Leonard Groover and I live right here. I'm the one who called."

Floyd asked, "Mr. Groover, can you tell us what happened, why you called 911?"

"Sometimes I can't fall asleep. I was sitting at my second-floor window late last night, or I should say early this morning. I noticed a lot police activity here and also on Spring Street. I saw patrol cars circling the block.

A short time later I saw a drunk, at least I thought he was drunk, staggering up the sidewalk. He had trouble walking, bumping into parked cars, street lights, and once fell against the front of the building he was passing. When he got here, he crossed the street, then fell down against that grey car. He then sort of rolled underneath it. I kept watching, but he never came out from under that car. I thought one of those patrol cars should check on him, before someone gets in that car and drives away. That's when I called 911."

"We think he shot a police officer over on 8th Street earlier. He wasn't drunk. He had been shot by the officer. He died under that car."

"How is the officer?"

"He was wounded, but he'll be fine. Mr. Groover, we'll need to get a written statement from you at police headquarters."

"Yes, that will be fine. But you will have to send someone to take me there."

"Will do Mr. Groover. Thank you for making that call."

CHAPTER

23

Hans Schultz took the call a little after 8:00 a.m. that same morning. Arnold Hurst immediately said, "I'm afraid I have bad news, Mr. Schultz. But being you have cautioned us not to discuss things of a sensitive nature over the phone, I'll make a trip to the compound. It's an urgent matter that will require your immediate attention. I am leaving now and should be there in a few hours."

Arnold Hurst, the satellite commander for Zealand, Virginia was dreading Hans Schultz's reaction when he broke the news. As he drove he had time to think. *"Will he hold me responsible for the actions of those dolts? Oh, why did it have to be those two? There's no easy way for me to tell him, so I'll just give him the facts and see what he recommends."*

When Hurst entered the compound office at noon, Hans Schultz, Otto Shafer, and Sheriff Luke Hayes were watching the TV news. *"…and shot him as he sat in his patrol car. Zealand police are not saying much about the incident, but we have learned that the officer survived multiple gunshot wounds and is being treated at the hospital. We also understand that one, or possibly both shooters might have been shot by the wounded officer. As reported at the top of this newscast, one of the neo-Nazi signs was found at the scene. The officer reportedly said there was a racial slur directed at him before the shooting started. The officer is black, the two shooters, white. We'll bring you more on this story as it unfolds."*

"Come in Arnold," said Hans. "What is so urgent that you drove all the way from Zealand to tell us?"

"That news report!" It's the result of an operation gone bad, and I don't know what to do about it."

Hans instructed. "Okay Arnold, start from the beginning. Don't leave out details."

"Well sir, you had directed the satellite commanders to use our discretion about what operations to conduct. Several weeks ago, we shot and killed a nigger cop in Zealand. It went smoothly... it got a lot of media coverage... our SS sign had a lot to do with it.

Last night we had another opportunity. We found out that this nigger cop who works the grave-yard shift, the cops call it the morning watch, parks his police car at a certain place, at a certain time, and just sits in it waiting.

There's a club, a strip club two blocks away on Spring Street at 10th Street. A lot of our boys hang out there. This nigger sits there on 8th Street and watches the light at Spring. When a car busts the red light, he pulls it over. He arrests a lot of drunk drivers coming from that club."

"Keep going Arnold."

"I chose three of my best men for the operation. Henry Gattis, Junior Porter, and Bobby Comstock. The three would drive in Bobby's pick up to that location and make sure the police car was there. Then Bobby would drop the other two a block away at Commerce Avenue and 8th. Henry and Junior would walk up 8th street and go to the driver's side of the car. If the window was closed, I told them, just tap on it and act like they wanted to tell the cop something, when he lowers it. Then you both shoot the nigger in the head. They were to put an SS sign through the patrol car window and walk back to where Bobby was waiting." Arnold Hurst stopped talking.

Hans Schultz asked. "What happened next?"

"I didn't know anything until sometime around 3:00 this morning when I got a call from Bobby. He was so shook-up that I could hardly understand him. He said while he was waiting, he thought he heard some gunshots. I questioned him about that. He said it was real quiet and he was only a block away. He said when they didn't return he thought about driving up the street to where the cop car was. But he was afraid to leave the pick-up location in case they had to make their way back another way."

Arnold continued. "Bobby told me that all of a sudden, police cars, fire trucks and ambulances came from everywhere. He said lights were going on in the houses on the block, and people were running up the block. The two still hadn't showed up yet, so I got out of my truck and walked up to where the crowd was."

Arnold looked straight at Hans, and said to him, "Mr. Schultz, what he told me next is why I came right over here. He told me that Junior was down on the sidewalk, and they were working on both legs which were bloody. They were also working on the nigger cop who was also bleeding. He said he didn't see Henry anywhere, and then Junior and the nigger were loaded into ambulances and taken away.

Bobby stayed there with the crowd for ten or fifteen minutes, when suddenly several police cars tore out of there. That's when they found Henry under a parked car a few blocks away. People in the crowd were saying that he had also been shot. Bobby told me he heard that Henry was dead." Arnold Hurst stopped talking again and sat just staring at the floor.

Hans said, "I get the feeling, Arnold that you've not told us everything, and the rest is the real reason that you drove all this way. "Please tell us…" raising his voice, "and tell us now!"

"The first meeting that you summoned the satellite commanders here to the compound, Henry, Junior and Bobby were with me. As I said, they were three of my best men." Arnold again looked at Hans and said, "When you and Mr. Shafer came to Zealand, you planned that operation where we rounded up all those old Jews from their shitty little church. When we took them out to the field to dig with the shovels, you were giving all the orders, including the order to fire. The reason I'm telling you all this is that those same three were there too. And that includes Junior Porter, who was shot in the legs, and is now in police custody."

Arnold took a few deep breaths and continued. "Junior knows where this compound is located, and that you three are the leaders of 'The Steel Swastika.' The cops would do anything to know who and where. The question is, will Junior keep his mouth shut, and maybe get the needle, or will he turn rat?"

Arnold now had their full attention and kept talking. "The cops and the D.A. will offer him one hell-of-a sweet deal, at least a very minimum sentence. But he knows what will happen to him if he opens his mouth. The Aryan Brotherhood will be waiting."

CHAPTER

24

There was another meeting taking place two hundred miles away, at Zealand Police Headquarters. Present were Zealand Police Chief Lansing, Deputy Chief Watkins, Lieutenant McGee, Detectives Lincoln and Washington, Ridgewood County D.A. Dick Donahue, Ridgewood County Sheriff Bert Logan, and FBI Special Agent Fred Roman. New to the Task Force was Joyce Morgan, U.S. attorney for the Western District of Virginia.

The formal greetings, and opening remarks by Chief Lansing were concluded. Coffee and donuts from a side table in hand, they settled into their seats around the conference table. "With your permission Chief," said Lieutenant McGee. "I'd like for Lincoln and Washington to brief everyone on what's occurred in the last twenty-four hours." In response Chief Lansing nodded.

Detective Harry Lincoln said. "I'll keep it short and to the point. Most of you probably have already heard the latest. Early this morning there was an attempted assassination of Zealand Police Officer Maurice Willis as he sat in his patrol car. He was shot three times… He survived. He is now in the hospital recovering. The two shooters, white males, we believe are members of 'The Steel Swastika' the neo-Nazi, white supremacists gang committing brutal hate crimes across the country." Lincoln thought for a minute, and then said, "I realize that you know about this bunch and what they have been doing."

"What you also probably know, is that the officer was able to return fire striking both shooters. One was hit in both legs, falling to the ground, unable to get up. The other, although hit, was able to run from the scene. He was found a short time later a few blocks away, under a car... Dead!" Harry stopped talking and looked at Floyd. "My partner, Detective Washington will bring you up to speed on the significance of this incident."

"And significant it is," said Floyd. "Of all the known hate crimes committed by members of this gang in the many places around the country, this is the only time we'll have an opportunity to interview one of them. Someone who might be the key to their downfall. His name is Junior Porter. He has an extensive rap sheet. Detective Lincoln and I went to see him in his well-guarded hospital room." Floyd went on to explain that they knew it was too soon after the treatments of his gunshot wounds to talk with him. They were anxious just to have a look at him.

"He was lying in the bed hooked up to the monitors, still somewhat under the influence of the anesthesia. As soon as my partner identified us as detectives, he raised his head up off the pillow and said to him in a low groggy, threatening voice, 'Get the fuck out of here and take your nigger with you.' We left without another word."

Deputy Chief Watkins addressed the group next. "As Chief of Detectives, I am deeply concerned about the seven hate crimes committed in Zealand by this gang. The eighth hate crime occurred less than a mile just outside the city limits in unincorporated Ridgewood County. It is being handled by Sheriff Logan's department. My first concern is why there are so many here in Zealand compared with the rest of the country? Are they headquartered here? Two of our officers were shot while on duty, one in the middle of the day, and the other in the middle of the night. One was killed, the other survived. Was the shooting of the police officers a new trend, or were they just targets of opportunity? Both were black!"

Deputy Chief Watkins took a moment to review his notes, then continued. "Chief Lansing and I would prefer that Detectives Lincoln and Washington be the lead investigators in the Zealand cases. They will make available any progress to Special Agent

Roman, keeping him in the loop. As we've discussed in our previous meeting, these crimes come under both state and federal statutes. We anticipate the prosecution of the wounded shooter, and any future suspects, will be worked out between District Attorney Donahue and U.S. Attorney Morgan."

***

Two days later Harry and Floyd went to the fourth floor of Zealand Memorial to speak with the doctor who was treating Maurice Willis. "I think it's too early to question Officer Willis," Dr. Ellin advised. "The bullet that grazed the back of his head caused a slight concussion. Maybe in a couple of days. However, a visit now would be welcomed, but keep it light and short."

They found Willis to be in good spirits, and not lacking for visitors. He said that in addition to family and friends, most of morning watch had come by, three and four at a time. When Floyd asked about the piece of equipment next to his bed, Willis answered, "That's a morphine drip for my pain. When they get ready to discharge me, I'm going to ask the doc if I can stick around for a few more days."

The next stop in the hospital was down one flight to room 308, where two uniformed police officers sat in the corridor next to the door. "Well if it isn't the presidents, I'm honored," said the older cop as he shook hands with Harry and Floyd. "I guess you're here to see that piece of shit. While in there, maybe pull out a couple of plugs. We'll never tell."

When they entered the room, Junior Porter stared at them with cold contempt. Harry stood at the bed and stared back at him. "Junior Porter, we are here to tell you officially that you are under arrest, charged with aggravated assault on a police officer. And to advise you of your constitutional rights. You have a right to remain silent..."

Harry finished, then asked, "Do you understand your rights?" Porter said nothing. Harry then showed him a paper. "This is a form stating that you have been advised of your constitutional rights and that you understand them. "I'd like for you to sign it." Porter refused the pen that was offered and continued to stare, not saying a word.

Harry turned to Floyd and said, "We're done here partner, let's go."

***

In the office of the Ridgewood County District Attorney. Dick Donahue asked, "How is Officer Willis coming along? It's been three days now since the shooting."

Harry replied, "He is recovering faster than anticipated. He should be going home in a few days."

Lieutenant McGee was anxious and got right to it. "Well Dick, did you and the new U.S. Attorney come to an agreement on which of you will prosecute that redneck mutt?"

"Yes Lieutenant, we'll prosecute him at the state level, from my office," answered the D.A. "As for any others here in the City of Zealand, and Ridgewood County, we'll look at them case by case… And Harry, what did Mr. 'white supremacist' have to say for himself?"

"Floyd and I went to see him at his hospital room yesterday. We advised him of the charges he was arrested under, read him his Miranda rights. He refused to sign the Miranda understanding form. He never uttered a word the entire time, just stared at us with contempt."

Floyd added, "We'll let him stew until he's released from the hospital, and then see if his attitude changes when he's sitting in a jail cell."

"Sounds good to me," said D.A. Dick Donahue.

CHAPTER

25

The following week, Junior Porter was released from the hospital. He took up residence in a 7′x10′ solitary cell at the Zealand City Jail adjacent to police headquarters. There were several interrogation rooms, each furnished with a metal table and four metal chairs, two on each side of the table, all bolted to the floor. The difference was the chairs on one side of the table sat higher than the chairs on the opposite side. It was common practice for the detectives to sit on the higher side, to give them a psychological edge. Watch any late-night TV talk show, and see the host sitting higher than the guest(s).

Harry and Floyd had Porter brought to one of these rooms. "You're in deep shit Junior," said Harry. "You could do twenty or more years for the shooting of Officer Willis. In addition, the district attorney might also charge you with conspiracy to commit other hate crimes with your Nazi buddies."

Junior Porter looked from one to the other, and then ignoring Floyd, said to Harry. "So, what are you telling me?"

"I'm telling you that when you finish serving time in the Virginia State Penitentiary, you will be turned over to the feds. Hate crimes are also felonies under federal law. They will try you, then you'll spend the rest of your life in some federal prison. You will never again breathe another breath of free air."

Porter sat and said nothing.

"Okay Junior, I'll get to the meat of this conversation." Harry continued. "We want to know who the leaders of 'The Steel Swastika' are, and the location of their main headquarters. Here's the deal. You give us what we want, and we'll talk with the Ridgewood County District Attorney and the U.S. Attorney for Virginia. If it proves you provided us good information, you will likely get significantly reduced sentences, both state and federal. There's no need to die in prison."

Porter thought to himself, *"No need to die in prison. Ha! No matter how short my sentence is, the word will travel fast if I turn rat. Wherever I'm sent, they will find me and kill me. The Aryan Brotherhood will first cut out my tongue, let me suffer for a few days. Later I'll be found dead with my dick stuffed in my mouth."*

The room was utterly silent for five minutes.

"Alright, I'll give you what you want," Junior Porter finally said to Harry. "But I can't go to prison, any prison, not even for a day."

***

The meeting was held two days later. Harry was asked to brief the members of the Task Force on the last conversation he and Floyd had at the city jail with Junior Porter. After Harry finished, he quoted Porter's final statements, then continued before anyone had a chance to say anything.

"With respect to you all, I'd like to give our take on the situation. My partner and I have concluded that we cannot walk away from his offer. On one hand, we have this cowardly neo-Nazi who might have committed many of these brutal, vicious crimes. None of which we can prove. On the other hand, is this same coward who shot a police officer, and can be prosecuted for it. However, the officer has survived, and will make a full recovery."

Harry looked around the table and saw that he had their full attention.

"Porter explained that he could not give up this white supremacist gang in return for a reduced sentence. He had been told, no matter the prison, state or federal, the Aryan Brotherhood would know he was the rat who brought down the organization. They would be waiting to torture and kill him. He said he would name names, sign statements, and testify in court, but only if he did not go to prison. We explained the witness protection program to him, and he liked that. 'But,' he said, 'how do I know that I give you all this stuff, and then y'all double cross me and send me to prison?' We told him he would get a written agreement signed by both the Ridgewood County District Attorney, and the U.S. attorney for Virginia."

By this time, they all knew where this was going, but kept listening.

"This is the break we've been waiting for, maybe the only break we'll ever get to shut down these monsters. Detective Washington and I would strongly recommend that District Attorney Donahue, and U.S. Attorney Morgan consider the witness protection program."

During a break there was quite a buzz around the conference room. The pros and cons concerning the fate of Junior Porter were debated vigorously. The debates stopped shortly as a courtesy extended to the final decision makers, Joyce Morgan and Dick Donahue. After some more discussion, both concurred with the proposal, agreeing that prosecution at the state level would be quicker. Task Force members each offered professional input and advice. By the close of the meeting, a plan was devised. To put that plan in motion, Detectives Lincoln and Washington were to meet with Junior Porter to get the critical names and locations. They would bring with them, the signed agreement to place Porter in witness protection, provided that his information was true, accurate and brought results.

***

The following day Harry and Floyd brought Junior Porter to the headquarters building, up to the homicide squad room, and straight into Lieutenant McGee's office. The homicide commander gave orders that they were not to be disturbed, and to hold his calls, then closed the door and sat down at his desk. He remained unusually restrained and quiet.

Harry said to Junior Porter. "Here is the paper that you wanted, guaranteeing that you won't go to prison. Instead, you will be placed into the witness protection program. It's signed by the two people who have the authority to make such a deal. Now you understand that it's stated in there it is only valid if the information you give us is true and results in what we are after. You also agree to testify in court against the people who are on trial."

Porter nodded his head and said, "yes I understand and agree."

"One more thing Junior," said Harry. "At the hospital, when I advised you of your rights, you refused to sign the form stating you were advised and that you understand them. I'm asking you to sign it now."

Harry handed Porter a pen. He signed.

***

Back at the West Virginia compound, Arnold Hurst was immediately ordered back to Zealand with firm instructions. "All operations will stop," bellowed Hans Schultz in a mild panic. "Get that word out right away to all your people. Also, no talking about the organization or any past operations. No war stories among each other nor anyone else. You never know who might be listening. And Arnold, if this Junior Porter is still being detained in their city jail, find a way for someone to get to him. Report back to me. Now go!"

Hans Schultz quietly, nearly whispering to Otto Shafer and Sheriff Luke Hayes. "It is critical that we silence that man before he tells all. He might very well keep his mouth shut and go to prison... we cannot take that chance... we just cannot! There's too much at stake. And what I said about Zealand also applies to all the other satellites around the country. All future operations will be put on hold until further notice."

CHAPTER

26

Harry said, "Okay Junior, this is where you start to earn your way out of prison. Tell us what we want to know."

"The Steel Swastika headquarters is in a compound in that strip of West Virginia between Pennsylvania and Ohio, about two hundred miles or so from here. I think it's Blanton County, and the sheriff there is Luke Hayes. Him and two others, Hans Schultz and Otto Shafer are the bosses of the Steel Swastika, although Hans Schultz is the top dog. He likes to be called 'Der Fuhrer', and for everyone to do the Nazi salute."

"How do you know all this, Junior?" asked Harry.

"Each city in the organization is called a satellite and every satellite has a commander. The commanders have meetings at the compound with Hans Schultz. Each commander usually brings two or three guys with him. I've gone twice with Arnold Hurst, the Zealand satellite commander."

Harry asked, "How many cities or satellites are there? Where are they? Do you know the names of those commanders?"

"There must be maybe a dozen or so. They are trying to get more. I've heard Pittsburg, Dallas, Miami, New York, Atlanta, Denver, St. Louis, Boston, Cleveland, New Orleans. As far as the commanders, I never paid any attention to names."

***

At the next meeting of the Hate Crimes Task Force, three new faces were seen around the table. Urgent calls to West Virginia had been made the day before, resulting in the presence of: Director Carl Sutter, West Virginia Bureau of Investigation, and Colonel Hugh Carter, West Virginia State Police, both traveled from Charleston, WV. The third, FBI Special Agent in Charge Gloria Walton from the Wheeling, WV field office.

District Attorney Dick Donahue addressed the group. "We have just had a major breakthrough in the Steel Swastika hate crimes. An attempted assassination of a Zealand Police Officer resulted in the arrest of one of the perpetrators. A tentative agreement was made to place him in the witness protection program in exchange for the location of the SS headquarters, and the identity of the leaders. In addition, and most important, he will testify at their trials."

Donahue paused for a moment, there were no comments or questions. He continued…

"Blanton County, West Virginia is where all these hate crimes have originated. There is some sort of compound on what used to be rural farm land. We've done some checking and found the registered owner of this property is Hans Schultz. Our information is that he is the leader of the Steel Swastika. He has two lieutenants, Otto Shafer, and hold on to your hats!!… Blanton County Sheriff Luke Hayes."

Director Sutter and Colonel Carter looked at each other with shock and disbelief. "That's hard to accept," said Sutter. "Hugh and I have known Sheriff Hayes for many years. Are you sure about this?"

Donahue assured them. "This informant knows that if we catch him in one lie, our deal with him is off and his ass is gone."

U.S. Attorney Joyce Morgan spoke next.

"We are in the process of completing the affidavits to present to a federal judge for arrest and search warrants. The arrest warrants will be for Hans Schultz, Otto Shafer, Sheriff Luke Hayes and his deputies. The arrest warrants will also include Arnold Hurst, the Zealand, Virginia satellite commander. The search warrants should produce information on other Steel Swastika individuals throughout the country."

She then added, "I've been in touch with the U.S. Attorney General and the Director of the FBI, both in Washington. This will be a coordinated effort among federal, state and local law enforcement agencies. The FBI will be the lead agency when the federal warrants are served."

CHAPTER

27

The mobilization began with a confidential briefing. Included were ranking officers and agents of the various units to be deployed. Not knowing how many supremacists would be there, and what kind of armed resistance they might encounter, law enforcement was going in with overwhelming force. FBI Swat teams from Quantico, and several near-by field offices. West Virginia State Police Swat teams, plus several dozen troopers. The U.S. Marshals Service personnel to be held in reserve. Once the compound is secured and under control, members of the Task Force will take over in a supervisory capacity. FBI agents and investigators from the West Virginia Bureau of Investigation will be instructed to recover all files and records, both electronic and hard copies.

***

Three days later, at 8:00 a.m., law enforcement personnel entered the Steel Swastika compound in Blanton County, West Virginia. They encountered several dozen men with holstered handguns. They were immediately disarmed, and handcuffed. Many others were found in a cluster of barracks type buildings. They surrendered without a fight, there was no resistance. The bully is stricken with a case of diarrhea when faced with superior force. When FBI agents inquired about Hans Schultz, they were directed to a nearby building. As they approached it, three men came out and walked towards them, two in civilian clothes, the third in uniform with a badge and holstered gun.

"What is the meaning of this, what is going on?" Insisted one of them.

"Identify yourselves." Insisted the agent in reply.

"I am Hans Schultz, owner of this property. This is my associate Otto Shafer. And this is Blanton County Sheriff Luke Hayes."

FBI Special Agent Gloria Walton stepped forward. "We have arrest warrants for the three of you."

To the other agents she said, "Please take the Sheriff's weapon."

Other Task Force members joined them. WVBI Director Sutter asked if there were a place where the group could sit and talk. "My office in right in this building," answered Hans Schultz. Once inside the three were searched for weapons and given the Miranda warnings.

After the three were given copies of their arrest warrants, Hans Schultz reviewed the search warrant authorizing the confiscation of all files and records relating to the Steel Swastika. It included all weapons, ammunition, and explosives in the compound. Several dozen FBI agents and WVBI investigators spent the remainder of the day filling trucks with all items seized. West Virginia state troopers went to the sheriff's office where they arrested Sheriff Hayes' three deputies and secured the office.

***

The following day, investigators scrutinized the seized files and records, and found the names of satellite commanders in fourteen cities and towns. Federal, state and local law enforcement personnel descended on these locations, resulting in the arrests of these leaders. From their files, gang members were identified and arrested.

***

In Zealand, Harry and Floyd led a SWAT team up the stairs

and knocked on the door of apartment 3B. Nervously, Arnold Hurst opened the door. "I knew you would be coming."

He was taken down the stairs and driven to Zealand Police Headquarters. In an interrogation room, Harry and Floyd sat across the table from a shaking Arnold Hurst.

Detective Harry Lincoln said menacingly, "Listen, you piece of shit, you're going to give us the names of all those red neck neo-Nazi punks in your so-called satellite."

Satellite commander Arnold Hurst said meekly.

"Yes sir."

CHAPTER

28

During the next few weeks, there were mass arrests in cities and towns across the country. Some, on state felony charges, such as murder, kidnapping, rape, aggravated assault, and aggravated battery. Others on federal conspiracy to commit hate crimes, and civil rights charges. Still others faced both federal and state felony charges.

Somewhere in the vast desert southwest, the U.S. Marshall Service planted Junior Porter in a two-room shack, just a chair in one room, and only a bed in the other. They also arranged for employment on a construction project doing manual labor for minimum wage. He would keep a very low profile, knowing the Aryan Brotherhood and other neo-Nazi gangs would be looking for him, for a very long time.

***

They stopped at Mike's Tavern after leaving the Homicide squad room, for a quick burger and brew. Floyd said, "What gets me Harry, during all the many arrests of the Steel Swastika gangs, not one of those supposedly tough guys put up a fight. They all surrendered meekly."

"It's the typical profile of a bully," said Harry. "They do these terrible things to innocent and helpless people, who can't fight back. But when faced with equal or superior force, they back down and whimper. I hate a goddamn bully Floyd, that's the main reason that I became a cop."

***

The next day, Homicide Detectives Harry Lincoln and Floyd Washington, along with Lieutenant James McGee were summoned to the Mayor's office. Police Chief Robert Lansing and most of the department's brass were there. Also present were Ridgewood County's District Attorney Dick Donahue, and Sheriff Bert Logan. It was a press conference, the local and national media in attendance. The mayor wanted to personally recognize the homicide squad.

"In particular," the mayor said, "Our two 'Presidents,' Detectives Lincoln and Washington, forged an agreement with a two-bit thug. This agreement resulted in the dismantling of the murderous white supremacists, neo-Nazi gang, who called themselves, the Steel Swastika. Those thugs who've committed numerous brutal hate crimes across the country, have been arrested, and are awaiting trial."

The mayor paused for a moment, turned and looked at the law enforcement officials lined up behind him.

"In closing, on behalf of citizens across this country, I'd like to say thank you to Lieutenant James McGee, your homicide squad detectives, and to the many law enforcement people throughout the country, local, state and federal, who worked together. Because of them, this cancer has been eradicated, and innocent people no longer have to live in fear."

Epilogue

Floyd Washington and Awa Senghor were married, officiated by Superior Court Judge Joseph Heller, in a simple ceremony at the Ridgewood County courthouse. In attendance as witnesses, were Harry Lincoln and Jessica Daniels. Harry felt this was the final step of Floyd's road to happiness and peace, after the tragic death of his wife some time ago.

At the airport as the foursome said their goodbyes, Harry informed Floyd that on their return, Lieutenant McGee was planning a party for them with the entire homicide squad attending. The newlyweds then left for their honeymoon at Niagara Falls on the U.S. - Canadian border.

Harry and Floyd were given a week off to rest and decompress, for all their time and effort in the Steel Swastika case. Harry chose to spend the week with Jessica in his father's cabin in the Blue Ridge mountains, where he felt a closeness with his late father, Ben Lincoln.

The Gold Shield

Prologue

It was after midnight when Homicide Detective Harry Lincoln drove away from Zealand Police Headquarters headed to the loft he called home. He had been working the evening watch, 3:00 p.m.- 11:00 p.m. When the shift ended, he stayed at his desk, entering into his computer the final details of the domestic homicide, that he and his partner had handled during the previous hours.

The streets were dark and nearly deserted, vehicular traffic sparse. Driving home in this relaxed atmosphere, Harry let his mind wander. *"I sure have been fortunate with the three partners I've had since being assigned to homicide. Jim Conte took this rookie detective by the hand and taught me the ins and out of working homicide. Then Jim took his pension, much to my dismay. Next, Liz Kovak took Jim's place, and cured any doubts I had about a female partner. She made sure I kept my feet on the ground, and my hands off some piece of shit thug. Liz left when she and her husband decided to have a family. And now my fellow 'co-president', Miami PD's finest, Floyd Washington."*

His thoughts suddenly interrupted by the screams of a woman! The volume increased as he lowered the car window. Harry slowed the car looking and listening. And then he saw them, a man and a woman. Harry stopped the car and jumped out yelling 'police' several times, holding his badge case in one hand, his 9mm service weapon in the other. The woman was backed up, cowering in the dark doorway of a closed store, the man standing over her, his hand raised holding an object. Harry shouted again identifying himself as a police officer as the man turned to face him... It was a meat cleaver! "Drop that and get down on your knees," Detective Lincoln ordered.

The man ignored the command and took a step towards the

detective. The two stood, only the width of the sidewalk between them. The man raised the cleaver and slowly took another step. "Drop the weapon and get on your knees," Harry repeated. "If you come any fuckin' closer with that cleaver, I'll shoot."

Still holding the cleaver high above his head, the man suddenly started to laugh and then charged. Harry fired twice, striking the man in the chest with both rounds, knocking him to the ground. The man did not move when Harry checked him. Not sure if the man was dead or alive, Harry took out his cell phone, called 911, gave his location, identified himself to the operator, and requested an ambulance, a patrol car and a supervisor. Harry also requested the pair of homicide detectives working the morning watch. He went to the store entrance to check on the woman, but she was not there. He called out to her, as he checked several doorways, but she was gone. The street was desolate, no people, no traffic. He then heard sirens in the distance. Violating the rules of conduct at a crime scene, Harry took out his handkerchief, picked up the cleaver by the corner of the blade, and was stunned… It was a plastic toy!

CHAPTER

1

Headline the next morning on the front page of The Zealand Times, *"Black Man Holding Plastic Toy, Fatally Shot by White Detective!"*

The Chief's office at Zealand Police Headquarters was tense. Police Chief Robert Lansing, Deputy Chief Glenn Watkins, Lieutenant James McGee and Detective Harry Lincoln sat quietly, wondering how explosive this shooting might become in the days ahead. "I don't doubt for one minute that the incident last night happened exactly as you reported it," said Chief Lansing, addressing Harry Lincoln. "But with the police shootings of unarmed black men by white police officers around the country, things here might get pretty nasty. However, I want you to know that the three of us, along with the rest of this department will stand behind you and support you. And Harry, in accordance with policy and protocol, the State Bureau of Investigations will handle the investigation. It will be examined closely. In the meantime, you are on administrative duty until this is cleared up. Your presence here will be required by the state investigators. Lieutenant McGee will explain how it will work." The meeting was then adjourned.

Detectives Lincoln and Washington were hastily transferred back to the day watch. This 7:00 a.m. – 3 p.m. shift was for the convenience of those who needed Detective Lincoln available during regular business hours, until the investigation is completed. Because partners stay together, Detective Floyd Washington joined him on the day watch. At lunch time on their first day back, Harry and Floyd left the building, and headed for a fast food drive-in window. They then drove to a park away from the headquarters building. "I don't know how long I'll be off the street," said Harry sitting on a park bench, biting into a tasty chicken sandwich, then washing it down with some ice-cold sweet tea. "But as you know partner, that's the way it is everywhere when a cop is involved in a shooting."

"Surely Harry, this has got to be ruled a good shooting," answered Floyd with a note of anxiety in his voice. "Being attacked by a guy with what you believed was a deadly meat cleaver, and who had just attacked a woman on the street."

"You would think so, but that woman, the only witness that we know of has disappeared, the guy I shot is dead, and all they've got is my account of the incident. And the wild card in the whole incident, that menacing meat cleaver was just a plastic toy. I've already given my written statement to the state investigators. I've got to tell you Floyd, it sure felt strange being on the other side of the table."

"Harry, our morning watch guys Dunbar and Forsyth have identified the man who attacked you. Maurice Fulton, black male, forty-two years old. Has a long history of mental illness. His rap sheet includes two arrests for aggravated assault, and five misdemeanor disturbances. They told me that he's from the neighborhood where it happened. In addition to the state investigators, McGee has sent some of our guys out to canvass the area for any witnesses. After I take you back to the office, I'm going out to beat the bushes also."

By the time they returned, a dozen or so protesters had already gathered on the sidewalk in front of Zealand Police Headquarters. Two vans from the local media were parked down the street. "Looks like it's started Harry. I'll drop you around back, so you don't have to run the gauntlet."

When Harry entered the 3rd floor squad room, instead of going to his desk, he headed for Lieutenant McGee's office, and went in, closing the door behind him. "Lieu, I need to take the rest of the day off. I haven't had a chance to hook up with two of my CI's, who have always come through for me. I think either one of them might find my missing woman witness. I'll stay away from the area where our guys are canvassing. Then I'll go straight home."

"Okay Lincoln, I think that's a good idea. She's the key to the whole damn thing."

***

Both confidential informants were a phone call away, and as soon as Harry got into his car, he made the first call. "Mule this is Harry, if you are free we need to meet, this is important. I'm in my personal car and headed your way."

"Okay Harry I'll meet you at the regular place. I'll leave right now."

At the bowling alley parking lot, Harry pulled up next to the CI's car. "Hello Harry, c'mon over and pull up a chair." Harry opened Mule's car door and slid into the front seat. "I read about you in this morning's paper."

"I read it too Mule, but the article left out a few details." Harry related the entire incident to him. "It happened in the area near the ball park, not far from your place. So far that woman has not been located, and she is the only witness that we know of who can back up my story. And Mule, because of the questionable police shootings around the country, the usual ones are going to make this a racial thing."

"I'll get started on it, put my feelers out. When I learn something, I'll be in touch."

"I'm on administrative duty now and will not get back on the street until this shooting is resolved. And as always Mule... thanks."

Harry's next call was to Ham, his other reliable CI. "I can't meet you for the next couple a hours Detective Lincoln, but whacha' got?" So, Harry gave him all the details of the incident over the phone. He then stressed to Ham the importance of identifying and locating the missing woman. "Okay Detective Lincoln, my ears to the ground… later."

He had just severed the connection from Ham's call, when his phone rang. It was Jessica. "Hi Jess, what's up?"

"What's up? Oh Harry, have you read the morning paper? You're all over the news on TV, the things they're saying about you."

"Yes Jess, I did read today's paper, but haven't been near a TV all day. I'd like to watch the evening news though and see what kind of spin they're putting on the incident. How about I pick up a pizza, you come over and we'll watch it together."

"That sounds good Harry, except for the pizza. I have some food in the fridge that I'll bring and put together dinner for us."

"Okay Jess, that sounds even better. I know it's early, but I'm on my way home now." said Harry.

***

They ate as they watched the news. *"… here at police headquarters the demonstrators are quite vocal, but so far peaceful. They are angry that, yet another black man was shot and killed, this time by an off duty white detective. The victim was holding a plastic toy when he was shot. The white detective has been identified as Harry Lincoln, who claims an unknown black woman witnessed the incident. This alleged witness was not at the scene when the first units arrived, and as of this time has not been identified, nor come forward. The detective has been placed on administrative duty until the state crime investigators can sort out this disturbing incident. We'll monitor this tense situation and bring you more as soon as we get it…"*

Harry turned off the TV, and both finished their dinners in silence. After a few minutes, Jessica spoke in a low voice, "Harry the way that reporter told it, you are going to be the bad guy."

"Yeah Jess, I wanted to see and hear just how the media was going to spin the story to the public. This is explosive stuff, with the recent uptick in police shootings across the country, where black men have been shot by white cops. Now I'm involved in this latest incident, and due to the spin of the media, the glare of the spotlight is on me. My truthfulness and integrity are now being questioned. It's very frustrating Jess, but there's not a damn thing I can do about it."

Harry refreshed their glasses with a bit more wine and said, "I'll climb down from my soap box now and offer my complements to the chef for the wonderful dinner." He took her hand and slowly led her towards the bedroom. "And now let's have dessert."

CHAPTER

2

There was a knock-on Mule's apartment door. When he opened it, he saw one of his associates standing there with a woman Mule did not know. After being invited in, the three took seats in the living room. The associate said, "This is Ms. Ella Jackson, the woman you wanted to talk to. She knows who you are and wants to talk with you about the other night." The man then got up, and with a nod from Mule, left the apartment. After telling her account of what had occurred in the incident the other night, Ella Jackson asked Mule what she should do.

***

In the squad room, Harry was at his desk struggling with mid-morning boredom, reviewing cold cases when his cell phone rang. The number on the caller ID was familiar. "Hello Mule, tell me something good."

"I have the package you wanted and would like to meet with you in some quiet, out-of-the-way place."

"Mule you are a prince, no make that a king. How about the rest area off I-81 southbound, just south of the city? At the picnic tables, in an hour. Floyd will be with me."

"A picnic sounds good Harry. We'll have a jug of ice tea with cups. You bring the vittles."

***

After a quick stop at the KFC drive-thru, Harry and Floyd waited at a picnic table. The rest area had the normal number of travelers coming and going. Their table was away from, and out of ear shot, of the other tables. Five minutes later, Mule appeared, carrying a thermos jug, walking towards them. Following was an attractive black woman, about thirty years old.

Mule handled the introductions. "Detective Harry Lincoln, this is Ms. Ella Jackson. I believe you two almost met the other night. And this other gentleman is Detective Lincoln's partner, Detective Floyd Washington." Mule paused as he poured himself a cup of ice tea, then selected a piece of chicken from the bucket. "Ella, tell these detectives what you told me about the incident, and don't leave out anything."

"I work the swing shift, 4:00 pm to 12:00 midnight at Glosser Industries, here in the city. At quitting time, I took the bus like I always do for the short ride to my stop. When I got off the bus I only have four blocks to walk home. There was nobody on the street except a man walking towards me. I was about to walk by him, when he grabbed me and pushed me into a doorway of a store. I screamed, and he told me to shut up or he would cut my head off. His hand was raised holding a meat cleaver... I learned the next day on the news that it was a plastic toy, that looked like a real meat cleaver... Anyway, I kept screaming. A car stopped, and a man jumped out saying he was a police officer. The man with the cleaver turned to him. I stopped screaming. I heard the policeman tell him to get down and drop the cleaver. The man kept walking towards him. The policeman told him again. Then I heard two shots and I panicked. I sneaked out of the doorway and ran away down the dark street. I didn't stop running until I got home."

Harry asked, "Ms. Jackson, did you know the man who attacked you?"

"No, I never saw him before."

"If you saw a photo, could you identify him?"

"I'm not sure, it was dark, and it happened so fast."

"Do you have to go to work today?

"Yes, I have to be there by 4:00 o'clock."

"I'd like you to come to the police station with us to make a written statement. We'll make sure that you get to work on time."

Harry turned and said, "Mule, I owe you big time...again. Thank you."

In the car, on the way downtown, Harry called another number. "Ham, you can take your ear up off the ground. We have the witness. Thanks."

They heard them before they saw them. "There must be several hundred of them," Harry said as they approached police headquarters. Noisy protesters filled the block, from curb to curb. News vans and trucks were lined up at the end of the street. Police in tactical gear blocked the entrance to the building. The end of the street was blocked off, but the detective car was waived through. Floyd drove around to the back, and the three went up to the third floor by a rear elevator. There they entered the Homicide Squad room.

Harry said to Lieutenant McGee, "This is Ms. Ella Jackson, my witness to the shooting the other night. She's agreed to come in and give a written statement. Ms. Jackson has to be at work by four this afternoon. I assured her we would see to it."

'I'm very glad you're here Ms. Jackson." And to Harry he said, "Have her meet with the state investigators, so they can conduct their interview, and get her statement. Tell them about her work deadline. Also tell them that I said, if they can't complete by then, they'll have to finish tomorrow. You and Washington make sure that she gets to work on time."

While Ella Jackson was with the investigators, Harry relayed to the lieutenant what she had told Floyd and him at the rest area. McGee looked relieved and said, "Well Detective Harry Lincoln, looks like you're off the hook."

Floyd, who had been quiet the entire time said, "Yeah Lieu, unless it becomes a racial thing, like in some of the cities where there have been police shootings. We all know that there are some people who would do anything to get their names in the paper, their mugs on TV."

***

Ms. Jackson's Interview was finished, and her written statement completed. The state investigators showed Ella Jackson a photo lineup. Included with Maurice Fulton's mug shot, were five other mug shots of black males similar to Fulton. She was unable to pick him out. Ella Jackson then left police headquarters with Lincoln and Washington. Fifteen minutes later Floyd pulled the car up to the front door of Glosser Industries at 3:50 pm.

As she got out of the car, Harry also got out. Shaking her hand, he said, "I sincerely want to thank you." And added, "You may very well have saved my career."

"And you Detective Lincoln, may very well have saved my life." Said Ella Jackson with tears in her eyes.

CHAPTER

3

The cage was opened, and the bird flew out. Homicide Detective Harry Lincoln was back in his natural habitat, the streets. "I know it's only been a few days Floyd," said Harry as the two drove away from headquarters. "But the restriction of administrative duty gave me time to think. I am a street cop. Whether I'm dressed in a suit investigating homicides, kidnappings, rapes and aggravated assaults. Or answering calls in a blue uniform preventing drunken husbands from killing their wives, to handling auto accidents, to breaking up bar fights, to writing traffic tickets. Or in jeans and an old sweat shirt working special operations. All of the many things that street cops do every day. It's why I love this job. If I wanted to sit at a desk for eight hours each day, staring at a computer, I'd get a job in some big corporation, with lots of cubicles."

When there was no reply from Floyd, Harry continued. "I was being punished, but I didn't do anything wrong. I told the truth about the incident. And after a few days, when the witness came forward, the state investigators agreed, concluding that due to the circumstances, it was a good shooting." Getting his emotions in check, he said, "Floyd, I remember my first day on the job. The silver badge I was issued to pin on that blue uniform, was more than just badge number 1479 identifying Patrolman H.B. Lincoln. It was a sworn promise to enforce the law fairly, to serve the public, and to protect the law-abiding citizen from the bad guys. Then, five years later, when I was promoted to detective, the gold shield replaced the silver one. I have no family, so this job is my life. This gold shield means everything to me. If they had taken it because of that shooting, I don't know what I'd have done."

Floyd spoke for the first time. "If it was me Harry, I'd feel the same as you, however I'd be bitter as hell. But think of the guy who is convicted of murder, and then sits in prison, maybe on death row. Then ten, twenty years later, it's proven that he is innocent. Someone else committed the murder. How do you think he must feel?"

"Floyd, I think about guys like him a lot. In all of the homicides I've investigated over the years, my worst nightmare is that one of my cases, turns out to be that guy." After a brief pause, Harry continued. "I believe the worst thing that can happen to anyone is to bury their child. The second… to be punished for something he or she didn't do."

They drove around the city, without any particular destination planned. Harry shaking off the indignities of the last few days, wanting to get his feet back on the pavement. After that brief exchange, they rode in silence, the only sounds… the constant chatter from the police radio in the background. When suddenly they were jolted out of their revere…

"Detective radio 199 to Homicide 134/136…"

Harry, riding shotgun, picked up the radio microphone… "134, go ahead 199"

Detective radio 199: "Go to 1401 Elm Street, in the 7th Precinct. Meet with the watch commander at that location."

I34: "Copy that, 1401 Elm Street in the 7th."

***

1401 Elm Street, a moderate private residence, in a middle-class neighborhood. When Harry and Floyd arrived, they saw three patrol cars parked in front. They were met at the front steps by a sergeant and a patrol officer. The sergeant said, "Lieutenant Forbes, the watch commander is inside talking with Mr. and Mrs. Baker. Go right on in, detectives."

Lieutenant Forbes recognized them, made the introductions, and told the Bakers that Detectives Lincoln and Washington will be handling this. The lieutenant then gave the detectives a brief account of the situation. "Mr. and Mrs. Baker have a seventeen-year-old daughter, their only child. They own a business in which both of them are required to operate. They close up each night at 2:00 a.m., and when they got home this morning a little before 3:00 a.m. they checked on their daughter who was asleep in her room. When Mrs. Baker got up about 8:00 this morning, her daughter was not in the house and the back door was wide open. They can fill in the details. No one has been in the girl's room except the Bakers. Do you want my patrol officer to remain here with you?"

"Yes, have him to go to the rear of the house and watch the back door until it can be processed." said Floyd. "Has a crime scene unit been notified?"

Lieutenant Forbes said he was leaving that to them. He and the sergeant then left.

Floyd got on his radio and requested the crime scene unit, giving the location.

The couple was quite upset; she was sobbing, he just stared out of a window. The four then took seats in the living room. Harry said to them, "I know you've told the other officers the reason that you called 911. You heard what little that lieutenant told us. We would like to hear everything from you this time. Start from the beginning. Fill in all the details. And don't leave anything out."

Carl Baker spoke up. "As the lieutenant said, we own and operate a small bar downtown. Florence and I handle it with the help of a waitress. We open at 4:00 in the afternoon, closing at 2:00 a.m. We have our regular customers, and on normal nights the three of us do okay. On busy nights we bring in extra help like one or two more waitresses, and another bartender to help me behind the bar. Sporting events, concerts, conventions, days of the week. That determines the busy nights. We usually get home by 3:00 o'clock."

There was a knock on the front door. Floyd got up and

admitted two crime scene techs. Floyd then asked the Bakers, who had been in their daughter's room in the last several days. A now composed Florence Baker answered, "Just Carl and me, and of course Sally, our daughter."

Floyd asked, "What about the police that were here? The lieutenant, the sergeant and the patrol officer. Did they go into the bedroom? And were they at the open back door?"

Carl Baker said, "I was with them the whole time. They looked into the bedroom but did not enter it. All three were looking at the back door."

Floyd said to the techs, "Come back here with me, and I'll show you the areas that need processing. They went down a narrow hallway, stopping at the first room. This is the girl's bedroom, and as always in cases like this, check the bed for forensics. Blood, semen, and pubic hairs. Then the usual; photos, measurements, and lift all the prints you find. Three police officers from the 7th were here. Their prints can be eliminated from those on file downtown. After you are finished processing, roll a set from Mr. and Mrs. Baker for elimination. Most of the prints should be from the daughter, seventeen-year-old Sally Baker. Process her tooth brush, hair brush and her hand mirror. And lift her DNA from those brushes. It's the unidentified prints that we want to look at. Examine all doors and windows around the house to determine forced entry, if any. After processing the back door, also check it for signs of forced entry. It was found wide open, but it might have been the way out."

Floyd returned to the living room where Harry was interviewing Carl and Florence Baker. "As I looked into your daughter's room it appeared to be in somewhat of disarray. As if there might have been a struggle." Said Harry.

"Well there might have been," said Florence. "I'm ashamed to tell you, but Sally's room always looks like that, unless I straighten it."

Harry continued. "Mrs. Baker, is it not a possibility that Sally might have gotten up and out before you checked on her at 8:00 o'clock? Then left through the back door and forgot to close it?"

"She has on occasion, but not this time. When I got in from work at 3:00, I looked in on her. She was sleeping but had kicked the covers halfway off. When I covered her, I noticed that she was wearing the pajamas I had gotten her for her recent birthday. Then later this morning at 8:00, I went in to wake her. She was not in her bed. I looked around the house and she was gone. The back door was wide open. I went back into her room and discovered her purse and wallet, her keys, and most shocking of all... her cell phone were all there! That phone is with her 24/7. And those pajamas she was wearing, were nowhere in the room, nor the bathroom. No Detective Lincoln, my daughter Sally did not leave this house voluntarily, on her own. She was taken by force!"

"Mrs. Baker," Harry asked. "Do you have a recent photo of Sally? Preferably one with a true likeness of her." Florence crossed the room to a desk and picked up a framed portrait of her daughter. She removed it from the frame and handed it to Harry. "Thank you, Mrs. Baker. We'll make copies and return this original. One more thing, we'll need a good physical description of Sally."

Floyd got out his note book and said, "In addition to her measurements, we'll need hair color and style. Eye color, plus any distinguishing marks or tattoos. If she wears glasses, describe them. Anything else to help pick her out of a crowd."

Florence Baker was very detailed and descriptive.

Harry and Floyd assured Carl and Florence Baker, that they would do everything they could to find Sally. And they would stay in touch. They exchanged contact information with the Bakers, telling them to call either one, night or day, should they hear anything. And of course, if Sally returned home.

CHAPTER

4

The crowd of protesters were still demonstrating in front of Zealand Police Headquarters. The size of the crowd had increased and was now estimated between three and four thousand. A young black man was inciting the protesters through a bullhorn…

… "Rodney King! You remember Rodney King. The black man who was beaten without mercy, some years back, by four white Los Angeles cops. They were tried before a lily-white jury. An' guess what?... Not Guilty! Then, when half a Los Angeles was burned down, the Feds come in and those four white pigs went to prison. Then in Ferguson, Missouri. That unarmed black teenager was shot and killed by a white cop for no damn good reason. His white ass walked away, didn't spend not one day in jail. Watch the news on TV, read the paper. It seems like every day, somewhere, another innocent, unarmed black man is killed by the white man in blue. Then all a them crackers be high-fivin' in the pol-ice station, cause they say it be a good shootin'. I say it be one more nigga ain't goin' home to his mama."

He had the attention of the crowd and kept talking. "An' now, right here in Zealand, Virginia, a off-duty white detective, shoots and kills a black man armed wit a plastic toy. A plastic toy! He say the nigga had gone after a black sista' wit a meat cleaver, an' then went after him to cut him up. That's when he killed him. He say the sista' seen the whole thing. But they can't find her, cause there ain't none. He be lyin' jus like the rest a them. And then some a his white pol-ice buddies investigates an say the killing of that black man be okay, was justified. Another one a them good shootins'. Well we want justice for that brother with the plastic toy. Call in the Feds and put that detective's lyin' white ass in prison. Or half a Zealand might burn down, just like Los Angeles."

He shouted into the bullhorn, 'cops are killers.' Then again, 'cops are killers.' And again, 'cops are killers.' The crowd started to chant with him, 'cops are killers,' 'cops are killers.' The chant became the fuel for the demonstration.

***

Floyd and Harry entered the police parking lot through a rear gate, guarded by six or eight police officers in riot gear. Once up in the squad room, they briefed Lieutenant McGee on the new Sally Baker case. Summing up, Harry said, "From what we've learned this morning, Floyd and I believe this seventeen-year-old girl has been kidnapped. Taken from her bed during the night, sometime after her parents got home from work about 3:00 a.m."

Lieutenant McGee listened intently to the briefing. He then talked about the demonstration. "So far, it's just been noise, but as the size of the crowd increases, and different agitators shout this racial stuff into bullhorns, that talk gets louder. It's just a matter of time before things turn violent, and people get hurt." Now, with a serious straight face, looking right at Harry, McGee said, "You know Lincoln, if we just throw you out to that pack of wolves, no one gets hurt, and everyone goes home happy." A shocked moment later, the three had a good laugh. Resorting to unexpected 'cop humor', McGee came out with that gem of which legends are made.

After the laughter, Harry and Floyd left a red faced, wheezing lieutenant, and went to their desks. Harry started the Sally Baker missing person/possible kidnapping case file. He entered all the information from Carl and Florence Baker that morning. At the same time, Floyd had initiated look-outs for Sally Baker, to local, metro, and state law enforcement agencies. The National Crime Information Center was also notified.

At this time, everyone in the building, both sworn officers and civilian employees were concerned. The huge, loud crowd in front of headquarters was unpredictable. Would the demonstrators just continue their boisterous noise, or would they turn violent?

These citizens had gathered to protest another injustice, as they saw it. "One more innocent, unarmed black man, shot and killed by a white cop," Came the voice from the bullhorn. Non-violent protests are legal and are monitored by law enforcement. Occasionally, a second group forms, who are opposed to the first. It is the responsibility of law enforcement to stand between groups and prevent violence. Insuring that all citizens have a constitutional right to non-violent protest and free speech.

Because this group of demonstrators numbered into the thousands, all sworn Zealand police officers off days were cancelled, and placed on twelve-hour shifts. Joining ZPD, were deputies from the Ridgewood County Sheriff, and several hundred state troopers. One shift was 12:00 noon to 12:00 midnight, the other 12:00 midnight to 12:00 noon. The enormous crowd started to drift to the adjourning downtown streets, with police still monitoring. The protesters, egged on by agitators, got louder, but remained peaceful and law abiding.

However, the wild card in this whole equation showed up... gangs of thugs from the adjoining neighborhoods... as they always do. These thugs are criminals, violent law breakers who have been arrested numerous times. Due to the large crowd of demonstrators, the thugs joined and blended in with them. Their rampage of looting and destruction started with parked cars, and then patrol cars. Windows broken out, then overturned and burned. Many store windows were smashed, thugs entering and stealing everything they could carry. Some stashed looted merchandise nearby and returned for more. As the looting continued, there were foot chases, and police arrested all they could catch. There were many fights during these arrests, and injuries were sustained on both sides. At the same time, opposing demonstrators started shoving and fighting the original crowd, causing more injuries. And more arrests.

When order was finally restored, the crowds of thousands dwindled down to several hundred. Counter demonstrators left, and neighborhood thugs had slithered back to where they came from, or were in jail, after receiving medical treatment. Damaged cars were towed away, debris from vandals was removed, and shattered plate glass store windows replaced. A reduced police presence was detailed at the front entrance of the building. And Zealand police returned to their normal three, eight-hour shifts, or watches, each day.

CHAPTER

5

On that first normal evening, Harry and Jessica were invited to Floyd and Awa's townhouse for dinner. Awa had warned that dinner would be an authentic Senegalese meal. "I'm not too sure about this," Harry said to Jessica in the car, on their way to the Washington's. "I've heard that some African cultures eat snakes, and even dog meat. And sometimes, ugh… cats."

"Oh Harry," said Jessica with a chuckle. "Even if that's true, I don't believe that Awa would serve any of that to American dinner guests. And even if she wasn't thinking, you know that Floyd would intervene."

***

Floyd answered the knock on the door. Upon opening it he said, "Please remove your shoes, and slip on these sandals."

"And hello to you too." Said Harry with a smile.

Awa appeared alongside Floyd, as he said sheepishly, "Sorry for my abruptness, but we've planned this as an evening in Senegal. I meant to give you a heads up before we left the office. Shoes are not worn in Senegalese households. Please come in, and welcome to our home." A foursome of warm hugs followed.

Jessica said, "Awa, this is very sweet of you. I am happy and excited to be here." Awa smiled and acknowledged in broken English.

They sat in the living room, each with a glass of red wine supplied by the dinner guests. This was the first time Harry and

Jessica had been in their home. As they chatted, Jessica was amazed at how well Awa was understood in her halting English. She thought, *"I don't think I would be able to communicate in French that well, that fast, in the same circumstance."* Awa left the others talking in the living room. In a short time, she called them into the next room for dinner. A low-slung table with four place settings on it, and large pillows all around it. They sat around the table on the floor, against the pillows. Jessica was glad she had worn jeans. Awa wore a floor length flowing skirt.

Awa placed a casserole on the table. Floyd followed with two more. Serving spoons were placed along side. The food in each of them appeared different, and the aromas were mouth- watering. In the center of the table Floyd set a large bowl containing scoop-shaped slices of dark brown bread. "Okay folks," said Floyd, feeling somewhat mellow after several glasses of wine. "There is an art to eating this food Senegalese style. I'm about to tell you how, so pay attention. Each of the casseroles has a different base. This one nearest to me has a beef base. That next one is chicken, and the third is fish and shrimp. Each one contains a variety of vegetables, and something like couscous. A small amount of appropriate gravy for each is added for moisture. It is seasoned with spices that I've never heard of. Earlier the three were placed into a smoker, and slowly cooked for several hours."

As Floyd took a sip of wine, Harry spoke up. "So far, so good Floyd. I feel somewhat calmed now since you didn't list boa-constrictor as a base."

"Once you taste it Harry, you would not care if it was. But let me finish up here, I'm getting hungry. You dip from the bowl or bowls, onto your plate. Then with the odd shaped bread looking slices, you scoop some food from your plate, and experience heaven on earth. If scooping is too awkward, there is silverware at your plates."

Harry raised his glass and said, "Awa, Floyd, we thank you for inviting us to dinner, and if the food tastes as delicious as it smells, it WILL be heaven on earth."

Dinner over, there were genuine compliments for the chef. They were having desert and coffee when Harry's phone rang. He did not recognize the number on the caller ID. He swiped open the connection and said, "Harry Lincoln," in a clear, low voice.

"Hello, Detective Lincoln," said the male voice. "This is Carl Baker, I haven't heard from Sally, or anything about her. But we do have something that might be important. Can you or Detective Washington come by the bar?"

"Yes, we both can. We can be there in about an hour. Unless it's urgent."

"No rush, an hour will be fine. And thank you Detective Lincoln."

Harry repeated the conversation to Floyd and said, "Why don't you ride with me Floyd? We'll drop Jessica at her place, it's on the way."

***

"Carl's Friendly Tavern" was located on Glenwood Avenue, in the older section of downtown Zealand. Rows of three and four-story buildings, dating back to the early 1900's, lined both sides of this old street. Mom and Pop shops of every description could be found, side by side at street level. Seven cafes with sidewalk tables, three bars, a dentist's office, and a U.S. Post Office, were in the mix. The upper floors were up-dated and converted into lofts. What made Glenwood Avenue's fourteen blocks unique, was the lack of fast-food joints, convenience store/gas stations, and department stores. Not a Walmart to be found.

When the detectives entered the dimly lit bar, Carl Baker hurried out from behind the bar to greet them. "Thanks for coming out at this time of night. Let's sit at that table in the rear." There were four patrons sitting at the bar, another eight or ten at tables. Florence Baker was now behind the bar and waved to Harry and Floyd as they walked back to the rear. Their table was away from the others.

"It's kind of slow right now, so Florence and the waitress can handle things while we talk. Can I get you both something to drink?" Asked Carl. "You're not on duty now, are you?"

"We're not on our regular shift," answered Floyd. "But we are here on official business, so no thank you, we'd better not. Tell us what you have for us."

"Well we didn't think about it the other night, but since then Florence thought of something that might be important. I had mentioned to you that on busy nights we hire extra help. I want to tell you about the bartender that's here on those nights." Carl stopped, and then said, "I think it would be better if Florence told you. I'll take care of the bar. I'll send her right over."

Florence arrived at their table carrying a tray. "Carl says you can't sit in a tavern without something in front of you," Florence said as she emptied the tray, containing two cans of coke, and several bowls of chips, nuts, and pretzels. "Sorry I can't offer you more, but we don't serve food here."

"That's fine," said Harry. "We both just finished a big satisfying dinner. "What is it that you want to tell us about the part-time bartender?"

"Sally will stop in here some days on her way home from school. She usually brings with her a hamburger, or something like that. Calls it her 'after school snack,' and eats it here. Sally and I have a close mother-daughter relationship. She confides in me, and I am very thankful that she does. Things that teen-age girls usually tell their best girl-friends, rather than their mothers.

Like Carl told you, our part-time bartender Fred, is here on our busy days. Sally and Fred have limited contact on those days. She's mentioned to me that at times Fred has said things to her that made her uncomfortable. Such as, *'I'd like to see you on the beach, I'll bet you fill out a bikini in all the right places.'* And, *'Most women believe that men think black lace panties are the sexiest. I like white lace panties better. Which do you wear mostly?'* This is a forty-three-year-old man, talking to a seventeen-year-old girl.

"There was also some physical contact. As you can see from

here, that narrow hallway leads to the restrooms. One evening, Sally was leaving the women's restroom and stopped to look at that large bulletin board on the wall. Fred was going down that hallway to the men's rest room. In order for two people to pass in that narrow hallway, both have to be sideways. She was facing the wall, and he passed sideways, facing the same way. When he was behind her, he stopped and pressed against her. She said to me, 'Mom he was pressing his thing hard against my butt.' He said to her, *'Tight squeeze eh, I like it tight.'* He then continued walking to the rest room."

Florence stopped talking, thought for a minute, and then remembered, "He's said things to her about her breasts. She's told me that he has patted her behind several times."

"We'll need his full name and anything else that you know about him," Floyd said.

"His name is Fred Mills. I'll get his employment application from the office. Everything we know about him is on it."

When Florence returned with the folder, Carl had joined them at the table. He said, "This whole thing has gotten us sick with worry. As time passes, it's gotten more difficult to work, to be pleasant to our customers."

Florence began to sob, "Detective Lincoln, Detective Washington, please find our Sally soon. Bring her back to us unharmed. I'm begging you." She was crying so hard, she could no longer speak. She left the table for the restroom.

Harry looked at Carl and said, "Detective Washington and I will stay on this, and do everything we can, for as long as it takes. As soon as we know something, you will know it. And if you hear from Sally, or anything about her, let us know right away."

After leaving the bar, Harry said to Floyd, as they were getting into the car, "Let's see what Mr. Fred Mills has to say for himself."

Twenty minutes later, after repeatedly knocking on the apartment door at the address supplied by Ms. Baker, a man came up the stairway saying he was the building super. The detectives showed their ID's and inquired about Mills. "I haven't seen Fred for the past three days, and that's unusual for him. He's never gone for more than overnight. Is he alright? Is he in some kind of trouble?"

"No nothing like that," said Floyd handing him a card, "we just need to speak with him. When he shows up, ask him to give us a call."

CHAPTER

6

Arriving at police headquarters early the following morning, Harry observed a sizable crowd already blocking the main building entrance, with scores more gathering by the minute. Day watch police personnel, sworn and civilian, showed their ID and were directed by officers in riot gear to the rear parking lot. After parking their cars, they entered the building through a door marked, "Employees Only." Harry went directly to the third-floor homicide squad room. Floyd had not yet arrived.

Ten minutes later, Floyd badged one of the helmeted officers, and then parked in the lot next to Harry's car. However, instead of entering the building by that rear door, he walked back out of the driveway and onto the sidewalk, making his way to the front entrance. He was amongst the large crowd consisting mostly of black males with a few whites, scattered here and there. No one paid any attention to him, he was just one of the crowd. Occasionally when he made eye contact with someone, Floyd would nod, and then get a halfhearted nod in return. There was no ranting and raving, just a low drone of conversation between two or three guys, and some laughter with high-fives from small groups.

Parked on the sidewalk near the front entrance, Floyd noticed several people clustered around the open hatchback in the rear of a large SUV. In it he observed several bull horns and microphones, in addition he saw six large speakers mounted on light poles and trees. He supposed these were used to fire up the crowd. Just then someone tapped him on the shoulder from behind. Floyd turned and recognized a TV reporter from Channel

10 News. "Aren't you Detective Washington?" The reporter asked as another man pointed a TV camera at both of them. "And isn't Detective Lincoln your partner? You know, The Presidents."

"Yes, Detective Lincoln is my partner."

"What do you make of all this Detective Washington," asked the reporter. "Can you give us a statement?" When Floyd nodded his consent, the reporter addressed the crowd, asking for their attention as Detective Lincoln's partner, Detective Floyd Washington wanted to speak to them. Within two minutes or less, the only sounds were the drone of traffic from the adjacent streets.

"Not long ago I transferred up here from the Miami Police Department where I had worked homicide, and was assigned to the ZPD homicide squad," began Floyd. "I was partnered up with Detective Harry Lincoln." He paused and looked out over the hushed crowd. He had their attention. "I would like to speak to everyone here, and to those watching at home." Several men had picked up and pointed those microphones from the SUV toward him.

"I grew up in the racially segregated state of Florida, as were the rest of the southeastern states. Like many of you, I had to endure the harassment, the humiliation, and the hatred of the Jim Crow world. Even after I became a police officer in Miami, the chances of my wife and I being invited to eat dinner at the home of any of the white cops that I worked with every day, was about the same as me becoming the King of England. So, what I'm saying is, I'm not just here talking the talk, I'm saying that I've walked the walk!" I might be a homicide detective in a major American city, but I am still a black man.

Floyd was handed a small bottle of ice-cold water, drank almost half, and then continued. "My first day on the job here was with Detective Lincoln, when half way through the watch we stopped at a small restaurant for lunch. After our burgers were served, but before our first bites I popped the question. 'Detective Lincoln, do you have a problem working every day with a black partner?' He said that the short answer is no, and the long answer is hell no." Floyd stopped talking to let that sink in, while he drank some more water.

Floyd continued after a minute. "He went on to tell me that he remembers crying only three times since becoming an adult. The first was at the funeral of his first partner, a black senior patrolman who was his training officer and taught him the ins and outs, the ups and downs to be a good cop. He contracted cancer and while being hospital bound, rookie officer Lincoln visited him every day after his watch. He died shortly after. Lincoln told me he bawled like a baby. The second time was at his father's funeral, also a homicide detective, to whom he was very close. The last was attending the funeral of a black female police officer who was attacked in a set-up ambush while on duty by two thugs, who raped, mutilated and murdered her. Lincoln promised her, while looking at her in the casket, that he would never stop hunting until he found them. And then cried while still standing there and had to be led away. Detective Lincoln never stopped hunting until he found them. Those two thugs are now on death row."

After catching his breath and drinking some more water, Floyd continued. "I've seen all of those 'officer involved' shootings of black men on TV just like most of you have. Some have appeared to me nothing less than plain murder, and those officers, black or white should be held accountable. Some have been justified and they should not be vilified. I know from personal experience that a lot of violent incidences seen on the TV news do not have all the facts or have them wrong. Sometime the media puts their own spin on situations which changes the way it's received by the public.

The original intended victim in all this is a black woman who had gotten off work at 12:00 midnight and rode the bus home which she does every work night. Once off the bus, she walks four blocks to her home. The only other person on the street at that time grabbed her and pushed her into the doorway of a closed store. He threatened to kill her with what she believed was a large meat cleaver. She started to scream. At that same time Detective

Lincoln, on his way home from police headquarters, heard her screams. He stopped his car, got out and saw the man standing over her. He identified himself as a police officer. The man turned away from the woman and advanced toward Detective Lincoln, now threatening him with what was believed to be a real meat cleaver. He was ordered to drop that weapon two different times but kept coming at him with it raised high. At that point, Detective Lincoln shot and killed him.

The woman has already given her statement to the state investigators. In it she gave the same account and believes that Detective Harry Lincoln saved her life."

Floyd drank some more water for his parched throat. He looked out at the silent crowd, the only sounds, a cough here, a sneeze there. He said, "The next time a police officer shoots a black man, true justice is expected, true justice is demanded… the general public does, all of you here do, I do, and so does Detective Harry Lincoln. But we all want true justice, not some Jim Crow lynching in reverse."

Floyd stopped again for a long thirty seconds. Not a murmur from the crowd. And then. "Okay I've said what I wanted to say, what needed to be said. Bear with me for another minute. It's been more than a year now, and I've gotten to know Harry Lincoln the detective, and Harry Lincoln the man. Harry Lincoln would no more shoot an unarmed man, or one holding a toy, whether he was black, white, green or purple, any more than I would. This shooting is being investigated, not by the Zealand Police, but by the State investigators. The feds will also monitor the incident should there have been any civil rights violations. Harry Lincoln and I have become the best of friends, both on and off duty. I know this has become a cliché, but I mean this… I would take a bullet for Harry Lincoln, and I believe he would do the same for me. I've seen the TV news about the shooting, and due to the 'spin' the media has put on it, they are doing Detective Lincoln a grave injustice. I know I am speaking to you as Detective Lincoln's partner, but I am also speaking as a black man, I am asking each of you to do what's right and stand down." Floyd then walked around to the rear of building and through that back door.

Within the hour most of the crowd had gone, leaving a few of the usual rabble-rousers, and the hard-core who hated all cops. Those remnants were quickly disbursed by mounted police officers.

CHAPTER

7

Harry picked up the phone on the second ring. "Homicide, Lincoln." After listening for a few seconds, he said, "we'll be right down for them, thanks for calling." Turning to Floyd he said, "that was the ID section, they've got the results of the prints lifted at the Baker house." The elevators were too slow, so they hurried down the four flights of stairs to the basement of the headquarters building.

"We have identified four sets of prints from the girl's bedroom at 1401 Elm Street." The ID tech started to explain, having their rapt attention. "Most of them were probably Sally Baker's, and I say probably because of her age, no prints were on file for comparison. But it's safe to assume that the prints taken from items such as her cell phone, the water glass for her tooth brushes, and the faucets in her shower were hers. So most of the prints lifted in the bedroom matched those." The tech continued, "We had rolled Mr. and Ms. Baker's prints for comparison, and both of theirs were in the bedroom. The fourth set belonged to Fred Mills. His prints were on file with his application for his bartender's license. No other unidentified prints were found." The report with the results was handed to Floyd.

***

After knocking several times on the apartment door of Fred Mills and getting no response, Harry and Floyd went to the basement and found the building super in his shop. "He was here yesterday. I saw him out back, loading his truck. Gave him your card, told him to give you a call, that you needed to speak with him. He asked what for, and I told him that I didn't know."

"What was he loading in his truck? Asked Harry. "And what kind of truck?"

"I noticed a couple of large duffle bags, an overnight bag, and a backpack, didn't see what was in them. He drives an older model grey pickup, with a crew cab."

Harry thanked him for the information, giving him another card saying, "give us a call when he comes back, but don't say anything to him."

In the car, they were headed back to headquarters for the daily briefing with Lieutenant McGee on the missing Sally Baker case. Both with morose feelings, not looking forward to the verbal abuse that was coming, when suddenly the police radio snapped them out of their doldrums.

"Detective Radio 199 calling Homicide 134 and 136:"

"134 go ahead."

"199 to 134: Go by the IHOP on Valley Boulevard in the 7th. Meet a gentleman with a beard and glasses wearing a red jacket, sitting in a booth alone."

"134 copy that."

***

Ten minutes later Harry and Floyd entered the IHOP and spotted the man sitting in a rear corner booth. They slid into the seat across from him and identified themselves.

"Thank you for coming. My name is Martin Johnson and I might have some information for you on the missing Baker girl."

"Well Mr. Johnson we can use all the help we can get," said Harry with a look of anticipation. "We are all ears." Floyd sat still, his perfect white teeth shown by the grin on his face.

"I've been a regular at Carl's Friendly Tavern for quite some time now, and Carl and I have since become friends," said Mr.

Johnson. "One night I walked in and much to my surprise I see Fred Mills behind the bar mixing and serving drinks. I've known Fred Mills since we were both in the army some years ago. We are not close buddies but do keep in touch now and then."

The waitress came over and took their coffee orders. "I was in the bar last night and Carl told me about his missing daughter. I've never met the girl. When she occasionally drops by the bar it's right after school, and I usually get there later in the evening. I understand from Carl that Fred Mills might have something to do with it. I haven't seen him in about three weeks or so, and don't know much about him. However, I do know where he lives, but understand that you have his address. He drives a grey pickup and has a cabin in the mountains."

"Do know where that cabin is?" Asked Harry.

"No, I've never been there, but from little he's told me it's south on I-81 somewhere around the Wytheville area. He made it a point to say that it is kind of isolated, away from any nosey neighbors with prying eyes and ears."

"Mr. Johnson, you've been a big help, and my partner and I thank you. Should you think of anything else, please call us anytime night or day" said Harry as the three finished their coffee, paid their checks, and left the restaurant. In the parking lot, the three exchanged contact information and shook hands. "It's getting late Floyd, but if we hurry we'll catch McGee before he leaves for the day."

***

Back at the squad room Harry briefed Lieutenant McGee, while Floyd was at his desk typing an affidavit for a search warrant. "We contacted the Wythe County Sheriff's Department and spoke with Chief Deputy Ross who is in charge because the sheriff is on vacation" said Harry with a note of excitement in his voice. "He knows Fred Mills and has been to his cabin. On the way here, Floyd had called superior court judge Hardin who is waiting in his office to review our probable cause, and if it meets the standard he will issue the warrant."

Floyd entered the office and said to Harry, "It's completed, let's go and get the judge's signature on it."

"We need to go down this afternoon Liew, not wait until morning. If he's got her in that cabin, let's not give him more time to abuse, or whatever he's doing to her. Assuming she's still alive!" Harry put the emphasis on that last word. "We are to contact Chief Deputy Ross when we get south of Pulaski, and he will talk us in from there."

"Okay guys hit the road and good luck. By the way, when is the last time either of you got more than three, four hours of sleep. That's the price you pay to work homicide in our ideal, model city, this utopia according to our politicians. I'm proud of both of you," McGee said with an uncharacteristic quiver in his voice.

***

Several hours later they met in the parking lot of a closed strip mall. Chief Deputy Ross was there with three other uniformed deputies, one being a female. Harry and Floyd showed their ID's and the search warrant. "We are hoping to find Sally Baker, a seventeen-year-old white female, or any evidence of her presence. Fred Mills is the subject who is suspected of kidnapping her," Harry told the group.

Ross spoke up, "The cabin belonging to Fred Mills is about three miles from here. We'll go in dark and quiet, three vehicles with two of us in the lead SUV. You Zealand detectives in the second car, and the other two deputies bringing up the rear. It's very dark up there and when I turn my lights out, you do the same. Before we announce ourselves, the two in the last car will go to the rear of the cabin. We don't know if he'll offer any resistance, but just about everyone up here has some kind of weapon, so stay alert. Okay let's go."

***

They approached the cabin quietly and in the dark, the only lights were from inside. Ross and another deputy poised at the front door with a battering ram. Ross knocked with authority and a loud, clear voice announced, "Sheriff's Department, open the door!" There were the unmistakable sounds of scuffling, and then screams from a female voice, "Help! Help!!" The battering ram took down the front door and they rushed in slamming Mills to a wall. Sally Baker was in a hysterical state, screaming, crying and shaking all over. Harry and Floyd tried but could not console her. The female deputy came in through the rear door and went to the girl, wrapping her arms around her, trying to calm her. Sally Baker was chained to a pipe coming out of the wall. "Will someone get a key from that monster, so I can unchain her?"

Fred Mills was now face down on the floor, hands cuffed behind him. Harry did the honors, "Fred Mills you are under arrest for the kidnapping of Sally Baker. Other charges may be added after she is examined by a doctor. You have the right to remain silent..."

***

An ambulance was dispatched, and Sally Baker was to be transported to Zealand Memorial Hospital. The female deputy rode with her, the only one able to restore some semblance of calm. Ross called a crime scene tech to the cabin to collect evidence, physical and forensic, and to take photos and measurements. Fred Mills was shoved into the back seat of the detective car for the trip back to Zealand. "Keep your mouth shut," warned Harry. "If you utter one fuckin' word I'll come back there and kick all your teeth down your godamn throat."

"Chief Deputy Ross, my partner Floyd Washington and I don't have the words to thank you and your crew for the job well done. For the able assistance you gave us in rescuing that young girl and removing that piece of shit from the streets and hopefully to face the music. Again, a sincere thank you from us both."

"Detective Lincoln, Detective Washington it was an honor to serve with 'The Presidents.' Yeah, you guys are famous all over the state of Virginia. And we were glad to do it like the big boys, we don't get to do much of that down here."

"Well even the big boys in the NYPD or the LAPD could not have done it any better," said Floyd. Then with a round of handshakes, they got in their car and headed north on Interstate 81. Floyd riding shotgun got on the phone. "Mr. Baker this is Detective Washington, I've good news for you; We've got Sally! Yes, she's alright, quite shook up but by all outward appearances in good shape. She's being transported by ambulance to Zealand Memorial to be examined by a doctor and should be there in two or three hours. Yes, a distance from Zealand. Fred Mills did have her, and that piece of garbage is in our custody and being returned by us to Zealand Police Headquarters." Floyd stopped talking while Carl Baker relayed all this to Florence Baker, and then waited until all the screaming and shouting died down." No, after we drop Mills off Detective Lincoln and I need to get some sleep. We'll get with you later in the day and fill you in on all the details. See you then." As he put down the phone Floyd looked over at Harry. Looking at each other no words were spoken, the words were in their eyes. *We've earned the Gold Shield once again!*

CHAPTER

8

Two days later Harry and Floyd were sitting in the chief's office. Chief Lansing, Deputy Chief Watkins, and Lieutenant McGee were also there. "So, Lincoln, Washington tie up the loose ends for us," said the chief.

"Well," began Harry. "Most of it you already know from our report, and yes there are a few loose ends. The doctors determined that she had been raped numerous times both vaginally and anally. She had been smacked around, no broken bones, but lots of cuts, scrapes and bruises. There were deep bruises on her throat indicating strangulation. She spent two days in the hospital for observation, at least one parent always at her bedside, she went home this morning.

The first of the felonies, kidnapping occurred here in Zealand, Ridgewood County. The sexual assaults and other felonies were committed in Wythe County. District Attorney Donahue and the Wythe County DA will have to decide who does what, and where."

Floyd took it from there. "The cooperation and professional assistance we received from the Wythe County Sheriff's Department was the best. The Sheriff was away on vacation, so leading the charge was Chief Deputy Ross. Starting with his knowing where Mills' cabin was and following up with the rescue of Sally Baker and the apprehension of Fred Mills. But it does not end there, when the female deputy was able to calm the hysterical girl who was on the verge of a stroke, she rode in the ambulance with her all the way to Zealand Memorial. We put her up at the Holiday Inn Express. Then today the Wythe County crime scene tech arrived at our ID section to share all the evidence that was collected from the scene. That female deputy then rode home with the tech."

Harry finished up. "We've had Mills on ice in a holding cell for two days, no one has spoken to him since I gave him the Miranda warnings in his cabin when he was placed under arrest. Floyd and I will start his interrogation this afternoon. And that's all we've got so far. We should know more when we can interview Sally Baker."

Chief Lansing spoke, "I personally want to commend you both again on another job well done. You just can't beat the Presidents." Causing some smiles and a few chuckles around the table. "But before I adjoin this meeting, I want to address a few remarks to Detective Washington." The questioning looks went around the table landing on Floyd, who just shrugged his shoulders, his eyes wide.

"Before the Sally Baker kidnapping our biggest concern throughout the department was the large raucous crowd protesting the Detective Lincoln shooting. It grew larger each day, blocking the entrance to the building, and then closing the street. The usual loud mouths firing up the crowd with bullhorns and microphones connected to several large speakers. ZPD on full alert, the same for the neighboring law enforcement agencies, twelve-hour shifts, and off days cancelled." The chief stopped talking to catch his breath and drink some water.

"And along comes Detective Floyd Washington pushing into the teeth of that hostile mob, stopping at the front door. He is recognized by a local TV news reporter. The reporter asks if he is Detective Lincoln's partner. Washington affirms that he is. He starts talking to the crowd and also to the hundreds of thousands watching at home, and in the many bars, restaurants, TV and print newsrooms. He has the attention of thousands, maybe millions. I have to tell you, I have listened to hundreds of speeches, most of them read from a tele-prompter, or the speaker reading from a speech written by someone else. Washington starts speaking, no notes, or other speaker's devices. They sensed that he was not some slick talking politician. He was speaking from his heart. He's speaking to the good people, the decent people, those who make up most of the crowd. He connects with them; the majority have had the same experience growing up under tough conditions. As he talked there were many nodding their heads and shouting YES, YES! He won them over by telling the truth, they knew he was being sincere. As I said I've heard many speakers on many subjects, but I've not heard any of them being as sincere as Detective Floyd Washington. I'll leave it there, saying Floyd, you probably averted a mass riot with some officers being injured. I thank you Detective Floyd Washington and speaking for the ZPD we all thank you. Meeting adjoined!"

***

And so it went. The 'atta boys' mixed in with the 'oh shits. The too few of the former, nullified it seemed by the latter when delivered by a red-faced, scowling, out- of- control, Lieutenant McGee. However, behind all the bluster was a commander pushing his homicide detectives to the limits of their abilities, in a very stressful assignment. The missed sleep, the cold, on the fly meals, the strain on family and relationships. The upside-down world of the homicide detective. Only the most dedicated would choose such a demanding assignment. So, the kind words, the 'atta boy' spoken by the chief of police meant a lot to Floyd and by extension to Harry, both personally and professionally.

They left headquarters in the calm before the storm…

"Any car near The Real Pines housing projects in the 3rd," came the excited voice of the despatcher on the city-wide radio frequency. "Multiple signal 25's (gunshots) in the area. Cars on the way be advised signal 63 (officer needs help), the beat car is pinned down in the cross fire!" The overwhelming acknowledgement of the responding units, cutting each other off causing radio traffic to be jammed, creating communications inoperable.

"They'll do it every 63," shouted Harry over the screaming

siren as he and Floyd raced toward the 3rd precinct and the Real Pines. "Dozens of cars on the radio at the same time to report they are responding, and all the despatcher hears is a bunch of static." By the time the two detectives arrived at the projects, the shooting was over. The scene is covered with flashing blue lights from the many police vehicles. They managed to find the 3rd precinct commander amongst all the chaos. It was determined to have been a drive-by shooting in a turf war by a rival Hispanic gang against the black gang in the Real Pines public housing project.

"Glad you guys are here," said Major Hogate as several ambulances arrived. "Looks like five were shot among the warring parties. Too bad there weren't more. We should take those gang members out to the range and teach them how to shoot. However, on a sour note, a stray round went through an apartment window and grazed a five-year-old girl, and she was also cut from flying glass. That first ambulance is for her, and her mother will ride to Zealand Memorial with her. You can catch up with those other mutts at the hospital, I'm sending several uniforms with them."

***

Later at the hospital ER, Harry and Floyd were getting the results of the damages caused by the shoot-out. "The five adults brought in with gunshot wounds are non-life threatening with all five," said Doctor Deutch. "The bullet that grazed the arm of the five-year-old caused a minor scratch, and she had seven minor cuts from the pieces of glass, none of which required stiches. She is about to be released, and to state the obvious she is one lucky little girl."

"Thanks for the run-down doc," said Harry as they were leaving the ER.

Floyd had been on the phone with Lieutenant McGee. To Harry he said, "Lieu wants the gang unit to handle the shoot-out and they are on the way now. He wants us to call it a day."

***

On his way from the station in his personal car, Harry dialed his phone. "Hello Jess, how about meeting me at Ralph's Steak House, I'm in the mood for one of Ralph's rib-eyes."

That's sounds good Harry, anything exciting happen today?"

"No Jess, just another day at the office."

CHAPTER

9

"What a beautiful day Harry," Floyd said as they drove along the outskirts of the city. "Look at those mountains, it just doesn't get much better than this."

"Yeah, you grew-up looking at the ocean, but I've always had the mountains. And today is about perfect, the winter sun is shining, no snow or ice and everything is calm and peaceful."

They continued on at a leisurely pace taking in the splendor, without any particular destination. The only sounds, chatter on the police radio with information and instructions directed to other units. After several more miles Harry broke their silence, "Well Mr. President, let's enjoy it because at 2400 hours this sunshine will become moonlight. We begin our month on the morning watch."

***

Reporting for duty that night at the midnight hour, Lincoln and Washington had the squad room all to themselves as the last of the evening watch detectives went off-duty. "It's not like we've never worked the morning watch before, you in Miami and me right here." Said Harry. "But living upside-down from the rest of the world screws up sleeping, eating and so much more."

"Yeah Harry, I agree with all of that, but what the hell, It's only for a month."

"Okay Floyd, the Presidents shall protect and serve, without the bitching!"

They each grabbed a radio from the charging rack, made their way down to the detective parking lot, into their assigned 'Crown Vic' and pulled in service. "To put a positive spin on it Floyd, it's not all bad. The traffic is very light enabling us to get anywhere in the city in record time. And all the brass are at home asleep in their beds, instead of looking over our shoulders, waiting for us to screw up." But no matter how much they tried to brighten the coming days (nights), the mean dark streets would be their world for the next month.

***

At about the same time, car 1306 left the 3rd Precinct driven by Officer A.D. Martin. His partner was out with the flu, as others were, creating a manpower shortage in the precinct. Officer Martin would work this eight-hour shift… solo! It was just after midnight and there was still traffic on the main thoroughfares, enough to make a traffic case or two. *'Sergeant Young has been on my ass about me not making enough traffic cases. I'll sit on the light at Alpine Avenue and Eastern Boulevard which should be good for two, maybe three, before it gets too late and everything goes dead.'* It was just shy of 2:00 a.m. when he completed the third ticket for running that red light. Officer Martin then headed toward the donut shop for some coffee.

Zone 3 Radio: "Car 1306, at 481 Hendrix Street, Signal 29 domestic disturbance, reported by a next-door neighbor."

1306: "Copy that, 481 Hendrix Street Signal 29 domestic."

When Martin arrived, he was met at the curb by the caller. "Officer, he has beaten up his wife before but never in the middle of the night. They were keeping everyone awake with all the screaming and yelling."

A man opened the door after Martin knocked. "Sir, we received a report of quite a loud disturbance at this address, do you live here? And who else lives here?"

"Just me and my wife, Officer."

"I need to speak with your wife," said Martin as he entered the house.

"Oh officer, she's sleeping."

Martin shouted, "Ma'am I'm a police officer and I need to speak with you."

A woman stepped into the room wearing a bathrobe. She held a bloodied tissue to her nose. One eye was red, and half closed, and her face was red and puffy.

"Is this your husband?" Martin asked. "And did he do this to you?"

"Yes officer, he is my husband and he kept punching my face."

Martin ordered the man to put his hands up against the closed front door. He searched him for any weapons, and finding none, cuffed his hands behind his back. Martin then took his radio mic from his shoulder. "1306: Send a signal 82 (patty wagon) on call." Just then a second patrol car pulled up in front of Martin's, two officers got out and entered the house through the front door. "Hey Andy, we knew you were working solo tonight, so we came by in case you needed backup."

"Everything is under control here. This tough-guy only punches women, but thanks for the backup guys."

The wagon arrived and transported the prisoner to the city jail. By the time Martin completed the paper work and was clear of the Hendrix Street call it was almost 4:00a.m. *'Damn if it isn't lunch time. I think I'll head over to the IHOP and break bread with a couple of the guys."*

On his way there, he noticed how quiet it had gotten in the last hour or so. He was stopped for a red light and had rolled his window down, so he could listen to the quiet. The light turned green and he had just rolled into the intersection when he heard it... rap music louder than he'd ever heard before. And then he saw it... swinging into the intersection just missing the patrol car because Martin was standing on the brake pedal. This late model grey BMW sedan took off at a high rate of speed. Martin attempting to follow was now standing on the gas pedal.

"1306 to radio, I'm in a chase!"

Zone 3 Radio: "Copy that 1306, all other cars stand by. Go ahead 1306."

1306: "South on Empire Boulevard from Bushwick Avenue, a late model grey BMW."

Zone 3 Radio: "Cars on the south end of Empire Boulevard, 1306 is in pursuit of a grey BMW coming your way."

1306: "BMW turned left into side street, Green Street. It stopped in the second block. Hold me out with Virginia tag 14-WRN3."

Martin got out, the rap music was still blasting, and as he approached the car, observed several people in the car. The last thing Officer A. D. Martin heard other than the loud music was five gun-shots, before he fell to the ground… dead!!

Zone 3 Radio: "1306… Radio calling car 1306!" No response.

Zone 3 Radio: "Cars on the way to the chase on Empire Boulevard, check Green Street, two blocks east of Empire Boulevard, the last known location of car 1306."

1302: "I'm code 26 (arrived) on Green Street with 1306, he's down in the middle of the street. Start Fire Rescue, code 3 (rush call). He's bleeding and not moving, looks like signal 50 (person shot). The BMW he was chasing is gone."

1307: "I'm code 26.

1310: "Code 26."

1301: "I'm 26."

Zone 3 Radio: "Cars on Green Street, 1350 (Lieutenant) and 1355 (Sergeant) are on the way."

Five minutes later… 1350: "Fire Rescue advises that 1306 is signal 48 (person dead). Start homicide and the medical examiner. Place a city-wide lookout on that BMW with that license plate number. Also give the lookout to Ridgewood County, the other surrounding counties and the State Police.

Zone 3 Radio: "Copy that 1350."

***

Detective Radio 199: "Calling Homicide 134-136."

136: "Go ahead 199."

199: "In the 200 block of Green Street off Empire Boulevard in the 3rd precinct, signal 50/48 on a police officer. The medical examiner has been notified. The watch commander and the sector sergeant are on the scene."

136: "Okay we are on the way, should be 26 in ten minutes or less. Start a crime scene unit."

Harry looked over at Floyd and said very slowly. "It's the one call none of us want to get. But if it had to happen, at least I know that you and I will not stop… will not quit… will not rest… until whoever did this, gets the needle and then spends the rest of eternity burning in HELL!!!"

"My sentiments exactly Harry, however I could not have said it more eloquently, and I sincerely share your passion."

***

As Harry and Floyd turned off Empire Boulevard onto Green Street, all they saw for two blocks were flashing blue and red lights, police vehicles, fire rescue truck and ambulance. To get to the crime scene, they had to walk those two blocks. Green Street was a quiet, blue collar, residential street with street lights spaced far apart. It was not yet 5:00 a.m. and lights were on in some of the houses. The medical examiner had not yet arrived, so the body was not touched, except for fire rescue EMT's to confirm that Officer A. D. Martin was dead.

Harry and Floyd identified themselves to the lieutenant and sergeant and asking what was known so far. "All we can tell you," said the lieutenant. "Is that Officer A.D. Martin car 1306, was chasing a late model grey BMW, Virginia tag 14-WRN3. We've just learned that car was stolen two days ago from a downtown parking deck. We have no idea who was in that car, or how many."

The sergeant added, "Several of our cars were going to head

off the chase. When 1302, the first car arrived here, Martin was down in the middle of the street, not saying a word, probably already dead. And the BMW was gone."

When the crime scene techs arrived, they were directed by the detectives about the usual elements: photos, measurements, sketches and the collection of evidence. The medical examiner was through with his examination went over his notes with Harry and Floyd. "From my preliminary exam, looks like he was shot six times. One in the right temple, one in the right eye, and a contact wound at the base of the skull, the other three in his vest, chest high. Obviously the head shots killed him. We'll know much more after the autopsy, and ballistics tests."

Harry called his attention to Officer Martin's gun. "His gun is in his holster and it is snapped shut."

"While my observation was on bullet wounds, blood and other injuries, I hadn't noticed that," the ME said, "but it sure is."

Harry called one of the techs over. "Be sure you get a close-up photo of the officer's gun snapped securely in his holster."

"Lieutenant," called Floyd. "How about keeping the street blocked until after daylight? We are sending another team of crime scene techs to assist those who are here. We don't want to miss anything in the dark."

"Sure detective, Sergeant Wilcox will remain here with a couple of units and stay until the techs are finished. Unfortunately, I have to leave to meet my boss and the chaplain. We must go to the Martin residence and notify his wife and two children. I'd rather take a beating." He then got into his car and left.

Harry's phone rang. It was Lieutenant McGee. "Lincoln, when you and Washington can clear the scene, come on in to the chief's office for a briefing on the Officer Martin homicide."

Later that morning, the clock showing a couple of minutes before 10:00 a.m., a somber group sat around the chief's conference table: Chief Lansing, Deputy Chief Watkins, 3rd Pct. Major Willis, 3rd Pct. Lieutenant Sommers, Homicide Lieutenant McGee, Homicide Detective Lincoln, and Homicide Detective Washington.

Chief Lansing broke the morbid silence. "Needless to say, the murder of Officer Martin is the number one priority in the Zealand Police Department. Now, to be certain that we are all on the same frequency, I would like to hear from several of you how we got to this point. But before we get to that, 3rd Precinct Commander Major Willis, please tell us how it went with the death notification to the Martin family."

Major Willis talked slowly in a hushed tone. "As some of you who have done it in the past know how difficult it is, but for the family there is nothing worse. As Ms. Martin opened the door and saw us standing there, she knew. She backed away into the house screaming no, no, no, and sank to the floor on her knees. Her children, a twelve-year-old boy and a nine-year-old girl were eating breakfast getting ready for school. They ran to her crying. We were able to get them up on the couch, where they cried and hugged for the next five to ten minutes. When things settled down some, we answered some of her questions, and then we left. A female detective stayed with them, to try to get some family members to come to the house."

***

A fifteen-minute break was called, and coffee and donuts were brought in and placed on a side table. When time was up, Chief Lansing called the meeting to order. "Lieutenant Sommers, please get us started."

"It was about halfway through the watch when car 1306, Officer Martin came on Zone 3 Radio that he was in a chase south on Empire Boulevard from Bushwick Avenue. He said he was chasing a grey late model BMW. Shortly the BMW turned off Empire Boulevard onto Green Street heading east, with Martin right behind. Within two blocks the BMW stopped, and Martin pulled out giving the Virginia tag 14-WRN3. Zone 3 radio dispatcher could not get a response after calling 1306 several times. Cars headed for the chase, when 1302 first to arrive found

Martin down in the middle of the street, his patrol car with the blue lights flashing and the driver's door open. The BMW was gone. In a short time, it was learned the BMW had been stolen from a downtown parking deck two days before. Fire Rescue arrived and pronounced Martin DOS (Dead on the Scene). Those two blocks of Green Street were overloaded with vehicles, mostly 3rd Precinct patrol cars. Sergeant Wilcox and I had most of them to return to their beats, a couple remained for support. Also, on the scene was Homicide, these two detectives, the medical examiner, and crime scene techs."

"That was an excellent oral report Lieutenant Sommers," said Chief Lansing. "Please reduce it to a written report." Then turning to Lincoln and Washington asked, "Detectives, what is your take?"

"Officer Martin was shot six times, one in the right temple, one in the right eye, a contact wound at the base of the skull, and three times in his vest." Harry began. "We will know more after the autopsy. Ballistic tests will tell us what type of weapon was used and if there was more than one. We noticed that Martin's service weapon was snapped securely in his holster. After the shooter, or shooters are apprehended and on trial, he, she, or they can't claim self-defense, and shot the officer because he was about to shoot."

Floyd continued, "One of the first things that needs to be done is a house-to-house canvass and speak with every household on those two blocks of Green Street. That being a working-class neighborhood, we think the best times would be in the evenings after the dinner hour."

"Okay gentlemen," said Chief Lansing after thirty seconds of silence in the room. "This is how it's going to be. Detectives Lincoln and Washington will take the lead in the Martin homicide, which they have already done being on the morning watch detail. Lieutenant McGee, they will not be assigned any new cases. Their hours will be flexible, as needed under your supervision. Assign another team to this month's morning watch detail. As I've said, this tragic case has top priority, with the support of the entire Zealand Police Department. Whatever they need, they get. Lincoln, Washington... Good luck to you, and keep in mind, every member of the ZPD will be rooting for ... The Presidents. You will update Lieutenant McGee with daily briefings, who will then pass that information on to Deputy Chief Watkins. Meeting adjourned!"

***

After a few hours' sleep, a refreshing shower, and a quick snack, Harry met Floyd on Green Street going from house to house. In most, the story was about the same: "I woke up from a sound sleep to the loudest music I ever heard, and with the music was a police siren. There was a bunch of gunshots, and then a car takes off down the street, flyin'!"

At the seventh house, somewhat more detailed. The detectives identified themselves, and the man introduced himself as George Walker. "It was about thirty minutes before I get up for work. There was some kind of commotion in the street right outside my house. Some very loud music mixed with a police siren. I jumped up, looked out the window and saw a car stopped, with a police car right behind it with the blue lights flashing." The man paused for a moment, then looked right at Floyd and said, "Detective, I'm not a racist and mean no disrespect but that was rap music, and I never heard any kind of music that loud, it was awful. Anyway, I saw the cop get out and walk up to the driver's side window and shout something at the driver. The music stopped and then I heard gunshots and saw the cop fall to the ground. Three or maybe four guys got out of the car high-fivin' and talking loud, and almost dancin' in the street. That's when one of them bent down over the cop and I heard another gunshot. They got back in the car, turned on that loud damn rap music and left burnin' rubber."

"Mr. Walker," Floyd said, "no offence taken about that damn rap shit, I refuse to call it music. Whenever I hear it, my ears are offended. Rappers have a negative effect on black youth, as they look to them as role models. Even gang members dress, talk and act like them. I am embarrassed and sometimes apologetic when with my colleagues and blasted by that rap shit." Floyd stopped talking, and then said to Mr. Walker, "once I get wound up on that stuff, I find it hard to turn it off. But now back to business: How many gunshots did you hear, and were those guys white, black, Hispanic?"

"It seems like four or five shots real fast, maybe even a half dozen. Then when they got out of the car, just that one leaning over him. It was dark, and I couldn't see what race or nationality they were."

"Mr. Walker," said Harry. "We'll need to get a written statement from you down at police headquarters. You can ride with us, and we'll bring you back."

***

The next day, Harry and Floyd were notified that the stolen BMW was found in a shopping mall parking lot about an hour south of Zealand. Harry called the Sheriff's Department and was told they had not yet impounded that car. Arrangements were made for a Zealand crew to go down and bring it back. "It was used in the murder of a Zealand police officer, and we want to process the interior for prints and other forensic evidence." Harry had one more request. "If there had been a vehicle stolen from that same parking lot in the last twenty-four to thirty-six hours."

The deputy answered. "Why yes, a car was reported stolen from that lot about twelve hours ago. A black 2018 Chevrolet Impala North Carolina license plate H62-835."

Floyd placed a nationwide lookout for that car. And to ensure that it was given top priority he added, 'Wanted in connection with the murder of a Zealand, Virginia police officer!'

***

Here they come!! Something to behold! This seemingly endless convoy of law enforcement, led by thirty motorcycles, with patrol cars spaced throughout the funeral procession. City officials and police brass in plain cars following the hearse and limousines carrying family members. State police bringing up the rear, so no vehicles can overtake and break into the procession. At the cemetery, the casket is carried to the grave site, as the somber bagpipes blows the mournful sounds of, "Going Home." Mrs. Martin and the children are seated at the grave site, along with family members. There is a multitude of law enforcement personnel present.

Some in civilian clothes, most in uniform, mostly blue, the agency or department identified by the shoulder patch sewn onto that uniform. The array of colors (other than blue) and style of these uniforms varied the same as those wearing them. What did not vary, not by the slightest degree, was the strip of black tape placed horizontally across the center of the badge or shield regardless of one's rank.

The police chaplain read from the Bible and directed some comforting words to Mrs. Martin, and other family members gathered there. The Zealand police honor guard fired off the twenty-one-gun salute, a fly-over of six police helicopters, with one peeling, off in the missing-man formation, and a lone bugler blew the sorrowful sound of Taps. The honor guard folded the American flag from atop the casket and gave it to Chief Lansing, who walked over and handed it to Mrs. Martin as she sobbed softly. In a short time, the crowd thinned-out, car doors opened and closed, motors started, and vehicles left on their own.

***

Two days later the canvassing along Green Street was completed, and three more written statements were taken, however not much more was learned. Harry and Floyd spent time in the squad room keeping the file currant. The phone rang, and Harry picked it up. "Homicide, Lincoln."

"Detective Lincoln, this is Lieutenant Roper, Savannah, Georgia Police Department. On your lookout for the 2018 black Chevrolet Impala, North Carolina tag H62-835, wanted in connection with the murder of a Zealand, Virginia police officer. We have the car and four subjects with it."

"Lieutenant, that's music to my ears. How did you catch them? And what's it going to cost us to bring them back to Virginia?"

"They had just held up a liquor store and we got them coming out. And you can have them free of charge, with our compliments. We'll hold on to them until you or someone comes down to get them. In the meantime, we'll get them before a judge for an expedition hearing."

Harry and Floyd almost ran into Lieutenant McGee's office to give him the good news. McGee immediately picked up the phone and called Deputy Chief Watkins. Within the next hour, the four sat in Chief Lansing's office discussing the best way to bring those four felons from Savannah, GA to Zealand, VA. After going over all the options, it was decided to use the U.S. Marshall's Service. "They have their own planes," said Lieutenant McGee. "They do it all the time. We'll just have to pick up the tab."

Harry and Floyd drove to the airport, left their car in the police parking area, then boarded a flight to Savannah for the expedition hearing. They were picked up at the Savannah airport by Lieutenant Roper and on the way to police headquarters, the story was told. "That liquor store is across the street from a restaurant where two officers were eating lunch at a table by the window. They see a car pull up and double park outside the liquor store. They were attracted to it because of the loud rap music coming from it. Three black males get out, the driver stays in the car. As the three go in, they pull down face masks, and one of them is holding a handgun. One of the officers gets on his radio and calls in a 'robbery in progress'. Three patrol cars get there within minutes, blocking the car. The two officers from the restaurant pull the driver out, and when the other three come out, they are confronted by six officers with drawn guns. End of story!"

"That's quite a story," said Harry. "We would like meet those two officers and shake their hands."

"That'll be no problem," Lieutenant Roper told them. "But first the Chief would like to say hello," as he parked the car in front of Savannah Police Headquarters.

Walking through the door marked Chief of Police, the man sitting behind the desk got up and walked across the room to meet them. Lieutenant Roper made the introductions, "Detective Lincoln, Detective Washington, meet Savannah Police Chief Lane Hagin."

Shaking hands, Chief Hagin said, "I'm finally getting to meet 'The Presidents' and yes, you two are famous clear down here to Savannah, Georgia. After some chuckles and smiles, he continued. "I am very proud that two of our officers were alert and acted appropriately, resulting in the apprehension of those no good, low down cop killers. But right now, you'll need to get over to the court house for the extradition hearing. Lieutenant Roper will take you, and the two officers will be in court. And when you return to Zealand, please give my deepest condolences to Chief Lansing for the murdered officer."

At the court house, Harry and Floyd met with those two officers, shook hands and thanked them sincerely for their alert actions which led to the apprehension. The hearing lasted a few minutes, and the judge ordered the four prisoners extradited to Virginia. They were transported to the airport by paddy wagon, where the U.S. Marshalls airplane was waiting. Lieutenant Roper drove Harry and Floyd to meet the plane. They carried with them a duffel bag containing four unloaded handguns plus the ammunition from them, and the face masks. The prisoners were in handcuffs and leg irons, seated in a closed, cage like area. In addition to the pilot and co-pilot, there were two armed marshals, plus Harry and Floyd. After take-off and the plane leveled at cruising speed, Floyd spoke to the prisoners from the outside of the cage. "Now listen up, you no good pieces of dog shit. 'You have the right to remain silent'..." They were given the Miranda warnings. When asked if they understood, there was no response.

When the jet landed at the Zealand Airport and taxied to a restricted area, waiting on the tarmac was a patty wagon and two patrol cars. The four prisoners were loaded into the wagon and taken to the county jail, escorted by two patrol cars. Harry and Floyd hopped a ride to the police parking area, got into their car and drove downtown to police headquarters.

The following day Harry and Floyd along with Lieutenant McGee briefed Chief Lansing and Deputy Chief Watkins on the details of the arrests in Savannah. Later the two stopped off at the medical examiner's office to pick up the slugs recovered from the dead officer's body and his vest. They brought them to the crime lab, along with the four handguns and ammunition taken from the arrested suspects in Savannah. There they will undergo ballistics tests. Fingerprints lifted from the interior of the stolen BMW will be matched with the four suspects. They spent the rest of the day in the squad room putting together the case file. When they were finished, both left the building and headed for some R & R.

While driving, Harry thought, *I haven't spoken with her in almost a week, and this is the first chance I've had.* "Hello Jess, yes it's really me, and I'm headed for the pizza place. If you're not busy how about meeting at the loft and we'll share."

"Harry, I'm so glad to hear from you, I know how busy you've been. I've tried to keep up with it all on the news. I feel so bad for the murdered officer's wife and children. Tell me all about it tonight over pizza."

After a relaxing evening, Harry sitting in his recliner, with Jessica sitting on the couch across from him, looking at each other. Harry said in a low voice, "Jess, since we've known each other, the best part of so many twenty-four-hour days is when we are here together, and then you spend the night. And that's what I had in mind for tonight, but Jess I've got to pass tonight. These last few days have taken a heavy toll on me, both physically and mentally. I just want to flop into bed and pass out. Also, I've got an early morning meeting with the district attorney."

"That's fine Harry, I can see that you're not yourself. Next time when you are not so involved we'll have a special date. I enjoyed the pizza and your company, call me in a few days." Jessica left, and Harry did flop into bed.

***

Early the next morning Harry and Floyd met with Dick Donahue, the Ridgewood County District Attorney. "Come on in Guys, good to see you both, there's coffee and donuts in the back of the room. I've read the preliminary reports and see where you've done your usual good job."

"Well Mister DA, said Harry, "it was Savannah, PD who did the good job. We're just doing the paper work and connecting the dots."

"Yes, I understand that, and if those dots connect with positive results from the crime lab, then we've got a hell of a strong case, and I'm going for the death penalty for those lousy cop killers!"

***

The jury was out for less than an hour, and when they came back it was with a guilty verdict. That same jury unanimously voted the death penalty for the four. It would take some time before it would be carried out, as the appeal process ground its way through the courts.

***

Harry and Jessica, with Floyd and Awa were eating dinner in the roof-top restaurant atop one of the tallest buildings, overlooking the city. The dinner was to honor the late Officer A.D. Martin. "It gives Floyd and me such satisfaction," Harry said to Jessica and Awa, "and a tremendous sense of accomplishment to bring justice to victims of thugs and bullies."

"And partner," said Floyd. "We'll keep doing it as long as we carry these gold shields.

CHAPTER

10

It was the incessant rumbling, the terrifying roar that had Harry scared. When was it going to blow? Could he make it out in time? He slowly opened one eye, the green numbers staring at him read 4:20 a.m. Opening the other eye, he saw his cell phone lit up and vibrating on the night table next to him.

Answering the phone in a sleepy, somewhat shaken, "hello."

"Detective Lincoln, this is Conway in communications. I'm calling you because you are this month's on-call hostage negotiator. Sir, we have a situation."

Coming awake instantly and turning on the lamp, Harry grabbed the pen and pad on that same night table. "Go ahead Conway, I'm listening."

"It's Chief Lansing sir, he and his family are being held at their house by two men. Deputy Chief Watkins requested you to meet him in the park a block from the house."

By this time Harry was sitting on the edge of his bed. "Conway, do you have any details?"

"No sir, except the emergency response team is also being notified."

"Okay, I'm on the way!"

Putting the phone down and muttering to himself, *'why do these things always seem to happen in the middle of the night? Get out of my nice warm bed and into the freezing January night. Oh, stop your bitching Detective Harry Lincoln, you wouldn't have it any other way. So, put on your long johns and get your ass in gear!'*

***

Arriving at the park Harry saw chaos and confusion; blue lights flashing, loud police radios, and louder voices barking orders. In the middle of it all, the mobile command post. Harry entered, and the chaos continued in the confined space of this converted motor home. When Deputy Chief Watkins saw Harry, he ordered non-essential personnel to step outside, and said, "Harry grab yourself some coffee and doughnuts over there on the counter." Remaining in the command post with Chief Watkins was the special operations commander, the SWAT commander, the commanders of the 2nd and 5th precincts, and this month's on-call hostage negotiator Detective Harry Lincoln.

"I'll try to keep this as brief as I can," said the Deputy Chief, having their full attention. "Through the years, most of us are familiar with the Tabor brothers, the oldest of the three, Earl Tabor sits on death row at the state penitentiary scheduled to get the needle at 12:00 noon today for the rape and murder of a twelve-year-old girl." He looked at his notes and continued. "Several hours ago, just after midnight the other two Tabor brothers broke into Chief Lansing's house and took him and his family hostage. The Chief, his wife, his sixteen-year-old-daughter and twelve-year-old-son. One of the Tabors calls 911 and tells the operator what they have and demands to speak to someone in charge. I am awakened and after a short explanation I am connected with Tabor who demands the governor issue a stay of execution of Earl Tabor. If not, and they execute his brother, the chief and his family will also die." Watkins pauses for a moment, and then continues. "I manage to get a sleepy and grumpy mayor on the phone and explain the situation. The mayor in turn tells the governor and the stay is granted."

***

The deputy chief then turns to Detective Lincoln saying: "The special operations commander has the inner and outer perimeters locked in, and neighbors within the inner perimeter have been evacuated. The SWAT commander has sniper teams set up in vantage points around the house, and SWAT entry teams standing-by, ready to go on the green light. An area for the media is set aside within the outer perimeter with a police-media rep for the dissemination of information. All is ready Harry, for you to make contact."

Harry dialed the Lansing's home phone, and a strange male voice answered. "Yeah who is this?"

"My name is Detective Harry Lincoln with the Zealand Police Department. Who am I speaking with?"

"Well Detective Harry Lincoln with the Zealand Pig Department, my name is Buster Tabor with the three Tabor musketeers. The second musketeer, Mort Tabor is here with me as guests in the home of the Zealand police chief."

Is everyone alright in there? Asked Harry with his fingers crossed. "Maybe put Chief Lansing on the phone so I can be sure."

"Let me tell you something pig, no he ain't coming to the phone, I'm the only one you're gonna talk to. And yeah, everyone's okay in here… so far," said Tabor in a menacing tone.

"Look, why don't you call me Harry, and I'll call you Buster? We got the governor to issue a stay of execution for your brother Earl. So why don't you leave the chief's house? We'll guarantee you and Mort safe passage out of here."

"Look Lincoln, how fuckin' stupid do you think we are, safe passage my ass! Now let me tell you what's gonna' happen. You pigs are gonna' get my brother Earl sprung from that prison and then brought to the house here. When he gets here, have an SUV big enough that will hold seven people; gas tank full, keys in it, with a working police radio on all channels parked in front of the house. Then the three Tabor musketeers with the chief and his family will drive away for places unknown."

"Buster, we don't have authorization to have someone released from prison, especially one under a death sentence."

"Well then get the governor to do it like he stopped the needle. And if he can't or won't do it, then the president can pardon anyone he wants to." Buster's tone changed when he said, "and tell them that four lives are the trade off."

"Okay Buster, I'll get on it and see what I can do, but something like that is going to take some time. Meanwhile we stopped Earl's execution, so how about letting one of the children out, you know tit for tat, I scratch your back, you scratch mine? You still will have three more in there."

"No one is leaving this house until my brother Earl walks in here without a mark on him," Buster sneered looking at the chief. "You got that Lincoln?" Buster said into the phone.

"Yes, I've got that Buster, but before any arrangements can be worked on for Earl's release, we have to know that the four that you are holding in there are okay, and not being mistreated. Send out one of the children so we can be assured, otherwise the people with that authority say, no deal."

The SWAT commander alerted all within the inner perimeter that one of the hostages may be coming out. Within the next five minutes the front door opened, and the twelve-year-old-son of Chief Lansing walked out and was hastily taken to a van within the outer perimeter and questioned by a sociologist. When it was learned that conditions in the house was as good as could be expected, Deputy Chief Watkins gave Harry the thumbs-up.

"Okay Buster, my back doesn't itch anymore, so now I'll scratch yours. I'm hanging up the phone so I can start working on the deal about Earl. I'll call you back soon, but if you need to speak with me before then, call me at this number, 206-848-1302.

***

All conversation with Buster Tabor had been heard over the speaker phone by the few that were in the command post, and they looked at each other for several seconds. Deputy Chief Watkins broke the silence. "Well, that's one less Lansing we'll have to worry about. Good job Harry. Now we have to see to it that no harm comes to the other three." Watkins paused and there was silence in the command post until he continued. "He certainly made his demand very clear, but I think it would take at the very least a superior court judge to order his brother's release. I'll have someone to check on that, very confidentially because at this stage we don't want that demand to get out."

***

Meanwhile, nearly one hundred miles away at the Virginia State Penitentiary another drama was rumbling. Thomas Sinclair the father of Anna Sinclair the twelve-year-old girl, who had been raped and murdered by Earl Tabor, was at the prison to witness the Tabor execution. When he learned it had been postponed, Thomas Sinclair was stunned and shocked. From the beginning it was a lesson in frustration and anxiety. First it took police a couple of months to investigate, arrest and charge Tabor. And then several more months before the D.A. put him on trial where he was found guilty of rape and murder, receiving the death penalty. Then the appeals process oozed through the courts for almost two years. Thomas Sinclair was livid as he sat in an outer office waiting to be called to speak with the warden. *"How could this happen?"* He thought. The longer he waited the madder he got!

Master Sergeant Thomas Sinclair retired from the military after a thirty-year career. His last combat assignment with the Third Infantry Division in the gulf war led to the defeat of the Iraqi army, earning this U.S. Army Ranger the Silver Star for gallantry under fire. He returned to civilian life with a severe case of Post-Traumatic Stress Disorder. "How could this happen?" which is what he asked, aloud this time, now sitting across from the warden.

"Mr. Sinclair," replied the warden, "I was as surprised as you and don't have an answer, but that's not the worst of it. I have been notified that efforts are under way for Earl Tabor to be released from this penitentiary where he will be transported to the City of Zealand. Don't ask me why because I don't know."

The color drained from the face of Thomas Sinclair, and found it hard to breath, he sat just staring at the warden. "There must be some mistake." He pleaded, "Please warden, please tell me there's been a mistake."

"I would like to tell you," a somewhat shaken warden said, "that this unprecedented action will not happen. But keep in mind, I'm just the warden of this prison, the ultimate decision makers are way above my pay grade." Both men stood and shook hands and as they approached the front gate the warden said, "You have my word that I'll do everything I can, such as it is to stop this insanity."

A defeated Thomas Sinclair walked slowly across the parking lot, got into his car and headed for Zealand, instead of home more than halfway across the State of Virginia.

CHAPTER

11

Zealand's mayor was at a loss when notified of this latest demand and called the city attorney for legal advice. "There is no precedent that I know of for this kind of action. Maybe the governor has that authority."

"A stay of execution is one thing," said the governor when asked, "but releasing a death row inmate from prison because of a situation like this one, is quite another. I suppose this would be handled through the courts."

On day two of the hostage situation, the superior court trial judge who imposed the death sentence, reached out to the Commonwealth of Virginia's Supreme Court. After a lengthy conference with two of the justices, the trial judge handed down a ruling authorizing the release of Earl Tabor from the Virginia State Penitentiary. This action was taken due to the threat of death of the three remaining hostages.

***

When word came down from the court, Harry got back on the phone. "Okay Buster, it looks like they are going to release your brother Earl, but they said before that happens you have to let the chief's wife and daughter out of the house."

"I don't know Lincoln that's two for one."

"Look Buster, they said that was non-negotiable and you are dealing with some very heavy hitters. That's the deal and if you don't take it, not only doesn't Earl go free, but he gets the needle!"

"Oh shit I gotta think Lincoln, I'll call you back."

The SWAT commander advised all units within the inner perimeter that two females might be coming out, and to have them brought to the debriefing van.

Five minutes went by slowly, and then the phone rang, "Okay Lincoln, I'm gonna let them both out. But if those heavy hitters are lying and change their minds, you're chief gets a fuckin' bullet in his Goddamn head."

Ms. Lansing and her daughter were met by SWAT officers and escorted to the debriefing van in the outer perimeter now containing the sociologist, a female detective and a chaplain. Their ordeal had mother and daughter very upset, crying on the verge of hysteria. They were given some time to calm down and assurances that in the end, "your husband, your dad would not be harmed." What was needed from them was the conditions in the house, how many and what kind of weapons did you see, and if anything should be sent into the house.

***

Back in the command post there was a round of high-fives, and a few Atta-boys thrown Harry's way. "You know Harry," said Deputy Chief Watkins, "If this ends well, the chief makes it out okay, the three Tabor brothers are behind bars, and then he learns who got his family out safely, he might just give you my job." Laughter in the command post, a lot of the pressure was relieved.

"Now back to business," continued Watkins. "For the next phase we must develop a strategy. Once they leave in the SUV that we provide we must attach a tracking device to it. And it has to be hidden where they are not likely to find it. We cannot lose them."

Harry spoke up. "Chief, can we have my partner Detective Washington to come to the command post? I have an idea along those lines and he would be part of it." Deputy Chief Watkins put out the order for Washington and cleared him for entry into the command post.

Word came from the van that no one in the house had been physically harmed, but there was verbal abuse and threats shouted in a vile, nasty way. Both bad guys had hand guns, but they didn't know what kind, although they were black and looked like the kind that police officers carry. They also took the chief's two handguns, both black semi-automatics. All the utilities were working so the house was warm. Ms. Lansing also said there was not much to eat in the house. She said that her husband would like pizza, and of the toppings he liked.

***

Harry got on the phone and Buster answered. "Don't tell me that they changed their minds already Lincoln."

"Nothing like that Buster, I wanted to let you know that I'm sending in a couple of pizzas for the three of you, until Earl arrives. When the pizzas get here, they will be brought up onto the front porch by two SWAT officers and left at the front door. They will then leave."

"When the hell will Earl get here Lincoln, or are you just jerkin' me off?"

"Earl will get here, but with a deal like this it's going to take some time.

***

Detective Washington entered the command post within the hour. He was introduced around to those who didn't know him. Deputy Chief Watkins wasted no time. "Okay Harry lets have it."

Harry had the floor. "Hiding a tracking device in that SUV is imperative. Now assuming they don't find it, and we know they will be looking, and if nothing happens to the SUV, we can pinpoint wherever they are. But I think we should have an insurance policy. My idea is to have a second tracking device on Earl Tabor himself. As we all know, when prisoners are released from prison, all their personal belongings taken from them when they went in are then returned to them."

Harry pauses for a moment and then continues. "Now, the warden is to be told by someone in authority, either the Director of the Bureau of Prisons or a Superior Court Judge or maybe even the Governor, someone with a lot of juice. He is ordered to follow the instructions of ZPD Detective Floyd Washington concerning the release of Earl Tabor. Floyd will go in low key and be very respectful, explaining why this is so critical. He will have the latest hi-tech, miniature tracking device hidden in the hollowed-out heel of a pair of new work boots that he will bring with him. These will be given to Tabor upon his release. Tabor will be told that the footwear he came in with was stored in the basement level, and with all the rain and flooding lately, his along with all the others had been ruined."

Harry looked at Deputy Chief Watkins. "Chief if you would call the warden and get Tabor's shoe size and explain what's going on. We'll get a pair and have our lab to install the tracking device."

The Deputy Chief looked at the four high-ranking superior officers in the command post and said, "I want you all to speak freely and truthfully. You heard Detective Lincoln's plan, now I want each of you to state the pros and cons." The four went to a closed off area on the far end of the command post. Fifteen minutes later they joined the others. The on-scene commander, a major said he was speaking for the four. "We kicked it around pretty good and all agreed that it is a terrific plan and we endorse it 100%! One thing that we would add, instead of one tracking device on the SUV put two. They will probably look for a device so put one where it might be found and hide the second where it should not. If the first one is found chances are they will stop looking."

"This plan is taking shape and looking good," beamed Deputy Chief Watkins.

Harry got on the phone. "Hey Buster, the pizzas are here and will be at the front door in a few minutes."

***

Deputy Chief Watkins left the command post and went to his office where he put in a call to the prison warden. He explained the situation concerning the police chief and his family and outlined the plan. He told him that when Zealand Police Detective Washington arrived at the prison, he would go over the plan in detail with him. "But first, warden it is critical that you get me Earl Tabor's shoe size, ASAP. Please call me with it, I'll be waiting by the phone, and thanks for your help." He then called the lab asking if they had three of the latest hi-tech tracking devices. They did! "Detective Washington will bring with him a pair of work boots, and an unmarked SUV, and he will explain what it is that I want done. This is top priority by my authority"

While waiting for all of the elements to be worked and come together, a schedule was set on a rotating basis for personal assigned to this operation to go to their homes, eat something, freshen up and grab some sleep. Harry stayed in the command post resting on an army cot, close to the phone.

***

Everything was in place and the operation commenced first thing in the morning. All units including the state police plus all law enforcement agencies around the state had been told that any radio transmissions concerning this operation was to be over the tactical channel. (The police radio in the SUV had the tactical channel blocked.) Floyd Washington was on the way to the prison with the doctored work boots. Upon Earl Tabor's release, the state police would transport him to Zealand.

CHAPTER

12

While all this was going on, Thomas Sinclair arrived in Zealand and checked into the downtown Holiday Inn Express. "Mister, you just hit it lucky this is the last vacant room in the house." And as Sinclair was filling out the registration form, the desk clerk asked, "are you with the news media also?"

Sinclair answered, "No why, what's going on? I noticed the traffic was pretty heavy with news trucks and police vehicles. There is also lots of people on the streets."

"Seems like some guys broke into the police chief's house and are holding him and his family hostage. It's all over the TV."

When Sinclair opened the door to his room, he immediately turned on the TV and sat on the edge of the bed, still holding his luggage. There it was! The commentator was summarizing the situation. "Chief Lansing, his wife and two children held hostage in their own home, by two men who broke in on Monday. Now two days later, wife, son and daughter have been released, but Chief Lansing remains a hostage. Police are being unusually tight-lipped in this case concerning demands made by the hostage takers. Our news team will stay on the scene of this hostage situation, and we'll bring you any new developments as we learn them."

Sinclair went back to the office and asked the desk clerk where this hostage situation was going on. "It's not far from here," the clerk told him. "It's in midtown, when you go out the door turn right and go maybe five, six blocks then turn right again for another three, four blocks and you'll come to a park. Just follow the blue lights."

***

At the prison, the warden was very cooperative, and things went smoothly. He had received his instructions from high up in his chain-of-command and had a better understanding after Floyd Washington explained everything to him. Upon his release Earl Tabor had no suspicions, glad to get the new work boots, and beyond that very glad to be getting out of prison. He was loaded into a marked state police SUV with two state troopers and transported to Zealand, Floyd leading the way in his car.

Upon reaching Zealand, Washington and the state troopers with Earl Tabor aboard were stopped at the outer perimeter. "Call the command post, Deputy Chief Watkins will clear us," Floyd told the officers at the barricade. After a minute or so on the telephone the blocking patrol cars were moved, and they were waived through. Once in the command post Deputy Chief Watkins thanked the troopers and after each had a cup of coffee, he relieved them. Then after a quick nod and a thumbs-up from Floyd, Harry got on the phone. "Okay Buster, Earl is here but before we send him in I want to speak with Chief Lansing to be sure that he's alright and hasn't been mis-treated. After that I'll put Earl on the phone."

"Not so fast Lincoln, how do I know you ain't lyin' like most cops do? If Earl is here, put him on the phone first, then I'll let you speak to your chief."

"Hello Buster," Earl said into the phone, "Yeh I'm really here so let him speak to whoever he wants to, so we can get the fuck outta here."

"Hello, this is Chief Lansing. He keeps calling you Lincoln, is this Detective Harry Lincoln?"

"Yes, it is chief, and just to make sure I'm speaking with Chief Lansing, very quickly what is my partner's name?"

"Detective Floyd Washington, who I commended recently for

speaking to that unruly crowd about you. Thank you so very much for getting my family out of here. I'm alright, they have not physically abused me and even shared the pizzas with me."

"Is there anything that you need or want that we can send in for you?"

"No, nothing that I can't do without, just see to it that my family is taken care of"

"Two female detectives are with them and will stay with them until this situation is over. So chief, think positive and keep your head up. You know the entire ZPD has got your six!"

Earl Tabor was escorted to the front of the house by two SWAT officers. Two other SWAT officers drove the SUV to the house and parked it. Harry got back on the phone. "You got everything you wanted: The keys are in it, and the gas tank is full. The police radio is operating on all channels but put it on channel 8 if you want to talk to me." A few minutes later, four men came out of the house and boarded the SUV. Chief Lansing was in handcuffs. The SUV drove away from the house.

***

Thomas Sinclair had made his way to one of the outer perimeter barricades where several of the cops were talking freely to the curious who had gathered there. "All we know is that these two guys got the chief as a hostage, and when some inmate from the prison got here the four of them were going to leave in an unmarked police SUV. This inmate was on death row and should have gotten the needle several days ago. It sounds crazy, but if they didn't release him and bring him here, those guys were going to kill the chief and his whole family."

A police sergeant rode up on a motorcycle shouting, "move those blocking patrol cars out of the street, here they come!" Floyd drove up behind him, parked and got out of the car. In the next minute the SUV appeared, drove past the crowd without slowing down, and was gone!

Floyd noticed a man in the crowd pushing his way to the front, and then talking to one of the cops. He looked familiar but could not place him. The man was becoming agitated, raising his voice and waving his arms. There was something about the guy, and the more he looked, the more convinced he was that he knew him, but from where? He thought that he might be a guy he once arrested in the many cases worked in the past. Floyd grumbled to himself about how his memory was starting to fail as he was growing older. He was almost to his car when suddenly it hit him. *'Oh man, could it be him? Could it really be him?'* Floyd made his way closer and shouted over the crowd noise, "Top, hey Top!" The man was still ranting. Floyd shortened the distance and turning the volume up several clicks, tried again. "Hey Top… Top… yo Top!"

The man turned and their eyes locked. Neither spoke, they just stared. Then finally, hoping this was not one of those PTSD dreams the man asked, "Wash, is that you? Tell me this is you Wash."

"Yes Top, it's me: Corporal Floyd Washington, U.S. Army, 44th Ranger battalion, Third Infantry Division… Iraq…The gulf war!

Close enough for a handshake, each grabbed the other in a vicious bear-hug, back-slapping harder than they should. Both overcome with emotion they could not let go, two pairs of eyes filling with moisture, then rolling down cheeks. Tender moment over, Floyd pushed back holding Sinclair at arm's length, finding his voice said, "Top, this is better than a kid's Christmas morning, but I didn't know you lived in Zealand."

"Wash, this past week has been a downer, but seeing you has made the clouds part, and the sun shine. And no, I don't live here in Zealand I'm on the coast, Portsmouth. Is this where you live? I thought you were going back to Miami."

"Well it's kind of a long story, and there is so much for us to catch up on, but I really have to run. I have to get in my car over there and take the same route that the SUV busted out of here a few minutes ago. If you are free and if you want to… take a ride with me."

"Wash if one of the guys in that van is Earl Tabor, I am free and would very much like to take a ride with you, let's go!"

***

In the car Floyd asked, "Top how do you know about Earl Tabor, and what's your connection?"

As they drove Thomas Sinclair relayed the whole story, getting emotional when saying, "He raped and murdered my little girl!" And getting very angry about the cancelled execution and the release from prison. They traveled several miles, neither one talking, the only sounds coming from the police radio giving driving directions.

"There are four people in that SUV, Earl Tabor plus his two brothers, and Zealand Police Chief Lansing who is their hostage. There is a tracking device on that vehicle giving its location at all times. Those signals are received at the command post, and once the barricades around the house are opened up, the tracking of the SUV will switch over to police headquarters," Floyd explained. "My assignment is to follow those driving directions, staying a mile or two behind the SUV. It is done this way because they will be looking to see if they are being followed. We have dealt with the Tabor brothers before and don't want to do anything to anger them and cause them to take it out on Chief Lansing."

***

"Okay Wash, you've told me several times that when you got out of the army you were going back home to Miami. You said that your plans were to join the Miami Police Department. So how did you end up a cop in Zealand, Virginia?"

"Well Top, that's just what I did when I was discharged from the army. I was a patrolman with the Miami PD for a time until I made detective. I worked vice and fugitive until I was transferred into homicide. That assignment must have agreed with me, my clear-ups were good, and I was being noticed. Noticed by the brass, by the media, and by other detectives. I had gotten married back when I was a patrolman. Lil and I were very happy and wanted to start a family, but that never happened. During the time I was working homicide, Lil got sick. Cancer! She died shortly after. It devastated me, and I had to get away, away from all the memories. Being in our house was painful, it depressed me. I started sending letters and resumes to major police departments. Zealand PD was interested, and here I am!

***

Back at police headquarters Harry and several others from the Special Operations Section (SOS) were monitoring the tracking devices. They saw that all three were working well, the two in the SUV and the one in the work boot. Floyd occasionally gave his location to verify that he was staying about a mile to a mile and a half behind the target vehicle. "I've got an idea chief," Harry said to Deputy Chief Watkins. "Why don't we send four of our plain-clothes SOS guys in a pickup truck to hook up with Washington. They haven't gotten that far, and if something should develop causing him to take action, he'll have some muscle with him." Watkins got on the phone and gave the order, Harry notified Floyd.

***

In the SUV Earl Tabor said with a sigh of relief, "well so far, so good." And sat back a little more relaxed.

"Well I'm not too sure about that," answered Buster Tabor. "They're makin' it too easy. They got these little things that they put on a car, so they can tell where you are goin'. Ain't that right chief? And what are those things called?"

"That's right, and they are called tracking devices."

Buster was quiet for a few minutes, just staring out of the windshield, and then said, "Mort, that gas station-convenience store up ahead, pull in there and park out of the way." It was a busy place, but Mort drove in past all the hub-bub and parked away from it all. Buster then said, "Earl, lets you and me get out and see if they put one on, we can find the damn thing."

They were looking and feeling all along on the outside of SUV when Earl yelled, "hey Buster is this what you are talkin' about?" In his hand he held a small metal object taken out of the wheel well above the right rear tire.

"Yeah Earl, that must be it," shouted Buster.

Back inside, Buster dialed channel 8 on the police radio. When Harry answered he said, "Hey Lincoln, maybe we're not so dumb as you think we are." And with a satisfied smirk said, "we found your little toy so now try and find us!" With that he went outside, threw down the tracking device on the concrete and crushed it with the heel of his boot. (Luckily Earl didn't help him!)

***

"Well the lab followed our instructions," said Deputy Chief Watkins to Harry monitoring the radio. "They put one where it would be easily found, and to find the other they would have to take that vehicle apart. What is Washington's location?"

"I had told him where they stopped, and he said they were near the I-81 entrance ramp." With that, the SUV left the gas station and entered the interstate, southbound. The SOS pickup not far behind blending in with the mostly pickup trucks and SUVs on the interstate. Floyd in his detective car, keeping his distance.

Fifteen minutes later the SOS pickup advised that the SUV was pulling into a rest area. Harry told them to enter the rest area, appearing as travelers and to keep an eye on them. Floyd copied all that and told Harry that he would park on the entrance ramp out of sight of the rest area, and there was a state police car with him, occupied by two troopers.

***

Once they got parked at the far end of the parking area Buster said, "man I gotta take a leak, my teeth are floatin'." Earl said he had to go with him. "Mort, you stay and watch the pig chief and if he tries to holla or give you any shit, just fuckin shoot him."

The SOS cops radioed the situation and were told by Harry for three of them to follow those two who will be armed, into the restroom and take them down. A uniformed state trooper would come in behind them. And the forth was to position himself near the SUV but out of sight, until a ZPD detective and a uniformed state trooper arrived.

Three SOS cops with badges on lanyards around their necks and guns drawn entered the restroom. "Police," they shouted at the two who were standing at urinals. "Don't turn around or you will be shot. Finish up and put your hands on your heads. Okay, now back up slowly." The two brothers did as they were told. "Now get down on your knees." With two of the cops covering, the third searched both Tabor brothers and removed their guns. The trooper had arrived and was at the door keeping anyone from entering.

At the same time, Washington knocked on the SUV door while the others were still out of sight. "Hey in there, you got gasoline pouring out of your tank, and it might start a fire!" Mort Tabor came outside and when turned to take a look, Floyd put his gun in Tabor's back. "Don't move and put your hands up. I'm a police officer and you are under arrest." The others came around the vehicle and disarmed him. Floyd rushed into the SUV and found Chief Lansing on the floor handcuffed to a pipe. The handcuffs were removed, the chief got up and put a bear hug on Detective Washington who then got on the radio. "Harry, we got the chief and he's okay. The three Tabor brothers are under arrest. Our location is southbound on the freeway, the first rest area south of the city. Send some crime scene techs to work the areas of arrests. And Harry, it might be a good idea to bring a doc to check out the chief."

The troopers cleared the rest area and roped it off. They put in a call for two more state police units to block the ramp, so no other vehicles could enter, except for Zealand police vehicles.

They all went into the office. The employees were told the rest area would be shut down for the rest of the day, and they could leave now. They should report back tomorrow at their regular times.

Detective Washington had the Tabors, one by one brought into a small office where he read each one the Miranda warnings... "You have the right to remain silent..." When asked if they understood them, neither spoke and also refused to sign the form saying they were given the warnings and understood them. They had been advised, and that's what was important. It was all recorded on video.

Thomas Sinclair sat out of the way and kept staring at Earl Tabor once he learned which of the Tabor brothers he was. His mind was in a turmoil. *"I want to kill him, that no good piece of dog shit. But if I do, I'll be the one who goes to prison, and it's almost worth it. But if I do, that will put Wash in a hell-of-a bind, after all he's the one who brought me here with him. I can't do that to him. But I just can't depend on the Commonwealth of Virginia to do it. I'll just bide my time and see what develops."* He sat and stared.

"Hey Top," Floyd said coming over to sit with him. "You are the only guy here except the Tabor brothers who isn't laughing or at least smiling. Why so glum? Is something bothering you?"

"No Wash, just watching you guys operate, and I'm impressed. I do have a lot on my mind, but that's for me to work out."

"Top, when this is all over we'll get together, and maybe I can help you with those things on your mind. After all I owe you one from our time in Iraq, and I'll never forget it."

Zealand Police Department vehicles entered the rest area, and more kept coming. Up and down the chain of command, various ranks and assignments showed up. It had the feel of a celebration, celebrating the safe rescue of the very well-liked and respected Police Chief Robert Lansing. Detective Lincoln and Deputy Chief Watkins arrived together and joined Detective Washington and

Chief Lansing in the small office. After hugs and high-fives, Watkins said, "Chief, this whole thing was a combined effort involving many people, but the loudest atta-boys goes to these two… presidents!"

"I want to hear all the details tomorrow or maybe the next day in my office," said a very worn out chief. After a cursory examination the doctor cleared Chief Lansing to go home and rest up for a few days. "And when I get there the first thing I'll do is hug my wife and children. Then I want to soak in a hot tub, and shower to get the stink and crud off me. After that I will devour a steak dinner medium-rare, then hop in my bed and fall into a deep, sound sleep."

Activity was slowly settling down in the rest area. Some crime techs, several uniformed police officers and a couple of state troopers remained. When the techs were through they headed back to the city along with the cops, and the troopers opened up the rest area before they left.

On their way back, Chief Lansing rode with Deputy Chief Watkins, so they could talk privately. Another car was occupied by Detective Harry Lincoln, Detective Floyd Washington and Thomas Sinclair. After Floyd made the introductions, he said, "Harry, let me explain who this man is, and why has he been with me on such an important assignment. I first met Master Sergeant Thomas Sinclair when I was in the army, in Iraq during the gulf war. We were both assigned to Charlie Company, 44th Ranger Battalion, 3rd Infantry Division. He was the first sergeant, the company Top Sergeant. I was a corporal. We were on a mission to take out an Iraqi ammo dump, about ten miles from our camp. A lieutenant was in charge of our twenty-man raiding party with Thomas, the second in command. The mission was accomplished as the dump went up and could be heard and felt for miles around. On our way back, we ran into some Iraqi infantry who outnumbered us about two-to-one. We engaged them in a fierce fire fight, however our lieutenant along with three other rangers were killed. Several were wounded but able to continue. I caught two in my leg, and could not stand or walk, but I could still shoot. Top here took one in his arm, and a second in the hand of the same arm. We had managed to eliminate their patrol but knew that enemy reinforcements would be coming shortly, as we were still in Iraqi territory, about six or seven miles from our lines. Top had our radio man to contact the battalion, giving our situation and location, and requesting they send a sizeable force to meet us, because the enemy might overtake our slow withdrawal due to our wounded. They were told that we had already sustained four KIA's." (Killed in Action).

Floyd got emotional and had to stop talking. After a long minute he continued. "Now Harry, get this picture... we can't just wait there for the cavalry to arrive because we are sure the enemy is coming after us, so we have to move. The next thing I know, Top has me up on his shoulders holding me with one arm because the other is useless. Top had given me his weapon before he hoisted me up, so now I'm holding two Thompson sub-machine guns. He is in a lot of pain, I'm in a lot of pain, and I'm thinking, why some of the other guys don't help Top carry me. And after I look around I see all the guys that can walk, are dragging those who can't. We are a rag-tag, beat-up bunch, but we're moving. We are moving two, maybe three miles with me on Top's shoulders. The cavalry met up with us with medics, stretchers and morphine. Our 3rd Infantry Division soldiers kept going and clashed with the enemy soldiers and beat them back."

With a tear running down one cheek Floyd continued. "I don't know how he found the strength in the condition he was in, but if Top hadn't carried me that distance, I would not be sitting here now, telling you about a heroic U.S. Army Ranger, Master Sergeant Thomas Sinclair!"

"That's quite a story Floyd," said Harry. "And I can understand the close bond between the both of you, but you've never mentioned him to me."

"Well Harry, here's the strange part." And Floyd related the course of events earlier in the day that led them to recognize each other, and them being together at the rest area.

Sinclair spoke up. "Detective Lincoln, I was at the Virginia State Prison the other day to witness the execution of Earl Tabor for the rape and murder of my twelve-year-old daughter. When it was cancelled, I learned that he was going to be released from prison because of the tense situation here in Zealand with the police chief and his family. As soon as Wash and I hooked up, he had to leave to follow the SUV with that murderer in it. I rode with him so we could get reacquainted with one another, but my mind was on killing that no good piece of dog shit in that SUV. After the arrest of the three brothers, I got thinking that if I did anything like that, it would all come down on you Wash, and I couldn't do that to you."

"Top, I'm very glad that you didn't you didn't do it. Yes, I would have been in deep shit, but you would end up doing serious prison time."

"And if I can put my two cents worth in," said Harry. "By the time the courts and politicians get through making their speeches, he will get the needle in record time. Floyd and I will be tied up for the next few days with all this, what's your plans are you going to be around?"

"No, I'm going to head home to Portsmouth in the morning. I've got a room in the Holiday Inn Express downtown, if you can drop me off."

At the front of the hotel they exchanged contact information. Harry and Thomas shook hands, and Floyd hugged him and then looking him in the eye said, "Top, you saved my life and I'll never forget it. I want you to know, I will always be your friend. Zealand and Portsmouth are not that far apart, so please let's stay in touch."

Epilogue

For the next few days Zealand Police Headquarters was not the same place. Within the confines of this historic building, just about all conversations centered around Police Chief Robert Lansing's ordeal. From deputy chiefs down to patrolmen, sworn and civilian personnel, male and female, black, white, Hispanic and Asian. It spread throughout the precincts, the units and squads, as well as to the patrol cars and detective cars where the partners hashed it out. From every level the consensus was relief, knowing through experience, how things might have turned out.

The half dozen lounged informally in a sitting area adjacent to the chief's office. They were a select group, chosen by Chief Lansing to resolve an issue of particular importance to him. In addition to Chief Robert Lansing and his adjutant Lieutenant Peter Forbes, sat Chief of Detectives Glenn Watkins. Rounding out the group was Homicide Lieutenant James McGee, Detective Harry Lincoln and Detective Floyd Washington.

"There are no words, at least not in my vocabulary, to express my profound gratitude to all who contributed to the safe release of my family. And of course, that would extend to my ability to sit here with you today. As I said there no words coming from my head... but feelings, strong feelings. Feelings from my heart... feelings from my gut!" Said an emotional police chief. "Once again I want to recognize two of our finest, however I don't want to leave it as one more atta-boy. They deserve more than that. I am offering to them both promotions to sergeant. Of course, that will mean transfers out of homicide, to the Uniform Division. I yield the floor to the Presidents."

Floyd spoke first. "Chief, I want to thank you for offering me the promotion, but if it's all the same to you I would prefer to remain a homicide detective, collecting those atta-boys. I enjoy coming to work every day. I would like to keep my detective shield.

And after a few minutes Harry took the floor. "A while back, a captain gave me some advice, he said, 'don't trade a promotion for a good assignment.' "Well I might regret this someday, but I'm not going to take that advice. Chief, thank you for thinking that highly of me, but I'd rather not trade my detective shield for sergeants' stripes. This Gold Shield means too much to me."

The meeting broke up, everyone leaving with satisfied smiles on their faces. Even Homicide Lieutenant James McGee.

About the Author

Harold B. Goldhagen retired as a Captain after serving thirty years with the Atlanta Police Department. Seven of those years as a Homicide Detective. He now lives with his wife in the North Georgia mountains

Other Books
by Harold B. Goldhagen

"Signal 63", Officer Needs Help
"Signal 50/48", Killing Atlanta's Finest
"The Lincoln Logs", A Detective Harry Lincoln Trilogy.

CPSIA information can be obtained
at www.ICGtesting.com
Printed in the USA
LVHW031950030521
686351LV00004B/57